Nate Grisham

Book 3
Revenge

WR Benton
Grady Clark

LOOSE CANNON ENTERPRISES
Paradise, CA

Nate Grisham, Book 3
2018 Edition
ISBN 978-1-944476-79-3

www.loose-cannon.com

Books by W.R. Benton

Nate Grisham, Renegade Trapper (Co-authored with Grady Clark)

Fur Seekers (Co-authored with Grady Clark)

Red Runs the Plain, Book 1 of the Plains Series

The Fall of America, Premonition of Death

Jake Masters, Bounty Hunter

Nate Grisham, Black Mountain Man (Co-authored with Grady Clark)

Missouri in Flames, I Rode with Jesse James

War Paint

War Drums (Sequel to War Paint)

James McKay, U. S. Army Scout

Blood Money

Alive and Alone (Young Adult)

Simple Survival, a Family Outdoors Guide (Non-Fiction)

Impending Disasters (Non-Fiction)

Bubba's Dawg Might be a Redneck (Southern Humor)

My Child is Missing: Based on the true story of Jared Ropelato

Buffalo Soldiers

Blood Mountain, Plains Series Book #2

Books by Grady Clark

Nate Grisham, Renegade Trapper (Co-authored with WR Benton)

The Widow Nancy Buck

Nate Grisham, Black Mountain Man

The Fur Seekers (Co-authored with WR Benton)

A Southern Moon Rising

The Long Ride Home (Co-Authored with WR Benton)

DEDICATION

To Susan Upton, Joani Moeller, Heather English, Melody Medders, Lynda K. Bundrant-Taylor, Wendy Hartman, and Tom Abeyta, good friends on Facebook. I thank God for having good Friends.

As a twenty-six year active duty veteran, I salute all that are currently serving, have served honorably, and will serve. Remember the motto: God, Duty, and Country.

TABLE OF CONTENTS

Chapter 1

Cotton Top and I are in a world of hurt right now, with ammo running low, both of us wounded and a new day dawning. Along about noon, the day before, the Blackfoot caught us near the base of mountain, and shot Cotton from his horse. Then, they stuck an arrow in my left arm just before dusk. I'd seen six bodies laying in front of us before sunset, but I strongly suspect I'll see none once we have full light.

"How are ya hangin', Cotton?" I asked and the effort to speak caused pain, because he was behind me and I had to twist my body.

"Rough doin's, but I'm still here."

"Did the bleedin' stop yet?" He'd taken an arrow in the upper left side of his chest and I knew it had to smart more than just a little.

Cotton sent a stream of tobacco juice to the dirt before he said, "It stopped deep hurting hours back, but now it's startin' to stiffen up on me a mite. Damned arrow hit me right above the collarbone, so it'll heal iffen I live long enough."

"Do ya reckon those Injuns are still out there?" I was anxious and fighting a bout of fear.

"It all depends on what they're willin' to pay fer our hair. We've kilt at least six of 'em, mayhap more, but I cain't figure out why they've not left yet   or have they?"

"We'll know in a few minutes. I pray they're gone, only ya can never tell about a Blackfoot."

"Yep, they're a determined bunch, only I wish they'd leave us the hell alone. Do ya realize this is the fourth time we've fought 'em in a month?"

I chuckled and replied, "Yep, I gave that some thought last night, but they've got some prime beaver land and iffen a feller can sneak in, do a little trappin' and then sneak out, he's made a bundle of cash. I know all they're doin' is protectin' their lands, but I wish they'd loosen up some on us, because I'm getting' tired of fightin' all the time."

"Be full light in about 'nother thirty minutes. Iffen they're gonna attack us, it'll be in this time period."

"I'm ready for 'em. Ya got all your guns loaded?"

"Now, what do ya think? This is it too, no more power."

"Well, I'm savin' my last bullet for me." I said, because I'd seen firsthand what Injuns do with captives, and it ain't a pretty picture. There is no way in hell I'll be taken alive.

"I'm thinkin' of doin' the same, but don't know if I have the bark to shoot myself."

"By God, I do, because I know what they'll do to me if they take me alive and so do ya."

"I got movement on this side."

"Shit, it figures." I felt my stomach tighten with dread.

Long minutes passed with the sun clearly seen slowly rising, and a few minutes later it was full light. I scanned the area in front of me and saw not a single person, but yet I'd seen no movement all night long.

"Do ya still have movement?" I asked just slightly above a whisper.

"Yep, but it's strange, because it seems to be movin' at a right angle to us."

"Mighten be a trick, so keep your eyes open."

"Sumbitch," Cotton said a few minutes later and then stood, "it's a deer feeding, so the Injuns are gone."

I stood and gave a mighty stretch to get the kinks out, and it felt good. *Damn,* I thought, *we're miles from the nearest help and in a mess.* I turned to Cotton and said, "We've lost all of our supplies, have one horse, and as far as I'm concerned we're in some serious trouble."

"Hell, we were both born to trouble. Here in a bit we'll look for the packhorse, your horse is gone, so if ya want 'em back ya need to start trailin' them Blackfoot."

I chuckled and replied, "I think not. They can keep my horse, but we do need to look for the packhorse as soon as we can. I don't think she's gone far, only it all depends how scared she got when the shootin' started."

"She ain't far."

We walked to Cotton's horse, which was tied to the cedar, and I said, "Ya ride, since ya have the shoulder wound and let's see if we can find some tracks."

Within minutes I spotted tracks and began walking after everything I owned in the world. While I didn't have much, it was all on this packhorse, I needed it and I'd walk a long distance for a ride and supplies.

After about an hour, I spotted the animal near a narrow stream and as usual, she was nipping at the tender grass that always pops up in springtime.

I turned to Cotton and said, "Let me approach her; the reins are hanging freely, mayhap it won't frighten her if I approach alone."

"Hell, I ain't goin' no place, yer the one on shank's mare, not me."

I simply walked near her, spoke in an even voice and gave her a pat on the head. She bumped me with her head, as if she missed me, and it was that easy.

Five minutes later, I approached Cotton and said, "Okay, now that I have a ride, let's move into the trees and have something to eat. I'll divide the gear and supplies, so each of us will carry some of it."

"I'm grizz hungry, so dig out that deer meat and get to cookin', I mean after we divide the gear."

An hour later, our meal complete, we loaded the horses, and both mounted. The weather was beautiful, with a light pleasant breeze, and not a cloud in the sky. I was without a saddle, but it beat walking.

"Do ya still plan on goin' to Butterfield's Tradin' Post?"

"Yep, or do ya have another place in mind?"

Pulling his hat off and then scratching his head, Cotton said, "No, I guess not, since I don't see where we have a choice. We lost every damned thing thing we had but what we've got right now, so this wasn't one of our better years, huh?"

"We can always get more plew, supplies can be replaced, but ya seem to forget we're still alive, and to me that matters a great deal."

"Oh, I know that, only damn it all! We worked all winter and don't have a thing to show for all that effort. The Blackfoot piss me off and one day they'll make me really mad."

"Chalk it up as experience, my friend, and learn from it. Besides, ya had all the Blackfoot ya could kill yesterday and I don't remember ya even bringin' this up at the time."

"I was too busy stayin' alive to get pissed."

"Enough naybobbin'; let's ride, and keep the noise down. I suspect those damned Injuns are still pretty close." I chuckled inside, because I knew Cotton was just making noise. Sure, he was mad, just like me, to have to start all over again, but like I said, we still had our lives.

The trail meandered around the side of a mountain and it was wide enough we could have rode side-by-side, only we rarely did that. If someone wanted to ambush us, they'd have to work a bit to do the job, but it had happened before. Two yahoos riding side-by-side were just asking to be killed.

The afternoon passed quickly and a couple of hours before dusk, I spotted vultures circling over an area off our left.

"See the vultures?" I asked.

"I see 'em. Let's mosey over that way and see what they're plannin' for a meal. There are too many for it to be a dead critter or a single man, or so I think."

"Uh-huh, I agree. Better get yer rifle out and rest it over your legs."

Ten minutes later, we neared the damnest thing I'd ever seen and it confused me. We were off a ways, mayhap three hundred feet, and in the gently sloping valley below was five wagons. Most had burned, but one looked to still be intact. I saw a good number of folks on the ground and none were moving.

"Unfork your horse and let's take this slow and easy," I said.

"Looks like Injuns hit these folks, but I can't tell what tribe yet."

I pulled the hammer back on my rifle, noticing the loud sound in the cool spring air. *Easy*, my mind was screaming, *There is something about this that ain't as it should be.*

"Ya stop and cover me as I move forward," I said and continued walking.

"Watch yer topknot out there, Nate."

The first body I saw a young woman of about twenty and when I realized she was black, it surprised me. She'd been used hard by only God knows how many warriors, and when they'd tired of her, they'd cut her throat. *Don't see many black folks out this way, so how did she get here?* I wondered as I untied her apron and covered her head. I didn't see enough cloth around to cover her naked body, so I did the best I could. Maybe I'd find something at the wagons.

The next body was a black man and he'd been opened

from crotch to brisket, scalped, and mutilated badly. His eyes were open wide, unseeing, yet reflecting pain and fear. Three arrows, Sioux by the markings, were in his chest.

Each body I checked was mutilated, scalped, and dead beyond a doubt. I was more confused by each of them being black, because there just weren't many of us out this way. It was not until I neared the last wagon I heard a noise. I thought I heard a voice, but wasn't sure, so I stopped. I turned to Cotton, pointed at him and then drew a circle in the air. He waved and began to circle the wagons. I remained in place, but heard no additional noise.

When his circle was complete, he walked to me and said, "I counted forty unshod horses leaving. It looks clean to me."

Whispering I said, "Someone is in that wagon."

Cotton shrugged and called out, "Ya, in the wagon, get yer ass out here or we'll leave ya where ya be, but the choice is yours. Don't come out with a gun in yer hands, or we'll shoot to kill."

I saw the double barrels of a shotgun poke out from the side of the canvas and went to ground. "We'll help y'all if we can, but pointin' a gun at us ain't real friendly." Cotton said from beside me.

"Who are you two?" A male voice from the wagon asked.

"Nate and Cotton Top, two mountain men. We were on our way to the tradin' post when we saw vultures in the sky. The Injuns are long gone, iffen that's what yer scared of, and it's not likely they'll be back."

"You a black man?"

"Yep, I am. Do ya have a problem with that?"

I heard a light snicker, "No, I don't, because all three of us are blacks, too."

A man's head poked from the back of the wagon, and I saw he was smiling to beat the band.

"Ya need to all come out of the wagon and let's move away from this place."

The man jumped from the wagon and asked, "We ain't gonna bury these folks?"

He was a short man, just an inch or two over five feet, and close to thirty or so would be my guess. He was thin, little hair left on his head, and wearing wire-rimmed glasses. He did have a warm smile, so I said, "No, we can't take the time to bury these folks, there are too many of 'em. And, what's your name?"

"Moses, and my kids are April and Thad." At the mention of their names, two young kids stuck their heads from the wagon. April I'd guess was close to ten, and Thad a year or two older. Both had bright eyes and intelligent looks.

"Moses, get yer kids and let's move. While the Sioux are long gone, the smell and sight of a killin' of this size makes me feel a bit unnerved. Let the kids ride my horse and Moses, ya can ride Cotton's for a few miles." I said, expecting the survivors were not only tired, but scared shitless. I knew Cotton hated to walk, but I'd have neither of us on a horse, when we had exhausted folks with us.

Cotton asked, "Any food left from these wagons?"

"Beans, flour and some cornmeal, but that's about it." Moses replied.

"Gather it all up and lets move. Oh, do ya have a weapon?"

"Shotgun and plenty of powder and shot."

An hour later, as we moved slowly over the trail the story came out of Moses, "Me and the kids were out hunting, when I heard the fight start. We'd usually go before first light and often we'd kill a deer and gather plants and roots on the way back to the wagons. This day, we heard shots, so we hunkered down in the woods and waited almost four hours before we returned. When we returned, everyone was dead, the horses were gone and four of the wagons were burning. I pulled what supplies I could from the burning wagons, but lost some stuff. Every single victim had their throats cut and were horribly mutilated. Why in the world would a body do that to another person?"

I didn't like talking on the trail, so I said, "Put a lid on all the talk until we make camp later. Remember, the Injuns that attacked yer wagons are still out here. Moses, if ya want to live to be an old man, learn to keep yer mouth shut as ya travel."

I thought I'd angered him, but he said, "I've much to learn and I understand the meaning behind your words, so you'll hear nothing else from me for a long spell."

The man was true to his word and never said another word, unless asked a direct question. Finally, near dusk, I said, "Cotton, move over to the oak trees on our right and let's get a camp up. I imagine these folks are hungry about now."

Within a few minutes we had a shelter up, fire started, and robes with blankets under a lean-to. Cotton pulled out a bit of deer meat, cut it up, and skewered some pieces with sharpened sticks. As the meat cooked, Moses made a batch of cornbread in our Dutch oven. I secured the horses and walked to a small creek and filled our water casks.

The kids were bushed, because they'd walked a good distance today and after supper, they quickly fell asleep. I glanced at Cotton and he nodded, so I knew it was time to ask Moses a few questions.

"Moses," the man's head came up and he met my eyes, so I asked, "What were y'all doin' travelin' in the Devils backyard? I mean, where were ya headin'?"

He gave a dry chuckle and said, "We honestly had no idea, except one of the men mentioned a Fort Atkinson. See, we used to live in Saint Louis, so we got together and decided to move west. It was a sudden decision too, because slave hunters were working the city and roundin' up whole families, as well as single folks, to take to the South. Anyone who didn't have a master was fair game for the hunters, too. I know of a good dozen folks that were freemen and women that were taken into bondage anyway."

"Couldn't you report it to the police?" Cotton asked and I knew he meant well, but I already knew the answer.

"No, sir, the police wouldn't give a black person the time of day and I think most were glad we were being taken away. Not all white folks give a damn about a black man." He said, and then glared at Cotton.

"Moses, Cotton and I go back for years and he's my partner, so pull in your horns. He's a good man, but has no idea of life of a black person back east. Now, what are ya going to do? I mean, y'all are a good forty miles west of Atkinson right now."

"West?"

"Uh-huh, west. Y'all missed the place completely. Did any of the men with the wagons have any experience in this type of country?"

"Abe, he was out this way in 1820, or I think that's what he said. Most of us were city men, used to working on the docks in Saint Louis, or others, like me, did accounting or were store clerks."

I met Cotton's eyes and he nodded.

"I guess Cotton and I'll take ya to Butterfield's trading post and leave y'all there. From his place ya can hook up with men heading to Fort Atkinson or Saint Louis. Now, some may not want ya along, but most won't give your color a thought. Iffen ya promise to work on the way back, they'll be more likely to take y'all along."

"I won't go back to Saint Louis, so it'll have to be the fort. I don't want April and Thad to grow up slaves, Nate, and I'll do anything within my power to prevent that. I was born a free man and, by God, I'll remain free."

Cotton asked, "Where's the momma for these kids?"

"Sara died of a fever about a year ago. She turned sick one night, fever got high, and by the next mornin', well, I'd lost her." Moses lowered his head and I saw tears on his cheeks.

"Death comes to us all eventually, but be happy knowing ya'll see her again." Cotton said.

Moses didn't reply for a long time, so I asked, "Don't ya believe in Jesus?"

"I believe, except the good Lord and me ain't been on speakin' terms for a long spell."

"Since Sara died, right, and ya blame Him?"

He nodded.

"I imagine you're mad at God because he took yer wife and left ya with two kids to raise on yer own, right? Yer a lucky man, or don't you see that? He could have taken yer whole damned family, only he didn't."

Giving a low sob, Moses said, "I loved that woman, Nate, loved her to death! Now she's gone, and I see her face each time I look at my children."

"Everything dies sooner or later, that's a simple fact of life. I don't know a person in this world that hasn't lost someone they love, but they don't blame God. The Injuns call it the circle of life and it's real."

"Nate's right. Ya need to stop living in pity, get yer shit together and start being a good father to yer children." Cotton said.

"What in the hell do you, a white man, know about how a black man feels? We're just a bunch of damned animals to you people anyway, but we have feelings too!"

"Moses, I warned ya once about Cotton Top. I don't know where in the hell ya get the idea that some white folks don't care and have no idea of our pain, but I can guaran-damn-tee ya that Cotton knows. I've been ridin' with this man for over ten years, so I know exactly the kind of man he is, and ya'd not make a hair on his ass. Ya bad mouth him one more time and the lot of ya will be left to fend for yourselves."

"You'd leave us out here over a white man?" He gazed into

my eyes and I saw him blink rapidly.

"Cotton ain't just *any* white man, he's my trappin' partner and like a brother to me. Now, I suggest, very strongly, that ya keep a civil tongue if ya want us to take ya to Butterfield's. I also think ya owe Cotton an apology."

Before Moses could say anything, Cotton bend toward the flames, picked up the coffee cup and said, "Injuns."

"Good God." Moses exclaimed and I could hear fear in his voice.

"Tribe?" I asked.

"Sioux, maybe."

"Hello, my friends. If you hunger come to my fire and eat. We have meat of a deer, coffee and sugar." I said in the Sioux tongue.

Silence.

After about five minutes a male voice asked, *"I look for white men who steal the land of the Sioux people."*

I thought I recognized the voice, so I asked, *"Dog Barking, is that you, my friend?"*

"It is I, Dog Barking."

"I am known among your people as Big Raven Man."

A warrior walked from the trees, approached the fire, but didn't speak until he sat in the dirt near me. He gave a weak grin and said, *"Big Raven Man, I have not seen you in many moons. I thought your fire might be of the ones who bring families onto our lands. This we cannot allow to happen. Our land has been ours since the beginning of time and we will keep it ours, forever."*

"That is as it should be, for all men. Do you have hunger?"

"No, I am not hungry, my brother." He squatted by our fire.

"Did your tribe kill the raven men half a days ride from here?"

"No, we have seen no raven men in many moons. I have heard Dull Knife and his group counted coup on one hand and four fingers of raven men, but that was two suns ago. The raven men had women, the white man's buffalo, their egg laying birds, and tools to stay on our lands."

"They do not know the customs of the Sioux."

"They will learn or they will die. We will allow no white men or raven men on Sioux lands to stay. Many like you do not stay, but come for the one who swims. Since your kind do not take our lands we are at peace with warriors like you."

"We are going to The One Who Trades and will soon move into the mountains to trap the one who swims. We wish only to travel over Sioux lands and we will use a little of your wood, water, and meat."

Standing, Dog Barking said, *"You may travel in peace over our lands."*

"Thank you, my brother."

"It is nothing." The warrior then walked into the trees and was gone in a few short minutes.

"I thought he wanted our hair." Moses said.

"Just a little small talk. He did say the Sioux will kill everyone who comes onto their lands looking for a place to make a home. He made it clear to me that Sioux land is not free land and they will fight to keep it."

"That's why they attacked us, I guess."

"Yep, but let's forget the Sioux for a bit, because we've been given safe passage. I'm still waiting for your apology to Cotton and I want an honest one, too."

I could tell Moses didn't like what I requested, but he needed to get to safety, so he said, "Cotton, I'm sorry and spoke out of turn. I have never been around any white folks that honestly cared about black folks and I assumed you were like them. I was wrong and apologize for my harsh words."

"I accept yer apology and suggest in the future ya get to know folks before ya start assumin' things about them. Nate and me go back fer years, and he's one of the best men I've ever met."

I said, "Enough said. I'll take the first half of the night and Cotton, the second half is yours. Moses, ya need to get some sleep."

"What about me?" Moses asked.

"Not on this trip. I want to get to know ya better and see how much ya know before I give ya a guard shift. On this trip, ya sleep."

CHAPTER 2

We arrived at Butterfield's Trading Post a week later, during a light rain, and the old man met us on the porch with a shotgun held ready in his hands. He gave me a huge smile and then said, "Light, come in and let me see what I have cooked on the stove."

We all entered and the heat from an old potbellied stove in the corner was overwhelming to me at first. All of us took a seat at the nearest table, as Butterfield made his way to his kitchen. A few minutes later, he returned with bowls of stew and a big plate of biscuits. He placed a pot of coffee in the center of the table, a bottle of rye beside it, and then sat down.

"So, Nate, who are yer new friends?"

"Moses and his family. April is the cute little girl and the young man is, Thad."

Thad nodded as April lowered her head and blushed.

I quickly told the story of the wagons and killings, then asked, "When do ya have some men going back east?"

"It'll be a spell, because I just sent some out yesterday. Next supplies ain't due in until just before fall."

Moses' head came up, he blinked a couple of times and then said, "That's over six months."

"Yep, it is, Moses. I don't get enough business to have a regular monthly shipment, so I resupply twice a year."

Placing his rough cast pewter spoon on the table, Moses looked around the table and asked, "What am I goin' to do? I have very little money, two kids to feed, and don't even have a place for us to call home."

"Don't ya worry about that none," Butterfield said, "I'll put ya'll up in some cabins I have, but you'll have to work to pay for yer board."

"He's an accountant, Butterfield, and not a man that knows

labor." I added.

"Well, then he can help me with the books a spell, help inventory my supplies, and clerk a bit. Then, on the side, he can split some wood, feed the chickens, and milk the two cows I got." Turning his head toward Moses, he asked, "Ya can use an ax and milk a cow, right?"

"I can split wood, never milked a cow, but reckon I can do the accounting easily enough."

"Well, you've got the job, but let me warn ya, and ya as well, Nate. I had a group of rough lookin' men ride in here not a week back, claimin' to be mountain men, but if they were, I don't see how they expect to trap a beaver with manacles. I think they're slave hunters and there was over a dozen of 'em. I'd guess nigh on fifteen or so, iffen I had to guess."

"They've never been this far west that I can remember," I said and remembered as a runaway, I was worth well over a thousand dollars.

"Well, I ain't never hear'd of 'em bein' out this far either, but they're here now for damned sure. The leader of the group was a big man, about your size Nate, with blond hair and beard. The men with 'em called 'em Blackie and his last name was Burke. He looked like a mean sumbitch to me, and the men with him were typical jaspers out for easy money. Another reason I knew they weren't mountain men was they had a pack of dogs with 'em."

"Hell, no mountain man worth his salt would take a dog into the mountains lookin' fer beaver. All it'd take is the dog to bark at the wrong time and ya'd be up to yer ass in Injuns."

"Well, if slavers are in the area, how are ya goin' to explain Moses and his family?"I asked.

"They were only here long enough to buy some panther piss, tobaccer, and powder. What or who I have workin' for me, they don't know and it's none of their business. If push comes to shove, I'll tell 'em Moses and his family are slaves of mine and that'll be the end of it."

"Say what?" Moses replied and started to rise from his chair.

"Sit back down and do the job now." I ordered.

"I ain't no man's slave!"

"Do ya have a better idea than Butterfield's?" I asked.

"Nate, I have my pride and I just— ."

"No man is makin' ya a slave, okay? It's a coverup in the

event the men question ya bein' here. If they think yer owned by Butterfield, then they'll drop the whole thing, because by law they can't do anything. Not that the law they use is any good out here anyway. Hell, we ain't even part of the states."

Lowering his head and shaking it, Moses replied, "I'll do it, mainly to feed my kids, but I don't like it much. But what about you?"

I laughed and said, "I'll be high in my mountains and if they want a piece of my ass, let 'em come for me. I think they'll let go fast enough when I kill a few of the worthless sumbitches. I was a slave once, but never again will chains hold me.[1]"

Butterfield glanced at April and Thad and then said, "Come with me, Moses, and I'll show ya to yer cabin. These young pups of yours are tired and with a full belly, they likely need some rest."

Moses and his family followed Butterfield from the trading post. As soon as the door closed, Cotton Top pulled the cork from the bottle and added a couple of inches to our coffee. I waited, because I knew Cotton well enough to know something was on his mind, but he'd speak when he felt the need. In the mean time, I'd wait.

My wait was a short one, as he said, "I don't like the idea of slavers out here. Hell, this land doesn't belong to the United States, so they really ain't got no legal right to be here."

"True, legally, but if they can gather up a handful of blacks out here and take 'em to the Deep South, they'll make good money. A healthy man like me is worth between a thousand and fifteen hundred dollars a head, as a field hand, while an educated man like Moses might bring a thousand more. Thad would be an easy thousand, and April might fetch well over two thousand."

"Why so much for a woman child?"

"They'd sell her to a sportin' house and since she's young, the owner would make big money until she caught the French pox or got sick on 'em. Sportin' houses are rough on women, no matter their color."

"Ya mean to sit there and tell me, they'd sell a ten year old child to a damned whorehouse? Nate, they'd have to wait for her to grow up first, right? Hell, when I want a woman, I want some bumps and curves, too."

---

1   See *Nate Grisham, Black Mountain Man*, published by W.R. Benton, 2013

"Yep, but they'll wait. Just taking her virginity might be worth a hell of a lot of money to some man. She's pretty too, which means men will line up, money in hand, to use her."

"Ya know, I can't say slavery is wrong, because it's in the Bible, but when white men want to enslave folks like ya and that little girl, it tell's me I might want to do some more thinkin'."

"I'll tell ya one thing, Bible or not, if a man comes—"

The small brass bell above the door *tinkled* and when I looked in the direction, three white men entered. They looked like mountain men, but lacked the tired eyes and narrow waists. I suspected they were part of the slavers, but prayed I was wrong.

I gave them a quick once over and saw the man in the middle was the dangerous one, because he carried two pistols and two knives. A knife fighter is not to be taken lightly, so if they started trouble, he'd be the first one I'd kill.

"Get yer ass up from the table, boy, and get some things I need." An older man on the end ordered and I knew he meant me, but to hell with him.

Cotton and I remained silent, but I thought, *I ain't nobodies boy.*

Walking to our table, the old man leaned over and placed his hands on the table top, and then said, "Didn't ya hear what I just said to ya, *boy?*"

Cotton glared at the man and replied, "Ain't no boys at this table, asshole."

"Why, ya sumbitch!" The man yelled and moved his right hand for the pistol in his sash.

A loud thump was heard, followed immediately by a piercing scream. When I glanced at the table, Cotton's big knife had pinned the man's hand to the top, and blood was starting to pool. Before I could pull my pistol, I heard a shot and the old man fell to the floor, taking our table with him, and started screeching. The pistol the man had pulled flew through the air to land near the counter.

Looking at the other two men, the dangerous one pulled his pistol, except by now my pistol was out, so I swung it in his direction and pulled the trigger. I saw dust fly from his chest, watched him fall to his knees, and then the third man moved toward me with a drawn knife.

I stood pulled my second pistol and pulled the hammer

back, but before I could fire, I heard Cotton's pistol explode. The man was knocked back hard against the door and I noticed he was bleeding profusely from his left thigh. He slowly slid down the door, leaving a trail of red blood, and ended in a sitting position.

"By God, that's three slavers that have learned a few manners." Cotton said.

The man I'd shot was unmoving but both of Cotton's victims were screaming and bleeding all over Butterfield's clean floor.

"Check the two of 'em by the door for weapons and take every damn thing ya find. Drag the one by the door away, too, because Butterfield will be here in a few minutes to see what the shootin' was about."

As Cotton moved, I checked the screaming man he'd shot. I pulled two more pistols, two knives, and a pair of brass knuckles from the man. I saw he'd taken a slug in the lights, so his death would be slow and agonizing, perhaps taking him days to die. I pulled my Green River knife, grabbed the man by the hair and pushed the blade to the hilt into his belly. I then moved the blade from side-to-side, as I twisted it. He have a loud gasp, his feet drummed on the floor, and his eyes grew huge. Finally, his eyes lost their focus, a rattling was heard in his chest, and his bowels voided. At that point I let his head fall to the floor and cleaned my knife blade off on his trousers. I figured I'd done the man a favor.

"The one shot is the chest is dead as hell, but this other piece of shit is still alive. It looks like the thigh bone was broken and he's bleeding like a stuck hog."

The door suddenly swung open and in walked Butterfield. He glanced at the blood and gore and then said, "Well, I see ya met some of those slavers I was tellin' ya about."

"Butterfield, get me some cotton so I can plug this boy up or he'll bleed to death all over yer floor." Cotton said.

Walking to his counter, Butterfield pulled two dirty towels and threw them to Cotton. "Is the bone broken?"

"Uh-huh."

"He'll lose the leg then."

I said, "Not here he won't. Cotton bandage him up and lets put him on a horse. He can just ride back to where he came from."

"It ain't likely he'll survive the trip." Butterfield said.

"Well, that ain't my problem." I walked to the slaver, squatted and asked, "Do you have a name?"

Through tightly clinched teeth the man said, "J . . . Jonas . . . Thompson."

"We're loadin' your ass on a horse and keep in mind, if I ever see ya again, you're a dead man."

"Blackie . . . will kill . . . you. Curtis . . . was his brother."

"Well now, Mister Thompson, which of these dead men was Curtis?"

"The one you . . . murdered . . . with the . . . knife."

"You tell the man my name is Nate Grisham and let him know I'm a runaway, too. Make sure he knows if he wants a piece of my ass, he can find me in the mountains." I said, knowing the only way to end this problem was to kill Blackie, so I wanted him to come after me.

"There, wrapped as well as I can do the job." Cotton said and then stood.

I turned toward Butterfield and asked, "Do ya have any laudanum and whiskey? I think it'd be good to give this feller a little to ease his sufferin' on the way to his friends."

"Ease his pain? Have ya lost yer mind?" The trader asked.

"No, not in the least. I want this man to live long enough to tell Blackie a black man helped kill two of his men. I want the slavers to come after me."

Bringing me a clay jug of whiskey and pint of laudanum, Butterfield said, "Hell, Nate, it's your funeral. I don't understand what yer plannin', but I'll do what I can for ya. Iffen I were ya, I'd just shoot the sumbitch in the head and be done with it."

Cotton took the laudanum from me, gave Thompson a small amount, and then made his way outside with the jug of whiskey. I knew he was tying it to a horse for the man. When he returned, we took the man outside and placed him in the saddle. I started to tie him in place, but then changed my mind, because his survival didn't really matter to me.

I could tell by the injured man's eyes the drug was working, so I asked, "Has the laudanum kicked in yet?"

"Yep, the pain is gone. When Blackie hears of this he'll skin your black ass alive, do ya realize that?"

"He knows where to find me. Thompson, go easy on the laudanum, because they'll need it when they cut your leg off. Besides, it's habit forming and ya don't want to end up with a nasty habit, now do ya?"

"What about the other hosses, guns and money my friends owned?"

"I think ya have all yer goin' to get for this trip. Chalk the loss up as a hazard of your job. Now get your nasty ass out of here before I change my mind and decide to lynch ya instead."

When he hesitated, Cotton said, "Go and do the job now!" He pulled his pistol and the sound of the hammer locking back was loud.

Pulling his horse to the right, Thompson left the trading post at a walk. From what little I knew of doctoring, I figured he'd be lucky to cover twenty miles. *If he dies, now that ain't my problem, is it?* I thought as I moved back inside.

Once we were inside, Butterfield said, "Besides the guns and horses, ya two have a little over a thousand dollars here. One jasper was carryin' about eight hundred and the other a little over two."

"Give the money, as well as the horses, to Moses and his family. Most likely the money came from slaves and it might as well be put to use by a black man."

Cotton met my eyes and nodded in agreement.

"Also, get a rifle outside from one of the horses and give it, along with two of the pistols in here, to Moses. Make damned sure you tell him to keep the pistols where folks can't see 'em. Tell him if he's seen carryin' one, one day he'll have use it. We'll leave a horse for 'em too."

"I'll do that for sure. Now what?"

"Well, bring us another bottle of whiskey and let's see if we can have a few drinks without havin' to kill somebody."

I stayed up late with Cotton, just talking of old times, prices of beaver plew, and nonsense stuff. Now, usually, I'm not much of a talker and it wasn't the whiskey that loosened my tongue. It was just one of those times, we all get them, when I enjoyed talking.

Two hours before sunrise we were on the trail moving toward the high lonesome, only this time we had two extra horses. I'd bought a couple of mares from Butterfield, to replace the one killed by the Blackfoot. One had a huge chest and I was well pleased with her. From the stuff the two dead men had, we'd found a couple of good sheets of canvas for shelters, some salt pork, a little lead and powder. The shirts and pants I'd given to Cotton, because they were too damned small to fit my big frame.

The day dawned beautiful, with a light warm wind, clear skies, and it was one of those rare days when I felt good just be alive. Birds were chirping, rabbits ran across the trail at times, as if playing a game of tag, and squirrels were out looking for nuts and choice grass seeds.

"We headin' up to Baldy?" Cotton asked.

"I've given it some thought, unless ya want to try another place."

"Naw, that's as good as anyplace else."

I brought up a subject I'd been thinking on since Butterfield told us of the slavers, "If those slavers get a hold of us, ya know what they'll do to ya, don't ya?"

He send a brown stream of tobacco juice to the trail and replied, "Yep, kill me most likely. They won't have much use fer a white man who runs with a black man as a partner. How-some-ever, they'll find out I don't kill easy."

I smiled and said, "No, I don't reckon ya do, but watch yer ass from now on, because they'll come for me. Hell, they have to know that we killed two of 'em and sent the other one back a cripple for life."

"Uh-huh, cain't be lettin' no lowly black man do that to three white folks, right?" His eyes danced, filled with mirth.

"Waugh, I'm Nate the black mountain man! I can out fight, out cuss, and out drink any man alive. I'm half grizzly bear, half alligator, and half panther. I can go weeks without water and months with no food."

Cotton sent another brown stream to the dirt, wiped his mouth off with the back of his hand and replied, "Bullshit. Now, enough naybobbin', 'cause we're on a tramp."

The day passed quickly, or so I thought, and I'd been alert for danger the whole ride. I knew it was just a matter of time before those slavers got on my ass, but when they did, I could make them let go quick enough, only that's not what I had in mind.

When those bastards get on our trail, I thought as Cotton pulled into some oaks to make camp, *I'll not stop until I kill every one of those men.*

"I've some beans, already cooked, that Butterfield gave me in some fruit jars, so I'll fry up some bacon and we'll have that fer supper, okay?" Cotton asked as he dismounted.

"That should be good, but do we have any bread?" I asked, since we never had much bread unless it was cornbread.

"He gave me a dozen biscuits."

I chuckled and asked, "That's enough for me, but what about ya?"

"To change the subject a mite, have ya given more thought to those slavers?"

"A bit, but not much. I don't think a one of 'em could find his ass out here, even if he started with his hands in his rear pockets. Oh, they'll want us now that we've killed a couple of them, but I really don't think they have the woods savvy to find us."

As we unloaded the horses, he asked, "Then how do they expect to find runaways, if they don't know where to look? I mean Able has a cabin in the mountains, Luke is trappin' with Short and his group, and Black Billy is, well, hard to say where he is, but it'll be close to women."

"Billy is likely near the Sioux this time of the year, he's taken by their maidens, so they'll play hell finding him. All together, not countin' Moses and his family, there are only about a dozen blacks out here. Give or take a few there might actually be a different number."

"It'd bring 'em some good money."

"Look, Cotton, stop chasin' the Devil around the stump and tell me what is really on your mind. I suspect ya want to take the fight to the slavers, but I don't see a need."

"I don't run good and neither do ya. I thought to put an end to this shit."

"Ain't no need to end it, because nothin' has started. I figure these men will ride around for a week or two, discover the mountains ain't filled with colored folks, and then go back home. I think they're a lazy group, used to chasing folks that are scared half to death, make little resistance when captured, and remain docile once in chains. But, if they come, we'll kill every swinging dick in the bunch."

"I don't like 'em around, is all."

I broke into a loud laugh and replied, "And ya think I do? Hell, I was told many times I was worth good money and I know there's a big reward for me. I also know if they catch me, I'll have a foot chopped off to keep me from running away again. Only, Cotton, I won't be taken alive. I'll fight slavery until my last breath, because I'll die a free man."

We'd been stacking supplies near where the shelter would go, when suddenly Cotton froze and said, "Don't move, and I mean not even a twitch. Less than a foot from your left leg is a coiled rattler."

Good God, not a snake! I screamed in my mind, because I hate snakes, but I replied, "Damn it, do something."

Cotton pulled his pistol from his sash, took careful aim, and when his shot sounded, I moved away as quickly as I could do the job. Looking at the ground where I'd just been standing, a huge rattlesnake was twisting and turning, with its head missing. I felt a shudder go through my body.

"Damn, help me load all of this again, we cain't stay here after that shot. Everybody and his brother knows someone is in the area."

CHAPTER 3

It's well past midnight by the stars and I'm guarding our horses. Unlike some folks, guarding never bothers me much and I like the time alone, so I can do some serious thinking. I'd been thinking of Georgia, the girl and not the state, when I spotted movement about a hundred feet from camp. I picked up a small stone and threw it at Cotton. I thought I'd missed him, because he didn't move, but when I checked a few seconds later, his robe was empty. The night sounds ended suddenly, so something or someone big was in the area.

Whatever is moving is good size, but it ain't no grizzly or painter, or I'd know already. Come on, get a little closer, so I can make out what ya be! I thought as I locked the hammer back on my rifle. As I waited, all movement stopped completely. *It's not a warrior, or he'd still be coming for us.*

Then, Cotton was at my side. Cupping his hands over my left ear, he said, "I think it's a person. Give it ten more minutes and then I'll go check."

I nodded, but thought he was a damned fool, because if it was a person, they were likely bent on stealing our mounts or killing us. It could be a hurt trapper, but that would be pretty rare doin's, since we were scattered to hell back in the mountains, but it did happen at times.

After about ten minutes, with no further movement, Cotton stood and moved toward the spot we'd seen movement. My gut tighten and I grew anxious as I waited some sort of response from him, but many long minutes passed before I heard him call out, "It's a woman. Nate, I need yer help."

I was shocked and thought, *What in the hell is a woman doin' out here? I'll bet I ain't seen five women in the last ten years out here, unless he means a squaw.* I stood and made my way to him, but kept my rifle at the ready. For all I knew, she might be a decoy for an ambush.

When I neared, I saw a black woman lying on her back, and couldn't tell the extent of her injuries. There was a pale moon out, but the light just wasn't enough in the bushes to see well. "She alone?"

"I circled and didn't see anybody else with 'er."

"How bad is off is she?"

"Can't really say right now, but she's lost a lot of blood. Near as I can tell she took a bullet to the upper back."

"Ya take our guns and I'll pack 'er to camp. Once there, we'll build a small fire and see what we have on our hands."

Once Cotton took my gun, I picked the woman up, placed her over my shoulder and made my way to camp. I suspect she might have weighed a hundred pounds, but she wasn't tall either, closer to five feet than six. I placed her on my robe near the fire pit and then pulled my possibles bag around, so I could remove my bandages and such.

When the flames came, I took my knife and cut her blouse from the tail to the neck, and pulled it open so I could see the wound. It looked as if the slug had passed through the meaty portion of her shoulder, only I didn't know if it'd hit bone or not. I pulled the ramrod from my rifle and started pushing it through the hole. I felt it exit clean on the other side.

I turned to Cotton, "Boil me some water, so I can clean 'er up. The bullet passed through clean, so I won't have any bone fragments to clean. While the waters cookin', bring me the whiskey and bottle of laudanum. I ain't never doctored a woman before."

Cotton gave a dry chuckle and said, "They ain't much different than a man, except in certain places. I'll bring one of my spare buckskin shirts too, because one of yours would fit her like a tent."

Granted, I'm a big man, but I was suddenly concerned about treating a woman. *How in the world am I goin' to wrap this shoulder and not see or touch her breasts?* I thought and felt a sudden wave of guilt flood over me.

"Here ya are." Cotton placed the items beside me and then added, "Now, when we wrap her up, just remember, it's got to be done and do what's required. Ya ain't takin' advantage of her or nothin', so keep yer mind clear of any guilt."

I grinned at him and said, "We've been ridin' together too many years, do ya know that?"

"Hopefully the good Lord will give us a lot more years to ride together."

"Now, I'm going to tie a whiskey-soaked rag on the end of my ramrod and push it in and out of the hole, because it's the only way I can clean it. I need ya to hold her down. If she starts to kick up a ruckus, we'll feed 'er a little laudanum."

I tied a rag to my ramrod, poured some whiskey on it, and then slowly inserted it into the path of the bullet. I twisted the ramrod as I worked it into the injury and when it came out the other side, I poured more whiskey on it and twisted it out of her back. While she moaned a bit, she didn't move or jerk on me. Once the ramrod was removed, I said, "Hold her tight now, because I'm goin' to pour some panther piss on the wound and it's likely she'll go ape-shit."

I poured the amber colored alcohol on her wound, but she didn't move at all. It concerned me enough, I felt her neck to see if she still had a heartbeat. Her heart was beating steady, but slower than I wanted to feel.

"Put my knife," I handed my skinning knife to him, "and yours in the fire to heat up. We'll cauterize her directly."

I poured two full cups of whiskey and as soon as Cotton turned away from the fire, I handed one to him. "Drink this, because I think in a couple minutes we'll need it for our nerves."

"Thank ya kindly fer the whiskey."

I didn't reply, but threw my drink back, wiped my mouth off with my hand, and then said, "It looked like a .45 caliber ball hit 'er, but she's lucky. Another quarter of an inch down or to the left and her shoulder bone would have shattered."

"Old Bob Kincaid has a left arm that is useless from a shot just like this-un here. Ya don't know the man, 'cause he lived back home, but he got the injury in the war of 1812. He told me the damned army doctor wanted to take the whole arm off."

"Couldn't he use the arm at all?"

"The fingers worked fine and he could bend his elbow a little, maybe a third of what a normal man could do, but he seemed to deal just fine with 'er."

"The blades will be ready in a minute or two. I want ya to hold her head up, so I can give her a little laudanum. I know she didn't jerk when I cleaned 'er, but I guaran-damn-tee ya, she'll come apart when a hot blade touches her. I ain't seen a person yet that can take a hot knife without jerkin' and screamin'."

"Uh-huh, she'll move." Cotton replied.

I fed her a little of the drug, looked at the fire, and said, "Hand me yer knife and I'll do the entrance hole first. Once I have the knife, ya get on her back pronto, so I can smear the flesh together before the blade cools."

Cotton handed me the knife, quickly sat on her back and held her shoulders to the ground. I placed the flat of the red-white blade against her injury, felt her buck hard, and heard a piercing scream fill the night air. Abruptly, it ended. *Good, she's passed out,* I thought as I pulled the knife from her.

"Let's roll her over and do the exit hole now." Cotton said.

When we rolled her onto her back, her breasts fell free of her blouse and I started to cover her, when Cotton said, "Don't worry none about here titties, we're here to do a job. Now, get that second knife and let's get her fixed up."

"Hold her down," I said as I turned and picked up the hot knife.

When the blade touched her smooth skin, she was motionless and not a sound was heard. I smeared the flesh together and noticed the bleeding stopped immediately.

"Lawdy, what a damned smell." Cotton complained as he poured whiskey into his cup. Taking a gulp, he added, "Now, get 'er wrapped up good and tight. I imagine it'll be tomorrow before we know what happened or how in the hell she got out here."

"I think she got away from those slavers."

"That's likely good thinkin' on your part, because I've never seen a black woman out here since day one. I still wonder why they're out here when there has to be easier slave money to be made back east." I started wrapping some cotton material around her, as Cotton held her up, and in a few minutes I had the job done. I know my face was red and I tried not to look at her breasts, but I'm a healthy man and my eyes were drawn to them like a bug to a light. I then covered her with a blanket, leaving the new shirt and old blouse beside her.

I said, "They have a reason, only we don't know it yet. Mayhap they're after me and decided to gather up all the black folks they can find along the way."

"Well, this creates a hell of a problem now. It looks like in a few days we'll have to take this woman to Butterfield."

"How's that a problem?"

"Shit, all we've done lately is take folks to him an' at the rate we're goin' we'll never get to the mountains."

I laughed and said, "We can leave her, iffen ya want."

Cotton looked at me as if I'd just slapped him and replied, "Nate, I'll leave no woman undefended and alone in rough country. My momma raised me better than that, and so did yours."

"I know that and I was just pullin' yer chain a mite. It'll be daylight in another hour; do you want to go back to sleep?"

"Nope, I couldn't sleep now iffen I wanted to do the job. Come light, I'll head out and make some meat. Since we'll be here a spell, we'll need more meat to eat."

Morning pasted slowly, with Cotton gone and the woman still asleep. Once full light was on us, I noticed our patient was a beautiful woman and I couldn't help but be attracted to her. She was the first black woman I'd seen out here, except for a couple that were killed with the wagons carrying Moses and his family. *Careful, old son, because you're married to the mountains and a woman is the last thing in the world you want or need.*

As I was adding a log to the fire, I heard a weak voice, "Wa —water."

Turning, I saw the woman was awake, "Here's a little, but don't take too much at first. I'll give ya more over time." I held her head up and poured a little from a cup into her mouth.

"Strong. Tastes like whiskey." She said after she'd swallowed.

"It's a mix of about half whiskey and water. It'll help ya sleep and keep the pain level down a mite." I chuckled a little, because I knew the alcohol was strong.

"Thank ya."

I nodded, thought for a second, so I could line up my thoughts and then asked, "What in the world were ya doin' out runnin' around in the woods at night?"

"I was taken by slavers about a hundred miles west of Saint Louis, right off the farm I was workin' on, and the owners were killed. I ain't a slave and never have been, so I was workin' for wages. There was three of us taken at the same time from the place. The Packards owned the place, but they were both shot down like dogs in the middle of the barnyard. After they killed them, they rounded up the three of us, and we moved out here. The leader, some feller they called Blackie, claimed he'd be sittin' pretty once he sold all of us in Mississippi."

"How many black folks does this man have now?"

"Not countin' me anymore, he's got seven."

"How many men with 'em?"

"Nigh on a dozen and some of 'em are blacks, too."

"Huh?"

"Some of the slavers are black men from a big plantation down South. I think they said Mississippi and they're lookin' for a runaway named Nate Grisham."

I chuckled, but felt a shudder go through me, because they were now a direct threat. "What's yer name?"

"Susan, but everyone calls me Sue. My last name is Wilson."

I nodded to her and said, "Glad to meet ya, Sue, I'm Nate Grisham."

"Why, you're the man those slavers are lookin' for, ain't ya?"

"Uh-huh, I'm the very one. Listen, I ride with a white man and he'll be back soon. He's out huntin' right now, so when ya see 'em, relax, he's good people. He's the one who found ya last night and iffen not for him, you'd be dead."

"Not all white folks are bad."

"Yep, and not all black folks are good either. We'll give ya a few days to heal a little, then we'll take ya to a tradin' post where you'll be safe for a spell." When she didn't answer, I glanced at her and saw she was asleep.

Cotton soon returned and immediately had the meat hanging from a rope in the tree. He walked to the fire and asked, "She come around at all yet?"

"Yep, she surely did." I then told him what I'd learned.

Removing his hat and running his hands through his filthy hair, he shook his head and said, "I say, by God, we take the fight to them. Now, I won't argue slavery with ya, but they have no legal right to a one of those folks. Hell, they killed them Packard folks just to take the black folks working fer 'em and that's murder."

"Cotton, I'm leanin' yer direction and pretty damned hard now too. See, if they didn't have those black folks, I'd simply go so deep into the mountains they'd never find my ass. After a month or so, they'd get fed up with the mess and go back home. But, they've killed folks, taken folks into bondage that are free, and who knows what else they've done. I'm a runaway and I expect someone on my ass, but free folks are just that and don't deserve slavery. As soon as Sue has healed enough, we'll take 'er to Butterfield."

"The Bible speaks of slaves and the makin' of slaves, but this ain't about slavery any way ya look at 'er. It's about killin' and kidnappin' folks and that's against the law in the old states. We need to put a stop to 'er."

A week later we rode to Butterfield's, but Sue wasn't sitting very straight in her saddle. I knew she was in pain, but after the first sip of laudanum the night she'd been shot, I'd given her no more. Laudanum grew to be a habit and while women often took it to settle their nerves and such, I didn't think anyone needed another habit. I'd handed her a bottle of whiskey before we'd started the trip and told her to drink it as needed for pain. So, it was either pain or drunkenness that had her sitting crooked.

The door to the trading post opened and out stepped Butterfield with a double-barreled shotgun in his hands. One of his eyes narrowed while the larger grew large before he asked, "Now, what in the hell are ya doin' back here so soon?"

I nodded toward Sue and said, "This woman wondered into our camp about a week back with a bullet hole in her back. Seems the slavers ya told us about shot her when she made a run for freedom."

"Well, bring 'er in and let's talk. This place has had a bunch of visitors since I saw y'all last time."

"Really?"

"Really. Now get her in here and put her in the last bedroom on the left. Then, get yer ass out to a table so we can talk."

Sue moaned as she dismounted and while I offered to carry her, she refused, saying, "I'm weak, not helpless. I'll get to bed under my own power."

Cotton and I walked to the bedroom with her and I placed the half empty whiskey bottle on a nightstand. "If ya get to hurtin' take a long snort of the whiskey."

Sitting on the edge of the bed, Sue said, "I hear ya."

I could see the pain in her almond shaped eyes, but whiskey was the best we could do for her. I turned and walked to a table. Butterfield brought a bottle of good rye to the table, pour all of us a drink and then said, "Those slavers never did come back here. I mean after ya killed them two."

"Maybe the man with the bum leg didn't get back to 'em." Cotton said, and took a sip of his drink.

"Maybe, but a group of a dozen white men showed up about three days after y'all left here. They were a mite pissed and lookin' fer the slavers."

"White men?" I threw my drink back and thought, *this grows stranger and stranger as time passes.*

"They claimed to be a posse out of Missouri, some little no-name town, which I don't rightly remember. Anyway, they said these slavers had killed and raped across the state as they'd traveled out this way."

"We know of two deaths, but heard nothing of rapes." I said.

Lowering his head, Butterfield said, "And, of course they stole the property of some men and they wanted to return the slaves to their rightful owners."

Cotton said, "Ain't this a mess. Sue told us the blacks were all free folks and none of 'em slaves."

"Cotton," I said and gazed into his eyes, "would you admit to bein' a slave? Ain't a one of those folks likely free, but they will be iffen I have my way."

"Ya know I won't fight to free a one of those folks. I just can't do the job, but I'll fight to see justice served for the killin's and rapes. What happens to the black folks after that, well, it ain't none of my business, now is it?" Cotton said, and then took a gulp of his whiskey.

Butterfield had been quiet, but then said, "Moses and his family must really be free because the men in the posse looked 'em over closely, too. I told 'em I'd hired Moses to do odd jobs around the place and they seemed to believe me, because they left 'em alone."

"Where are these white men now?" Cotton asked and then filled his cup and mine. Butterfield had hardly touched his drink.

"Out there," Butterfield moved his arms in a wide circle, "lookin' for the slavers, I guess. The last time I laid eyes on the boys they were movin' north on that old deer trail. Hell, ain't neither one of them groups know shit about the mountains and it's likely the damned Blackfoot will kill 'em all."

I sipped my drink and processed all the information I'd learned and it was likely the Injuns would kill some, if not all, of the men. But, that also meant the black folks would die too, and they were the innocents of the whole mess, runaways or not. *We need to find these slavers and free those folks. Once free, we can take 'em deep into the woods and hide for a spell. If they are really runaway slaves, then that posse will return them to their masters, so we need to avoid them. Damn me, even after we free 'em, what in the hell will I do with 'em in the long run? I need to slow down and do this one step at a time. If I get in a big rush, folks might die on me.*

Finally I asked, "Did ya get the name of the big bug?"

"Tom was all I hear'd 'em call the man."

I threw my drink back and said, "Butterfield, I need some supplies. Give me a pound of lead, the same in powder, another jug of whiskey, a half-pint of laudanum, and ten pounds of salt pork. I also need a small cask of black powder, the rough grade."

The trader moved behind his counter and asked, "Gonna do some blasting with that black powder, now, are ya?"

Chapter 4

This morning is cold, not just nippy, and as I ride, my capote is wrapped tightly around me. While it feels like snow, I know it's too late in the season for snow, until we get higher into the mountains. I hope it'll warm up as the sun moves, only I ain't sure, and can see my breath. I'm pissed too, which makes the ride uncomfortable to me, because Sue is riding with us. Just before we'd left Butterfield's, she'd come out of that bedroom demanding to go with us, but she wouldn't give me a good reason.

Finally, I'd said, "Iffen ya can't give me a good reason, by God, you'll stay here with Butterfield."

I was sitting at the table and she was standing beside me, when she said, "They raped me. Not all of them did, but two of them. I figure they owe me in blood for what they did to me." I'd expected her to break into tears, but that didn't happen.

I thought then, *just as I'm thinking now, ain't no woman that deserves to be raped.* Revenge is a healthy thing, if done after a great deal of thinking about it, but it's not a job to be rushed. Sue was entitled to her revenge, any woman would be in my eyes, only I wasn't no babysitter. She'd have to skin her own snakes.

"Okay, ya can go with us, but I'm warnin' ya right now, tear that shoulder open or fail to keep up and I'll leave yer ass, and then you'll go under. I've blackened my face, I have, and I'm on a tramp!" I warned her and meant every word.

"Huh?" She asked.

Cotton laughed and replied, "He said, if he leaves ya, you'll die. He also said he's goin' to war and he's rushin' to a fight. See, Injuns use the color black to show death, so by Nate sayin' he'd blackened his face, he meant goin' to war."

That was early this morning and so far she'd kept us with

us. I glanced back at her and she pissed me off by smiling at me and waving. *Damned women, it don't matter their color either, because they're all in control. Men, even big men like me, often do things for women that they'd never do for another man. See, they know those of us who've been raised right, can't refuse a request by a woman, as long as it ain't illegal. Back in the states, it looks like the men are in control, but they really ain't and my Injun buddies out here are in the same mess. I know who really runs a teepee, too. Red, black, yellow or white, the women are the real bosses.*

Cotton rode up beside me and whispered, "Nate, pull yer head out of yer ass and start watchin' the trail. I ain't sure what yer thinkin' on, but right now ya need to be payin' attention to ambush sites or we'll not live long on this tramp."

I nodded, grew mad as hell, but realized he was right.

Our noonin' was near a small stream that ran out of the mountains; the water was as cold as ice. I'd led the horses to drink and then moved to our small fire. Cotton was grinning and when I neared he said, "Nate, Sue here was tellin' me she loves this country."

I squatted, poured a cup of coffee and said, "It's pretty enough, but rough as hell. If the Injuns, weather, big critter, or bad man don't kill ya, an illness will."

"I suspect it's little different than back east," Sue said.

"Bullsh—."

Cotton interrupted, "It's a mite rougher out here, 'cause it's virgin land and people are few and far apart. Help ain't next door and may be hundreds of miles from where ya are."

"Well, I could get used to livin' here."

I chuckled and replied, "If the Injuns attack us, you'll change yer tune fast enough."

Sue looked me straight in the eyes and asked, "Nate, why don't ya like me? You've done nothin' but give me a hard time all day today."

I gave a loud sigh, shook my head and replied, "Sue, it has nothin' to do with ya at all, but the fact yer a woman. And, a hurt one on top of that. The men we're after are a rough lot, ya know that, so havin' ya along puts a damper on the whole she-bang. Now we have to worry about yer comfort and safety as well as our own."

Her eyes narrowed and her face flushed, just before she said, "Bullshit. I'll pull my fair share of the load, don't ya worry about that, and as far as comfort goes, I don't need anything the two of ya don't have."

"Well," I said with a smile and then continued, "then, Cotton put the fire out. From now on, until we locate the slavers, we'll have cold camps. I want no fires and no hot food."

Cotton objected, "Nate, she's a woman."

"Woman, my ass, she want's to be treated like one of the boys, so by God, we'll treat 'er like one of us. Ya spend the rest of this break checkin' her wound. I want to ride in twenty minutes."

For the rest of the day I got a cold shoulder from both of them, but I honestly didn't care. If we'd been alone, there would have been no fire at our nooning, and from now on, we'd move like we usually did when after a group of coldblooded killers.

Two hours after nightfall, I pulled into some pines and said, "We'll rest for the night here and leave two hours before sunrise. Iffen ya want to eat, there's creek water and jerky. Sue, ya take the first guard and wake Cotton near midnight. Cotton, ya wake me two hours later."

Cotton instructed Sue on what was expected of her and positioned her back in the woods, off to the side of us. Once finished with her, he joined me under the tarp we'd strung up between two trees.

"Sweet on 'er, are ya?" He asked from the darkness.

"Nope, but what makes ya think I am?"

"Nate, I been ridin' with ya for over ten years, and I can see it plainly with my eyes. Oh, ya might not admit it yet, but give it time."

I snickered and replied, "Yer wrong partner, this time fer sure. Now, don't misunderstand me, Sue has a lot to offer the right man. She's smart, good lookin' and got all those interesting bumps and curves, except I'm married to the mountains."

I expected a response, but instead all I got a low snore. The man had gone to sleep on me as we talked. I rolled over, closed my eyes and knew nothing until Cotton touched my ankle later.

"Any movement?"

"Nope, quiet on my shift. The night sounds are all there, so we're safe enough for now. Wake me, iffen ya get tired, because Sue went to sleep on guard. Between her injury and the whiskey she's drinkin' fer pain, she wasn't up fer the job. I don't want her pullin' guard until her shoulder is healed."

"When did she fall asleep, or do ya have any idea?"

"I never sleep when a new pilgrim is on guard and she's the first woman we've ever had, so I watched her fall asleep about an hour after ya rolled over."

"Cotton, ya snored while I was talkin' with ya."

"I must have woke up pretty damned fast then, because I saw her head nod. I woke her up, chewed her ass a little and sent her to bed. It was a dumb thing we did and all because ya want to be a hard-ass."

"She asked for it."

"I'm sleepy and won't argue with ya about it right now. How-some-ever, I want ya two to make up and get over this, so I can travel without worryin' about gettin' my throat cut one night. Understand?"

"I understand and agree with ya. I'll speak with her about this in the mornin'."

Cotton wrapped up in his robe and I heard him grunt, so I knew further conversation was over for the night. I picked up my rifle and moved to a huge pine tree where I could see the camp and horses. I spent a few hours thinking about nothing serious, but near daylight I spotted movement.

I moved to Sue, placed my hand over her mouth and whispered in her ear, "It's me, Nate. Yer fine, but take yer shotgun and move into the trees. I've got movement near us. Nod if ya understand."

She nodded, I removed my hand from her mouth, and once she'd started moving, I tapped Cotton on the ankle. His eyes flew open and he looked at me. I placed my hand behind my ear and knew he'd realize the night sounds were gone. He nodded and began to move.

By the time I'd moved to my position behind a log, both of them had gone to ground. I scanned the area, but didn't see a blamed thing, I mean nothing. Glancing up at the sky, I figured it was an hour to sunrise, so I'd wait.

It was right at false dawn when they hit us, and they hit us hard.

A loud scream filled the still morning air and three warriors ran toward our camp. I heard the blast of Sue's shotgun and all three fell to the ground screaming. Two others broke from the right and two from the left. I knocked one warrior down with a shot from my Hawken, and missed another with my pistol. I pulled my last pistol and killed another. I was reloading when I heard a pistol shot, another shotgun blast, and was struck hard by a running brave. I lost my rifle as I was knocked to the ground, so I pulled my knife and quickly stood. The warrior was Ree and in the dim light I could clearly see the hate in the man's eyes. He was an experienced knife fighter, because his knife was held with the cutting edge up and he was crouched over   ready to leap at me.

I took a swing at him, but before I could move, he'd sliced my forearm a good six inches. While not a killing wound, I'd lose blood and gradually grow weaker. I heard a noise behind and off to the side of the warrior and when I glanced in that direction, Sue walked from the trees.

She raised the shotgun, fired both barrels and the indian was kicked hard to the ground where he screamed. She immediately began to reload.

I neared the downed man and saw the shotgun had almost blown him in half. I grabbed his oily hair, and raising his head, I cut his throat. Blood spurted into the air and he started to choking on his own blood. Finally, his feet drummed on the dirt hard for a few seconds and then his body suddenly went limp. He was dead.

I heard Cotton call out, "Iffen yer okay, sound out with yer name."

"Nate and Sue, we're both fine."

"Well, I ain't and need some help. I took an arrow to my thigh."

Sue turned to me and asked, "Do ya want me to make a fire?"

"Hell, no, woman. We have no idea if other warriors are around. We'll wrap Cotton up and ride for a few hours. Then, we'll stop, doctor him up proper and move some more. We'll likely spend the next twelve hours in the saddle. Ya gather up all our gear and supplies while I get a bandage on 'em good and tight."

"You're a hard man, Nate Grisham!"

"This is a hard life, so if ya want to stay out here, toughen up a mite. Now, move like I told ya to do. I want to be on the trail in ten minutes."

It was well after noon before Cotton rode up beside me and said, "I need this arrow out and now. I can feel the edges of the head cutting my skin as we move. I've put up with the pain as long as I can. Iffen I go much longer, I think I'll pass out."

"Ya should have said something earlier. Pull off to the right, into those oak trees."

Once in the trees, I had Sue take her shotgun and keep an eye on our back trail. Cotton stretched out on his robe as I looked him over. It appeared stuck in his flesh, so I pulled a pair of pliers from my possibles bag, and placed them on the robe. I poured two cups of whiskey and handed one to my friend.

"I can't cauterize ya yet, not with the Ree mayhap on our asses, so that'll have to wait until this evenin'. Ya finish the whiskey and I'll pull the arrowhead out."

He threw his drink back and handed his cup out for more. I refilled his cup and then poured some whiskey on my pliers and skinnin' knife. I was ready to start the dance.

"We'll give ya a couple of minutes for the whiskey to start workin', then I'll get that arrowhead out of ya."

"Do 'er now and don't worry about me. Do the job right and I'll handle the pain."

I handed him a rolled up piece of rawhide and said, "Bite on this, 'cause this is goin' to hurt ya a mite."

As soon as the hide was in his mouth, I began to wiggle the arrow shaft and cut around it with my knife. I heard a few moans, but I knew he'd not scream. Less than five minutes after I started, the bloody arrowhead and broken shaft were both on the ground beside him.

Cotton looked rough, his forehead was damp from sweat, but he smiled and said, "Wrap me up tight and let's get movin'. Iffen ya don't mind, I'll keep the whiskey on my horse."

A few minutes later I helped him mount and called out to Sue. Once she was on her horse, we began to move again. About three hours later she rode beside me and asked, "When are we stopping for the night?"

"We'll stop for the night in the morning," I said, because I felt someone following me and I always listened to my inner voice.

Cotton said from behind us, "I hear'd ya, so don't worry 'bout me none. As long as I have this jug of panther piss, I'll get along fine."

About two hours after midnight, Cotton started leaning in the saddle and I knew it was time to take a break. I still had to take a hot knife to his nasty hide, but he was already pretty roostered, so it'd be better to do the job now.

"Pull over to the right near those trees. We'll move into the woods about a hundred feet and make camp. We'll have a fire long enough to cook, make coffee and for me to cauterize Cottons injury, then the fire goes out."

Cotton took to the hot blade like everyone does, poorly, and it was rough for a few seconds. He eventually passed out, so I decided right then to spend the night in this place. I put the fire out and covered it well with soil.

"Cottons a tough old coot, but we'll spend the night here and leave mid morning tomorrow."

"Do we need a guard here?"

"Yep, we need a guard here. The only place I don't have a guard is the trading post and tonight ya keep yer butt awake, too. Ya nod off like last night and I'll send ya back to Butterfield. We have to be able to trust each other out here and I mean completely. I know yer tired, we all are, but one of us has to be awake at all times or we'll lose the horses at best, or our hair at worst."

"Who goes first?"

"I'll watch until I get tired."

"Why not me?"

"Do ya want the truth?"

"Uh-huh."

I grinned and said, "Because I think yer more tired than I am. I'm semi-used to this kind of travel but it's not likely you've traveled this many hours or distance during one day in yer life. Plus, I still don't trust ya to not fall asleep."

"Back to me fallin' asleep, huh? This is hard on me and I'm not used to stayin' up at all hours."

"That's because most of ya back east are soft, like newly baked bread, and ya have all those comforts in yer homes, like beds and chairs. Well, let me tell ya, out here, ya root hog or die. So, which is it goin' to be with ya?"

She stood in the subdued moonlight, I knew she was pissed, and then she said, "I'll root right along with the rest of ya sonsofbitches!"

"Good, now get some sleep, because I'll wake ya in a few hours."

As soon as she wrapped up in her robe, I moved under a large tree and leaned against the trunk. I could see a million stars sparkling in the clear sky overhead and as I watched, a star fell from heaven with a long tail. My momma used to tell me, "Every time ya see a falling star, someone has just died." Now, I won't call my momma a liar, but seemed to me there should be thousands of stars falling on any given night. Hell, I was lucky to see just one a year.

Most of my shift was uneventful and I was a tired man. Finally, I woke Sue and moved to my robe. I was asleep in seconds. I have no idea how long I'd been asleep, when I felt a tap on my ankle. Looking up, Sue cupped her hand behind her ear. I listened, and heard nothing.

I had her stay in camp as I neared the trail we'd been on earlier in the day, I spotted a line of Injuns. It was still dark, so I knew they'd not see our tracks, and overhead I noticed a few clouds moving in fairly quickly. I heard one brave say something and another laugh, then a loud voice commanded in Ree, "Quiet!" I counted twenty-five warriors, then waited and saw two more bringing up the rear.

I hurried back to camp and said just above a whisper, "We need to move and do it now. If these clouds don't turn to rain within the hour, those Injuns will see our tracks."

"Can we move Cotton?"

"Cotton, can ya travel?"

"I'll sit lopsided, but I can move, need be."

"Help me pick 'em up and tie him to his horse. We're goin' to have move fast, with few breaks taken, for at least twenty-four hours."

I'd just finished tying Cotton to his horse when I heard a noise and turning, I saw a pair of Ree warriors rushing straight for me. I pulled my pistol, fired and the man on the left fell screaming, then I heard the loud boom of Sue's shotgun and the last one fell, unmoving, the whole front of his shirt stained crimson. I ran to the screaming brave and pulled my knife. My shot had taken him in the middle of the chest and he was dead, only he didn't know it yet. I squatted and stuck the full length of my knife under his ribcage and pulled it from side-to-side as I twisted the sharp blade. His eyes grew huge, he attempted to speak, but the words never came out. A few seconds later his eyes slowly lost their focus and I heard a loud sigh—he was dead.

I ran to my horse, mounted, turned and said, "We'll go overland for a few hours, it may buy us some time."

CHAPTER 5

Over the next three days we rode hard and fast, stopping every few hours to allow our horses to rest and to check on Cotton. Sue's injury was scabbed over and had no signs of festering, so I knew she'd live and Cotton was looking good as well. We'd had very little sleep, less than three hours a night and I knew we needed a break, so Sue and Cotton could rest a mite. Neither had complained, but I could see fatigue in the red rimmed eyes of both.

"Pull off to the right, into those cottonwoods and we'll make camp." It was near dusk, misting rain, and I'd had enough running. "Get a fire started, along with a hot meal, as I scout behind us a ways. Keep yer fire small, no larger than a coffee cup, and while that doesn't sound like much of a fire, it'll do to work with for now."

I spent the time until darkness checking our back trail and making a few traps that might, if we got lucky, kill or injure an Injun or two. I suspected they'd see the vines I used to trip the traps and simply ride around them. It's real hard to kill an Injun with a trap, but it has been done a time or two in the past.

When I neared our camp, I smelled no smoke and saw no light, and it was full dark. At first I thought I was in the wrong place, but then I heard Sue say, "That's close enough. Who are ya and what do ya want?"

"Sue, it's me, Nate."

"Come."

Either she was getting better or I was starting to show my age. As I neared, I saw she'd made the fire near one of the taller trees and the smoke was being filtered by the many branches.

"How's Cotton?" I asked, knowing he had to be in pain.

"His wound looks good, no red lines or foul odor, but it must be hurtin' 'em somethin' fierce. He took a big swig of whiskey right after you left and then fell asleep."

"What's in the pot?" I pointed to a cast iron pot on a bed of red coals.

"Cornmeal mush and I'll fry a bite a salt pork in a few minutes."

"We out of meat?"

"Uh-huh and I had to throw away what little we had because it went bad on us."

"Yer meal will do fine. Many a time I've had nothin' at all and other times I've ate dog, snakes, bugs, and even a few bird eggs with the baby birds already formed inside the shell. That was poor bull, that was."

"I ain't eatin' no damned dog."

"If we visit some Injuns ya might eat dog. Often they'll kill a young pup for honored guests and that's the only way ya want to visit Injuns—as an honored guest. By the way, how's yer shoulder?"

"I took a nip of whiskey, once I pried it out of Cotton's hand. Lawdy, did he have a firm grip on that bottle."

"He's in some serious pain right now, and our ride didn't help 'em much."

"I would have passed out, tied to a horse like that, and sufferin' like he was."

"Sue, he's a mountain man and fully understood why we had to get away fast and hard. He would have ridden like that until he died, and never complained."

"Who are we lookin' for right now, the slavers, or the white men that are lookin' for them?"

"It doesn't really matter which we find first. See, both are threats to not only me, but every black person out here. What you need to remember is we —"

"Hello the camp! We're white men, can we come to your camp?" An unrecognized voice called from near the trail.

"How many are in your bunch?" I called out, suspecting it was either men from the posse or some of the slavers.

"There are four of us, countin' me."

"Hold all yer rifles high in yer left hands when ya come. Agreed?"

"Ya ain't a very trustin' cuss, now are ya?"

"Do as I said, or ride on, because it doesn't matter much to me."

The voice chuckled and then he replied, "We're comin' in,

just don't shoot."

"A word of warnin' here, if ya move too fast or let yer rifle lower, I'll blow a hole through your breadbasket. Understood?"

"Oh, I understand alright, and we'll do as ya say. There used to be a bunch of us, but we ran into some Injuns a couple of days ago and lost a few men."

"Enough naybobbin, come!"

Turning to Sue, I said, "Get yer shotgun and move into the darkness."

"I have a pistol ready," Cotton said from his robe.

I moved into the darkness and cocked my rifle.

Four men approached our small fire and I heard Cotton order, "Put the guns on the ground behind the log. Then, put yer pistols on the ground near the coffeepot. When yer done doin' that, go sit in the dirt by the fire. Now, when y'all sit, line up in a row real nice, so our shotgun can take all yer asses out at one time, need be."

Once the men were sitting by the flickering flames of the fire, I walked from the darkness and sat on the log. Looking over my shoulder, I called out, "Keep the shotgun pointed at these jaspers until they answer a few questions."

I looked the men over and they weren't slavers, because each was clean and wearing bib-overall or canvas trousers. The shirts weren't homespun and looked to be store-bought. They dressed like a bunch of store clerks or shopkeepers, so I was confused. Two were of average size, nothing special about them, but another was short and as thin as a rail. The last man, who I noticed was wearing a tin star over his left breast pocket, was a big man, except most of it looked to be fat.

"Who are ya and why are ya in my mountains?" I asked, gazing into the eyes of the portly man. I assumed he was the leader.

"I'm John D. Jackson and I'm the ramrod of this outfit, or what's left of it."

"Well, ya answered half of my question."

"Nigh on two months back a bunch of slavers came through Springfield, Missouri and on their way out of town they stole every Nig—"

I pulled my pistol, cocked the hammer back and said, "Finish the word and I'll kill ya where ya sit. See, I don't care much fer the word."

His face turned crimson, his eyes narrowed, but finally he

said, "They took every darkie they could find, even the ones folks had freedom papers on. I'm the Sheriff there and while I was roundin' up a posse, I got word that they'd done the same thing in Saint Louis. Hell, a couple of those men raped some white women too. I come to fetch 'em, so I could take 'em back to Springfield fer a hangin'."

"If they'd raped black women, then it wouldn't have been a big deal, right?" I felt myself growing angry.

"Look, mister, I don't know who ya are, but blacks are property where we come from and we cain't have folks takin' things that don't belong to 'em."

"So, if you find these slavers, what'll ya do with the black folks that are free men and women?"

He thought for a minute and then said, "Why, I ain't gave that much thought. I guess we'd take 'em back to town and sell 'em."

"Jackson, yer a lard ass with no idea of what in the hell yer even doin' out here. I've half a mind to shoot ya where ya sit."

"Kill 'em all," Cotton said, and I heard his pistol hammer lock back.

"By God, ya cain't talk to me like that! I'm the law and what I say goes! Besides, yer colored and ain't got no say in this at all. You're just a piece of property, boy!"

My shot was loud in the night air and Jackson fell back to the ground. The other three men started to move, but Sue fired one barrel into the air.

"Nobody move." I said and then added, "Jackson took a slug to his right arm is all, but iffen y'all get froggy, I might aim better the next time." I then pulled another pistol from my sash.

Jackson sat up, his blood covered left hand over his injury. He glared at me through narrow eyes as he said, "I'll kill ya for this."

"Ya threatening me, Jackson? How in the hell did ya ever get to bein' a lawman, as dumb as ya are? See, I take threats seriously and normally I'd just shoot yer ass, but since ya ain't that smart, I ain't goin' to do that right now." While Jackson was mad, the other three looked scared shitless and they were the smart ones in my eyes.

"Make 'em ride shanks mare home." Cotton said from his robe.

"I can't do that, Cotton, they'd be dead in a day, but I have to do something."

"Jess let us go and we'll head back home right now. I mean right this minute, mister." The thin man suddenly spoke.

"I'd like to do that, but I honestly don't trust Jackson. See, I think he'll try to kill me, because he said he'd do the job."

"Well, I never said shit. I don't want no part of any of this anymore. You let me and the boys leave and like I said, we'll head back this minute."

I think he's telling the truth, but Jackson is still a problem, I thought, but said, "Okay, all four of ya can head back to Missouri territory directly, but by my rules. Either do as I say, or we'll start shootin'."

"Hell, yes, I agree and I promise ya, we'll head back tonight."

"Get all yer clothes off except yer long-johns. That means no hats or boots, too. Come on, get undressed. All of ya except Jackson."

"What about me?" Jackson asked, and now I could see fear in his eyes.

"I want you as naked as the day ya were born."

"What? By Damn, I'm an officer of the law and demand ya treat me as such."

"There ain't no law out here and Mister Lawman, yer authority ended when ya left Springfield, or did ya forget that? And, by the way, any black folks ya see out this way, they're free don't ya see? Yer damned slavery laws only cover the states and this land is unclaimed and untamed, as well. Now, ya either get naked, or I'll put the next ball through yer worthless head. Which will it be? Now, I hope ya'll tell me to go to hell, because I ain't killed a white man in over a week."

"He ain't pullin' yer chain either Jackson, so iffen I was ya, I'd start to shed some clothes." Cotton said in a serious tone.

"I'll do it, but iffen ya ever enter Springfield, I'll lock your black ass up! I'll not forget this."

As the man started undressing, I said, "I seriously don't think you'll make it back home, because I'm keeping all yer guns, but iffen ya do, you'd better think twice before ya tango with me. I'll take a lot of killin' and ya lack the sand."

Once the men were undressed, I said, "Okay, Cotton, ya keep 'em covered while I go get their horses. If one of these men sneezes or farts, blow a hole through 'em. Shotgun, stay where you are!" If Sue stayed in place I knew the men wouldn't move much, because I know no man, me included, who isn't scared of a scattergun.

Ten minutes later I was back with two of the horses and all the gear, including saddles from the other two horses, which I'd left tied by the trail. I added a few knives, shotguns, and clothing to the pile near the fire. Taking my time, I made my way to the log, sat, and then said, "Jackson, ya have two horses for the four of ya. I left ya one pistol with enough lead and powder to load it twelve times. I strongly suggest ya avoid all Injuns or trouble. Now, one at a time, turn and go to yer mounts. Once there, ride double or walk, it doesn't matter to me, but start down the trail. I'm only goin' to say this once, so listen very carefully, if I ever see any of ya again, I'll kill ya on sight. Now, Jackson, since yer the leader, move toward the horses."

He glared at me and I could feel his hatred, but he turned and started walking. He'd be lucky to ever reach Missouri territory and I was doin' him no favors, but I just didn't have the desire to kill the man. *Yer in for one hell of a rough trip, Mister Jackson,* I thought as I kept my pistol pointed at the man's back.

When the last man left, Cotton released the hammer on his pistol and Sue walked from the woods. She stood by the fire and immediately reloaded her spent barrel.

I walked to the horses and said, "I'm going to follow them a ways, just to make sure they move away from us."

"Use some caution, because they've been ridiculed and most men don't take that well." Cotton said and then took a sip of whiskey from a cup.

"Shotgun, ya keep guard until I get back," I said and then mounted my horse.

Sue laughed and said, "Hey, I like the new name."

"By God, the name fits, too." Cotton said.

I chuckled, tapped my horse gently and began to move toward the trail.

A few minutes later, in the faint moonlight, I saw the prints of two horses moving down our trail and I prayed that they'd not run into the Ree that'd been following us. If they did, the fight wouldn't last three minutes.

I followed the trail for over five miles, before turning back for camp.

When I neared our camp I saw no one, so I said, "Come out, it's just me, Nate."

"Are they gone?" I heard Sue ask from behind me.

"Yep, or at least were, only they might double back on us."

"That won't happen." Cotton said as he sat up from behind the log. "Ain't no grit in those men, and every damned one of 'em had no reason to be out here."

"Murder and rape is a pretty good reason, in my book, Cotton, but they're city men and should stay there."

"Will they get back safely?" Sue asked.

Cotton spurted, "Who gives a shit?"

"No," I replied, "I don't think they'll make it back, unless they have some really good luck. If they hole up during the day and move only at night, they might make it to Fort Atkinson, and from there they could travel with some other men toward Saint Louis."

"How bad was Jackson hit in the arm?" Sue asked.

"Well, he was hit pretty solid from what I saw by the firelight. I imagine at some point they'll have to take his arm off, because I'm sure the bone was shattered. They've one knife I left on a horse and if it don't fester on 'em, he'll live."

Sue sat by the fire and said, "You're a hard man, Nate."

I smiled. "No, I'm not hard at all, but I do have my personal honor and integrity. I'll not allow either one to be insulted. See, Sue, out here a man is what he wants to be, and he can be anything, as long as he can maintain his integrity and keep his honor. Why, without 'em, I'd not be Nate Grisham, mountain man."

"I can believe this, but your life must be hard."

"Missy, I was a slave once, before I ran away, and that life was much harder than this one. See, at that time I owned nothing, except my thoughts. Now, I am a free man, I worship God in my own way, I help those who need it, and I can be what I want to be here. Oh, I know I can die any day, but I'll die a free man."

"Nate, how about ya bein' my helper fer a minute and bring me another bottle of good whiskey?" Cotton said from this robe.

CHAPTER 6

Morning dawned chilly, with a brisk light wind from the west, and gray clouds that looked low enough to touch. Sue was sitting under a tree, her shotgun over her knees, and Cotton was sleeping, breathing deeply. I suspected the whiskey put him under, but until his thigh healed, I'll let the man drink. Seeing me up and moving, Sue nodded as I walked for the trees to do my morning toilet.

When I returned, I blew life into the gray ashes in the fire pit, added a few small pieces of dry tinder and then filled the coffee pot with water. Adding coffee grounds to the water, I sat the pot near the flickering flames to boil. I then sat in the dirt and watched the flames.

Sue neared and sat on the log.

"Looks like rain today or snow, but it's a little late in the year for snow." I made small talk as I waited for the coffee to brew.

She said, "About a half hour before daylight I heard gunshots to the south of us. It only lasted a few minutes, maybe two or three, and mayhap six shots all together."

"Why didn't ya wake me?" I asked, as I stood and dusted the knees of my trousers.

"Ya wouldn't have been able to do anything. I suspect Jackson and his bunch ran into trouble."

I shook my head and replied, "I suspect Jackson and his bunch met death. Instead of moving last night, it sounds like the fools stopped for the night. Most likely they ran into the Ree who were on our asses."

"What now?"

I gave thought to Jackson and his men. While I didn't like Jackson one bit, his men hadn't wronged me, except by riding with him as the leader, so they deserved what they got. *This might be a quick and easy way to teach Sue about Injuns and how mean they are in a scrap.*

"Did you hear me?"

"I want ya to saddle two horses and we'll go see what happened. Now, I have to warn ya, if the Ree caught those men and killed them, it'll not be a pretty sight."

"What about Cotton?"

"I'll wake him in a minute. Don't worry about him, he's a curly old wolf and will be alive long after ya and I pass on to the other side. Now, saddle the horses like I asked ya to do."

I woke Cotton, squatted and told him what was happening. I then added, "Iffen we're not back by noon, it ain't likely we'll ever be back. While we're gone, no fire, hide the best ya can, and we'll be back shortly."

"The Ree have moved on, so it ain't likely they'll come lookin' for us now. Odds are, they took what little Jackson had and returned to the village."

"Mayhap they did and then again, we'll not take any chances, okay?"

"I hear ya, but when I hide I'm takin' all the whiskey with me."

I slapped him on the shoulder, stood, and said, "We'll be back in the bit."

"The horses are ready to go." Sue said from the picket line we'd strung between two trees.

I walked to the horses, mounted and said, "Keep yer shotgun at the ready, all the time. While I suspect the Injuns are gone, I could be wrong."

She nodded in reply.

The trip to the location of the gunshots was short, with the distance less than three miles, but not right down the trail. Clouds dropped even lower and light misting rain began to fall. It was easy to track the posse, due to them riding double; the tracks were deep and a blind man could have followed them.

"They moved off the trail here and went into the woods. Now, I have to warn ya, any bodies we see will be scalped and mutilated."

"I . . . I can handle it."

"Stay behind me and scan the area closely as we move." I spoke, and then moved toward the camp.

The first body I saw was the thin man, and he'd taken three arrows to the chest and his now naked body was mutilated.

Both arms and legs had long deep cuts, his throat was cut, and he'd been scalped. His unseeing eyes reflected pain and fear.

I heard Sue puking, but said nothing.

Two other men were found pretty much the same way, except one had an injury from a lance in his chest. The men had body parts severed.

"Look, there is something in that man's mouth."

"Uh-huh, it's his pecker and balls. He must have made a poor fight of it, since all of his injuries are to his back."

Once again I heard her puking and realized we'd not found Jackson's body yet. "Spread out a bit and look for Jackson. He might have gotten away, but I doubt it."

Minutes passed and then Sue called out, "Oh, my God. Jackson is over here."

The Ree, and the arrows all had Ree markings, had played with Jackson a little. They'd strung the man upside down, from a big oak limb, and then started a fire under his head. His face had a melted look to it, his hair was gone, and his once white face was now black from the heat of the flames. He'd been opened from crotch to breastbone and long lines of gray purplish intestines lay near his head in the dirt. His privates had been removed and like the others, deep cuts were seen on both legs and arms.

As Sue leaned from her horse to puke once more, I said, "We've accounted for all of them, so let's head back to camp. We need to move today, and do the job pretty quick."

"You're not going to bury these men?"

"No, we'll not bury these men. The main reason is, I feel Injuns and think they're watching us right now."

"Good God, do you really think so?"

"I do, so turn yer horse slowly and follow me back to the trail. Once on the trail we'll waste no time returning. Once in camp, I want everything loaded and us gone within twenty minutes."

As we walked our horses toward the trail, riding side-by-side, I fully expected to be attacked any second and stomach felt like I had a badger gnawing on it. I scanned the countryside, only I didn't really expect to see anything amiss. *If they want us,* I thought, *they'll attack when we reach the trail. The area near the trail is wide open, so be ready then. Or, they might think we'll lead them to a larger group, so they might just follow us.*

At the trail, I spotted movement off my right, so I pulled the hammer back on my rifle, which I'd laid across my knees. I said, "Sue, move behind me and do it now."

"Trouble?"

"Uh-huh, directly, too."

I heard a loud war cry and four Ree broke from the brush. I fired, knocked one brave to the ground, pulled my pistol and heard it misfire. Casting my useless pistol to the ground, I pulled my last pistol, lined up a warrior's chest and squeezed the trigger. The man fell screaming and kicking. I heard Sue's shotgun and another warrior fell, but without making a sound. The last warrior held a lance and when he neared my horse he threw it at me.

I ducked, but the lance knocked my hat from my head. I fell from my horse, hit the ground hard, but quickly gained my feet. Pulling my tomahawk and Green River knife from my sash, I watched the warriors eyes as he neared. He hated me and I knew this was a fight to death, with no quarter expected by either side.

"Ya stay out of this one, Sue. This is twixt this warrior and me. Iffen I lose the fight, then blow his ass away with yer shotgun."

"I hear you."

The Ree rushed me and I felt the sting of his blade on my left arm. I grinned at him and said, "Is that the best ya can do, young pup?"

He replied in Ree, I guess, because I don't speak the language well. When he neared I kicked the knife from his hand and moved in close. He was an average size feller, but I'm a big man and wrapped my arms around him in a bear hug. I slowly began to squeeze. He groaned and moaned, as his feet kicked and his body quivered. I began to embrace the man as hard as I could and his moans turned into screams. Suddenly, I heard something snap, his body fell limb, and blood began to seep from his mouth, nose and ears—I'd broken his back. *Damn me, iffen ya don't die hard,* I thought as I threw his body aside.

Hardly out of breath, I picked up my hat, dropped pistol, mounted and said, "Let's ride and do 'er now. I want to move and do it quickly."

As we moved, Sue asked, "Why were those warriors there, when they'd already killed those men?"

"I think they weren't done mutilatin' those jaspers and our arrival put a stop to their fun."

"Why do they do that, I mean cut those men up like that?"

"Well, Injuns don't do it because they enjoy mutilatin' folks, only some might savor it, but the main reason is they believe they can meet men they've killed once they die. Now, don't ask me why, but they think they can fight men they've alreay killed and if they're mutilated, they'll enter Injun heaven that way. So, a man with hands missing, or legs cut off, isn't much of a threat to them in the afterlife."

"I doubt God would allow violence in heaven."

"They don't believe in a heaven or God as we know them to be. They call God the Great Creator or The One Above, or a number of other names. They don't have a Bible, so they're not Christians."

"Savages."

"Perhaps, but I think not. They pray daily, bathe daily, and feed the widows and kids. They have a government of sorts, and they are kind to those they call family or friends. It's unfair for us to judge them against our beliefs, because theirs works well for them."

We were close to our camping site, so I added, "Enough chatter, let's get everything loaded, including Cotton, and move."

The next day, as we moved up a winding trail on the side of a steep mountain, a warrior stepped out and stood in our path. I immediately recognized him as Shoshone and as far as I knew, they were a fairly peaceful tribe, and I spoke a little of the tongue.

I stopped my horse and said in Shoshone, *"Hello my brother, do you hunger?"*

"I have no hunger. Why are you on Shoshone land?"

"I look for two fingers and two hands of white men. The are takers of my people, the raven ones."

"You are known as Big Raven Man among my people, are you not?"

"That is true. Have you seen the white men?"

Many long minutes of silence followed my question and then, finally, the warrior said, *"Come to my village and we will speak to our chief. He has words for your ears that you must hear."*

"We're going with this man to his village," I said to Sue.

"Are we going to die?"

I chuckled and said, "No, these folks are good people and we're safe enough. The chief may know something about the slavers." I realized she'd had no idea what the conversation had been about, I thought and then said, "Cotton, did ya get all of this?"

"Most of 'er. I got enough to know we're goin' to the village." He said to me, but to the warrior he said, *"Lead the way, my friend and we will speak with your chief."*

The warrior said something I didn't understand and a good twenty or more braves stood from the brush and trees. I felt a shiver go down my spine as I thought, *Good God, I only saw this one man. If it'd been a fight it'd been over in less than a minute.*

The inside of the lodge was dim and it took a few minutes for my eyes to adjust. The structure was made of woven mats placed on support beams and then covered with dirt. A small fire burned in the center and a middle-aged man sat by the flames on a blanket. As we slowly approached the fire, my eyes began to see much clearer, and I noticed the chief was indicating for us to sit on his right side. I sat beside the older man, then Cotton and finally Sue. Not a word was spoken for many long minutes, as a pipe was packed with tobacco, lighted, and then positioned to each main compass heading. Finally, it was raised and lowered to indicated the sky and earth. The chief took a puff of the pipe and then passed it to me. When the pipe reached Sue, she coughed from the rough kinnikinnick tobacco, and passed the pipe back to the chief.

He tapped the pipe bowl onto his open palm and then sprinkled the tobacco in the dancing flames of the fire. He then placed the pipe on the blanket beside him. It grew silent once more.

Finally, the chief asked, *"Why do you search for the men who have the raven people?"*

"Would you not search for your people if they were stolen by others?"

"Yes, and I would kill those who took them as well."

I nodded.

"We have seen your people and they are but two suns from this lodge. My scouts tell me some of the takers are also raven men, so it is confusing to my mind how this can be."

"Raven people are like the tribes. We may look almost the same, but there are differences that only we can see. To you and The People, a raven man is a raven man, but they may not belong to the same tribe, so they are not the same."

The chief nodded in understanding and then asked, *"Will you kill these men who take your people?"*

"Yes, we will kill them."

"I see only three fingers of you, but many of the others. How will you kill them when they are many and you are few?"

"Like The People, we will do what is required to save our people, and their numbers are not important. We will hit them many times, always killing in small numbers, until they too are few. We have the Great Creator on our side and I have dreamed we will return our people."

"You have much medicine. But, let us speak of other things for a few movements of the sun."

"As you wish, father." I called the chief father out of respect for his position.

"You are known to us as the taker of the flat tailed one who swims, but others now cross our lands who have no interest in furs. Others make lodges on our lands and this is strange to us. Can they not see we live here and the land is ours? They rip the soil open so the land cries in pain and for what reason? Some look for the yellow rock, but others just make row after row of torn soil."

"They are farmers and they open the soil to plant seeds to grow food."

Silence as the old man gave thought to my comment.

"If they plant seeds, then they must plan to stay on Shoshone lands for a long time. They come with the white man's buffalo, birds that give eggs, and wild pig that they have

tamed. Do they not know they are on our lands?"

I have to watch my ass here, or I'll get a bunch of folks killed, I thought and then said, *"It may be that they do not know this is Shoshone land. They come, see no people, and think the land is good, so they stay."*

"My heart wants to think your words are true, but my mind tells me they are false. Do they not know that all land is claimed by one tribe or another? What is not Shoshone land is Crow land, or Ree land, or the land of other tribes. To take the land and not offer something in return is not a good thing."

I gave his words time to process in my mind and then said, *"Father, I do not know the minds and hearts of others. Can your brother speak for you? Do all warriors think alike when making war? I can not control others, but only my small group. We are only moving over Shoshone lands, in search of my people, and have no need of your lands. We carry nothing to stay on any land and all we have are weapons of war."*

"You men of the mountains have been among us many seasons and never stay on our lands. You come during the moon of falling leaves and you are gone once the moon of hunger has passed. But, others do not leave. I fear one day my people will grow tired of having our lands taken, and blood will flow like a river over Shoshone lands."

Damn, how do I give an answer to that? I wondered, but replied, *"A chief must always think of his people first, above all things. I hope the red river never flows, but I fear one day it may."*

"Would you like the people to help you get your people back, Big Raven Man?"

Lawdy, I don't want the Shoshone in this mess or the government will surely hear of it in some manner. I thought and then replied, *"I have had a powerful dream and a white buffalo told me I must do this battle with only three people. The buffalo told me to walk a sacred path and I would get my people back, but if I did not follow the path, many would die. I would like the Shoshone to show me where the men are and I will do battle with them."*

Giving me a solemn look, the chief said, *"As I said, your medicine is strong. Not many warriors dream of the white buffalo and you must walk the exact path given to walk. To move from that path may anger the Creator. I will respect your wishes. In the morning, before the birth of a new day, scouts will start with you and show where the white men are. Once your people have been spotted, they will watch, but not join in your fight."*

"Thank you."

"Now, one of the women will show you to the lodge that will be yours. This woman will also cook for you and see to your needs."

Once in our lodge, I explained my conversation with the chief to Sue, and she was surprised I didn't ask for help. "Sue, if these warriors help us and word gets back they've killed whites, the army will come in here and start killing. See, most folks from back east doesn't know a Shoshone from a Crow or Sioux, and they'll kill the first Injuns they run into. That will make the victims angry and they'll kill the first whites they see, because all whites look alike to them. It'd become one big killing circle."

An older woman entered, ladled out stew in wooden bowls and handed them to us. As soon as we were eating, she left.

Sue was really putting away the meal, when she suddenly stopped and asked, "What's the meat in this stew? It's good, but I can't place it."

I laughed and said, "Do ya remember a conversation I had with ya a while back about bein' the guest of honor when visitin' Injuns?"

"Of course, we discussed— "

"Foods, remember?" I took another bite of my stew.

As I chewed she said, "Oh, lawdy, no!" She started to gag as she gained her feet and moved toward the entrance.

Cotton laughed and said, "I reckon yer gal friend don't like the thought of eatin' dog, huh?"

"She's not my girlfriend."

"Well, ya could do worse. She's got all them bumps and curves, sharp as a tack, and as pretty as they come."

I laughed and replied, "Ya know I'm married to my mountains, so forget it. She's a city girl and not one to live the life we live out here."

"I don't know 'bout that, because she's damned good with that shotgun she carries."

"She is at that, but our life is not something I'd share with any woman. I like her, but don't love her, and that's important to me."

"Well, take 'er fer a roll in the robes then."

"I'll let that comment slide, because you've been in the

whiskey for about a week. Ya know me better than that, so change the subject."

Cotton took a long drink from his bottle and then said, "If we're leavin' before dawn, I'm goin' to sleep. And, I was just pullin' yer leg about Sue."

CHAPTER 7

Two warriors rode out from the village with us, but one immediately moved to ride about three hundred feet in front of us. The other rode beside me, and his eyes were constantly scanning the woods around us. I glanced overhead and saw clouds to the west of us, but not enough to concern me. Then, looking behind me, I saw Sue and then Cotton. Cotton was healing well and had reduced the amount of whiskey he drank each day a great deal. I noticed a stiffness in his leg, but figured over time it'd get back to normal.

We rode all day and a little before dusk, the warrior who'd been in front returned and led us to a good camping spot off the trail. Our meal was a deer the lead Injun killed with his bow earlier in the day and the meat was fine. We ate, then banked the fire, and all but the guards went to sleep.

The night was uneventful and I awoke remembering I'd not been awakened for a shift of guard. Making my way to the warriors by the fire, I asked, *"Who did the guarding last night?"*

The largest of the two braves said, *"Broken Bow and I guarded because we were not sleepy. We let our friends rest."*

"I thank you."

"Eat, and then we must leave. By the end of this sun, we will be near the men that keep your people. We will leave you then."

I nodded and replied, *"This I expect."*

The two warriors walked to the horses and Cotton said from the fire, "Ya know why them boys didn't wake us up, don't ya?"

"Yep, they didn't trust us to do the job right."

He laughed and said, "Well, I cain't say I blame 'em one iota, either. We had the best guards we could've had and ya know it, too."

I thought for a second, poured a cup of coffee and then asked, "Ya really up to this trip?"

"Not really, but I always finish what I start. It sounds to me like these slavers need a new job and those that don't want to look for work, we'll kill."

Sue was sitting beside the fire as well, sipping on coffee, and hadn't said much. Finally, she said, "They're a rough group and they'll die hard. I know because I've seen the bastards up close and personal."

"Little lady," Cotton said, "they cain't be no harder to kill than a damned Blackfoot and I've kilt my share of them over the years."

I saw movement near the trees and noticed one of the warriors waving for us to come to the horses, so I said, "Gather your gear and lets ride. If things go well today, we'll be near the slavers by dusk."

The clouds I'd noticed yesterday slowly moved toward us all day and by noon, they were overhead. There came a sharp crack of thunder, a gentle wind, and then a light rain began to fall. I pulled my hat down lower and continued to ride, knowing the Injuns wouldn't slow down unless it turned into a full blown storm.

Within an hour the wind was howling madly, and we moved back into some pines to make camp. While it wasn't cold, the rain fell harder now and the three of us had a hard time putting canvas up for shelters. As soon as our gear was stored under the primitive structures, I handed out jerky for us, while the Shoshone ate pemmican. I'd been out west for years, but had a hard time getting pemmican down my gizzard due to the fat. To me, it was like eating a grease ball, and I retched each time I ate the nasty stuff.

After we ate, everyone relaxed as much as possible to wait until the storm blew over. I pulled out a book and started reading. Cotton carved on the block of soft pine, while Sue watched me reading. Finally, I asked, "Do ya read, Sue?"

"Some, but I don't read much. I'm not very good at it, I guess, and don't see many books."

"Ya don't need books to read. Hell, I know many a mountain man that reads newspapers a year old, labels on can goods, catalogs in outhouses and just about anything that has print on it."

"I can't form the words and really don't know a big bunch

of words to start with. The Bible confuses me with all the thee and thou stuff, so I don't read it at all."

"Then why do ya speak so good?"

She laughed and replied, "Nate, back in Missouri I was hired to greet folks visiting the Packard's business and direct them to where they could get service. Mister Packard sent me to a school in Saint Louis for over six months, so I could learn to speak well."

"And, they didn't make ya learn how to read?"

"Readin' wasn't needed for the job, just talkin'. My brother Joshua is still employed by the company, and he was trained to do sums and keep the books."

I dog-eared the book I was reading and asked, "Would ya like to learn to read?"

She thought for a few minutes and then said, "No, I don't see where I need to read. I can read well enough to get by and have no interest in books."

Lawdy, how can she think like that. Books are the doorway to the world and full of excitement, I thought. *A person can learn so much from a book, even a bad one.* I finally said, "My offer stands if ya change yer mind later."

"That's not likely to happen, because once we collect the people the slavers have, I'll be returning home."

"Ya could learn a lot in that time, so if ya change yer mind, let me know."

Near midnight the winds and rain stopped, and looking up at the sky I saw the stars with no clouds. I hoped tomorrow would bring fair weather.

I spent a restless night, for no particular reason, and twisted and turned all night. As a false dawn was starting, I got up, started a fire and put the coffee on to brew. Of the two warriors I saw nothing, but that wasn't uncommon and, actually, if I'd seen them I would have been surprised. After making water, I returned to the fire and sat on a big rock.

A few minutes later Cotton joined me and said, "Leg's stiff this mornin', but the deep pain is gone. I think it'll take me a couple of months to get over the injury."

I simply grunted, not in the mood to talk, and I'm not much of a talker to start with, well, not like Cotton.

"What's got yer goat this mornin'?"

"I slept poorly."

"That'll do 'er fer me every single time. Ya ain't worried

about these slavers are ya?"

"No, not really. We'll deal with them when the time comes." I pulled the coffee pot from the fire and filled my cup. When Cotton raised his cup I filled it as well.

"We need to wake Sue and get ready to ride. I like the idea of finding those men in full daylight better than at dusk."

"Sue, ya need to get up."

"I hear ya and I'm awake." She stood, stretched, and then headed for the woods.

Cotton said, "She'll make some man a good wife, don't ya think?"

"Maybe, my friend, but it won't be me. So don't start on my ass again."

He laughed.

Sue returned and asked, "What's for breakfast?"

"Coffee." I said.

"No food?"

"Nope, I'm wanting to find those men before we have a hot meal. Once we locate them and move back a ways, we'll have a hot meal." I said and then added, "Here comes one of the warriors now."

Broken Bow walked to the fire, poured a cup of coffee and added eight teaspoons of sugar. He smiled after his first taste and said, *"We'll be close to the ones you seek when the sun is at its highest."*

"Good." I replied, and then picked up the small bag of sugar and gave it to the man. *"You may keep this as a sign of my friendship with you, Broken Bow. I will give Man Killer a small bag of tobacco as a gift."*

"I have no gift to give you in return."

"Your gift of taking me to the white men is enough. I thank you for helping me, and will call you and Man Killer brothers from this day forward."

"Man Killer will feel as I do   honored. It is but a small thing we do for you. All Shoshone would like to be called brother by Big Raven Man."

I shrugged and replied, *"I think it is not a small thing you have done. You have saved me the trouble of finding the man and that is worth something in return."*

"Come, we must ride now."

From the brush, I watched the slavers feeding their captives and suddenly felt a hatred I'd not felt in years. I tried to brush my anger off, but it remained smoldering just under my conscious thoughts. All the feelings I'd experienced as a slave flooded over me, with deep anger, fear, and frustration being the most apparent. I felt tears on my cheeks.

Broken Bow looked at me and asked in sign language, "Why do you cry, my brother?"

"I cry for my people," I lied using sign, except it was true in a way, because no man should be a slave to another. Simply seeing the slavers brought back horrible memories for me that had been locked inside of my mind for years, perhaps waiting for such a moment to come out.

"You are a true warrior. All warriors should feel the pain of their people, but most do not. I feel I have seen a sacred thing here today."

"It is nothing. Come, we must return to the others."

We moved like ghosts and were soon back at our camp, about two miles away in a dense grove of pine trees. I sat on a log near the fire as I told what we'd seen. I was less emotional now, having realized I was here to help the captives, but I could still see the whip in the hand of the white feeding the captives. Never again would the sharp bite of a whip touch my skin.

"We counted a baker's dozen slavers at the site and eight black folks. I also saw one woman that looked to be as white as ya are Cotton, which has me confused, because she wore chains."

Sue looked over the rim of her coffee cup and then took a drink. A second or so later, she said, "That's May, and she has very little Negro blood in her, maybe a fourth or less. Lookin' at 'er, you'd swear she was white."

Cotton asked, "She's a white woman, then?"

I shook my head, "Not by law, she ain't. Anyone with a tenth of black blood is a slave."

"She was a free woman, because I worked with her at the Packard's place. She took care of the baby and worked in the kitchen. She's a good woman, but she'll never have much, just like most of us."

Her words angered me, but I kept my big mouth shut. A person, regardless of color, could be something, if they wanted it badly enough. Of course, it's hard for some folks to understand the need to move out west or up north to be truly free. Some lacked the courage, while others lacked the funds to move.

Cotton asked, "How are we going to do this?"

"Tonight, once it grows late, we'll move among the slavers and instill some fear in them."

Cotton smiled, because he knew what I had in mind.

Man Killer said, *"My brother, we must return to our village. We would stay and watch the fight, but we feel the village needs us. If you have need of us, send someone."*

"When do you leave?"

Standing, the warrior said, *"Now."*

"May the Creator of All Things protect you both on your return."

The two men turned and moved toward their horses. As they left, I felt a little more vulnerable, knowing we were now on our own. Cotton and I have seen more than just few rough times, so I knew I could depend on him. So far Sue measured up well, but it remained to be seen if she had the sand needed in a real belly to belly fight.

I picked up a stick and started drawing the layout of the camp I'd seen and said, "The slavers were all in this area and the captives over on the east side. The fire was in the center, I saw no guard, and the supplies were stored here. Now, listen closely my children, because I'm going to tell you a tall tale of how we'll make their night one of pure horror.

It's a little after midnight and I've circled the slaver's campsite twice. While the moon was out, I had few fears because I'd seen no guard at all. Using sign, I spoke with Cotton, "No guard."

He cocked his head to the side and his eyes grew large as

he asked in sign, "None at all?"

"None. I counted thirteen men in the group and they are still positioned where I showed you earlier today with my drawing in the dirt."

"You still want to go in alone?"

"Yes, I will go alone, you scatter horses. We cannot help the captives yet."

He nodded and then turning to Sue he whispered, "Stay here. Cover us with the shotgun."

"You go left, I will go right." I signed.

We moved forward, avoiding sticks or twigs that would snap if stepped on and it was slow moving. I knew Cotton would wait for me to finish my chore or be discovered before he'd release the horses. I stopped at the edge of the camp and looked everything over closely. Nothing was out of place and I still saw no guard.

The men were scattered all over the place, and I could only guess where they were by the lumps in the darkness. I made my way to the first man and it surprised me when I saw he was black. I quickly clamped my left hand down hard over his mouth and cut his throat with my right. Blood spurted into the air, and I could feel the wetness on my hand and smell the coppery scent in the night air. His body jerked and quivered for a few minutes, then his bowels emptied, and he grew still.

The second man was a portly white man, with an empty whiskey bottle beside him. *By God, this is one hangover he'll never have to face,* I thought as I dropped my hand over his mouth. His eyes flew open, he saw me for sure, but before his hands could move, my knife tasted blood once again. He twisted and turned violently, to the point I grew worried he'd awaken the other men. I plunged my knife into his chest three times, feeling him stiffen with each thrust of my blade. Blood was still flowing freely from his severed throat when he finally stopped moving.

The next man was huge, bigger than me, so I skipped him and selected a tall skinny man. As my hand came down, his eyes flew open, saw me, twisted his head and shrieked. I brought my knife down with all of my strength and it entered his soft belly. The knife thrust brought a horrendous warbling scream from him.

I glanced around, saw a man about to stand, then heard a shotgun blast. The pellets struck the man in the head and he fell to the ground unmoving. I crawled into the darkness behind me. The shotgun boomed once more, then a pistol shot was heard near the horses.

From the camp a voice yelled, "The horses! They're after our horses!"

"Injuns!" Another voice screamed.

Cotton gave a loud Sioux war cry and it echoed through the trees. A few seconds later Sue yelled something, but I wasn't sure what in the hell it was, only it didn't sound like no Injun I ever heard before.

From the camp came one, two and then a third pistol shot, only I had no idea what in the hell they were shooting at. I know they can't see me, and Cotton is long gone. Sue, if she'd followed my orders, was headed back to our camp by now. I decided to hang around a while and see how these men reacted to our attack.

"What kind of Injuns took our hosses, Blackie?" A black voice asked.

"Red injuns, ya damn fool. Now how in the hell am I suppose to know?"

"I told ya we needed a guard! Didn't I tell ya we needed one, huh?" A different voice said.

"Ya mention guards one more time, Adair, and so help me, I'll shoot yer nasty ass where ya stand! Do ya understand me?"

"I hear ya, Blackie, and I'll not mention it again, but come first light, we have to get those hosses back or we're all dead. Hell, we'll not cover ten miles out here without a hoss." Adair said.

"Good idea, Adair, ya and Cummin's can go after our hosses then."

"Me? Hell, why me?" I could hear the fear in his voice.

"Simple, it was yer idea and ya pissed me off. Now, check the men and let me know who's been hurt. Rufus, throw some wood on the fire so we can see a bit better. Kill anyone too badly injured to ride."

Adair broke out laughing and said, "Ride what?"

As I watched, Blackie ran to the man and cold-cocked him with his pistol barrel. Adair collapsed to the dirt and lay unmoving.

"The next sumbitch that gives me a hard time I kill, understood?" I could feel the man's anger and knew no one would answer him; hell, he didn't expect a reply.

Rufus had the fire burning, then moved among the forms on the ground. He shook his head at each one, until he came to the man Sue'd shot. He moved to the side of the man, squatted, and said, "Looks like four dead and one injured."

"Can the injured man ride." Blackie asked.

"I'll ride."

"Ya'd better be able to ride, Jones, or I'll personally kill yer ass."

"I just told ya I'd ride."

"Nathan, ya and Rufus check our cargo and see if any were killed or injured." Blackie sat in the dirt by the fire, lifted a clay jug, and took a long swallow. Once done, he wiped his mouth off with the back of his hand and placed the jug at his side.

"We don't have anybody hurt among the prisoners." Rufus reported.

"Not a one? Now, ain't that strange?"

"Not when ya think about it. These red bastards are always marryin' runaways, so mayhap they plan to mix 'em in the tribe."

"By God, now that's an idea. From now on, we'll use them as a shield when we sleep, and I want guards out at all times. Wilson, move yer ass out a ways and keep an eye on us."

I smiled, because Wilson would be mine once he moved into the woods. Wilson was a thin black man, almost as dark as me, but a good foot shorter. He spat a brown stream of tobacco juice into the dirt near the fire and said, "I'll go, but I don't like 'er none."

"Who," Blackie raised the jug and said in anger, "gives a shit what ya like or don't like? Ya do what I say or I'll just add yer black ass to the captives."

"Marst Wilson wouldn't like that much, iffen he found out about it."

"Just get yer ass out there and leave me alone. Every damned thing is goin' wrong, and y'all are dumber than a basket full of horseshit. I just wanted to come out here long enough for things to cool down and to get Grisham. I get my hands on that big boy and I'm two thousand dollars richer!"

Mumbling, Wilson moved for toward the darkness and straight for me.

CHAPTER 8

Wilson made enough noise to wake the dead as he bulled through the brush and moved right for me. I remained motionless, knowing he'd never see me unless I moved, and smiled when the man sat on a log not three feet in front of me. *What was it this man said? Something like, Marst Wilson wouldn't like that much, so this man must be a slave. I wonder if he'd do this job if he had a choice? Let me find out,* I thought as I pulled my knife.

I moved swiftly and in a matter of seconds, had my arm around Wilson's neck and my knife point near his kidneys. I whispered, "Ya a slave? Use yer head to answer me. One sound and I'll drive the blade home."

He nodded.

"Ya gatherin' up black folks because ya want to do the job?"

He shook his head.

"Did yer master tell ya to do it"

He nodded again.

"Do ya want to be free?"

He nodded with enthusiasm.

"Now, I'm goin' to let go of yer neck, but if ya scream or make a noise and I'll shoot yer ass. Do ya understand me?"

He nodded once again, so I removed my knife, put in back in my sheath, and took his rifle.

I released him and said, "Move off to yer right and keep movin' until I tell ya otherwise. Ya got any bitches or complaints and we'll talk about 'em later; now move."

When we neared camp, I called out, "Sue and Cotton, it's me with another man."

"Damn, ya scared me being gone so long." Cotton said as he neared our small fire with his rifle held at the ready.

Sue walked from the darkness and said, "I figured ya stayed behind to listen and learn some things."

I smiled at her and replied, "Why, I did just that. This jasper is named Wilson and claims he's a slave bein' forced to do this job."

"I know 'em, and he's a slave." Sue replied.

I pushed Wilson forward near the fire and commanded, "Sit in the dirt."

I poured a cup of coffee, took a sip, and heard Sue say, "He's a slave, or so he claims. I've not seen him mistreat anyone, but he wasn't friendly, either. When May and I were raped, he had nothing to do with it, but the bastard didn't stop it, either. As far as I'm concerned, ya should have cut his throat."

"Since you've never been a slave, Sue, I'll pretend I didn't hear that last sentence. See, a slave ain't got much choice in what he does or doesn't do. He does what he's told to do, no more or no less. How long do ya think he'd have lasted standing up to those white men all alone?"

"It's doesn't matter! A real man would've died before he'd watch a woman raped."

Wilson lowered his head, and I suspected he was ashamed.

After a few minutes of stillness, Wilson said, "Sue, I wanted to help ya and May, too, but iffen I'd done a thing, they'd have killed me. I don't mean nothin' to Jackie and the rest, and ya know that as well as I do."

"You ain't much of a man in my eyes."

Wilson sobbed and replied, "Yer spoiled. Ya ain't never felt the sting of a whip on yer back, watched yer babies taken away, or had yer momma sold down river. The last slave Marst Wilson had with this bunch tried to runaway and do ya know what they did to him? Huh? The chopped one of his damned feet off and I had to hold the man as they slapped some hot tar on the stump. He lived, but he ain't worth a shit no more as a man."

"Okay, that's enough of this crap," I knew they could keep arguing all damned night, if I allowed it and I had some serious thinking to do.

Cotton asked, "How many men are left now?"

"We killed four and Wilson is here, so that means eight of 'em are still with the group."

"Well, they won't find no horses until daylight and they'll not find all of 'em anyway, or so I'd guess."

I thought for a second and then replied, "They don't need but eight horses now and we released many more than that, so they'll find enough."

"What are ya goin' to do with Wilson?" Cotton asked, as he looked at the man with disgust.

"I ain't decided yet, but I don't plan on killin' 'em unless I have to do the job." I looked at the skinny man and asked, "Do ya have a family back on the plantation?"

He shook his head and said, "I'm alone."

"What's goin' on here? I mean, I can understand ole man Wilson looking for his runaway slaves, but why the rapin's and killin' of others for their slaves?"

"I ain't rightly sure, but I hear'd Marst Wilson and Marst Grisham talkin' one day, years back, and Blackie had the idea of headin' into states and stealin' black folks. He claimed there was a fortune to be made with slaves and nobody in Mississippi would listen to no colored folks who claimed to be free. They been doin' this fer years now, but the brains and money 'hind it all is Marst Grisham. This last time, Blackie's plan was to go to Saint Louis, get supplies, steal all the black folks he could get his hands on, and then move west."

"Why west? Why not return to Mississippi?" It didn't make sense to me.

"Seems Blackie had some folks west of Saint Louis he had to get revenge on, and he wanted to end it all on this trip. This ain't the first time we've done this. Hell, they been stealin' folks for over ten years, but only a couple at a time."

"Ain't no money in taking one or two people at a time, is there?" Cotton asked.

Wilson said, "They usually took good lookin' women, and they bring top dollar at a whorehouse."

"I know y'all were lookin' fer me, but why? I've been gone fer years," I asked.

"Blackie met some white man in Saint Louis who said he knew of a black jasper living out this way, and he described ya pretty good. I reckon ya don't know it, but yer old master has a two thousand dollar reward for ya, and he wants to make an example of ya something fierce. Hell, when Blackie heard the amount, why, we were up and gone in an hour   headin' this way."

I grew silent, allowing his words some thought. Then after a few minutes, I asked, "Now, what am I to do with ya, Wilson?"

"When ya took me, ya asked me iffen I wanted to be free. Mister Nate, I'm alone in the world and ain't got no reason to head back home. I want to die a free man and if I have to do the job, I'll live in these woods."

"You wouldn't last long, because yer not tough enough," Sue shot out quickly.

Cotton met my eyes and I knew his question without asking, so I nodded.

"Wilson, iffen we let ya join us, do ya think ya could fight to protect us all? I want the truth now and not some bullshit answer." Cotton asked.

"I could do the job, but I have a lot to learn, because about all I can do out here is make a fire."

I extended my hand and said, "Shake iffen ya want to join up with us."

As we shook all the way around, Sue said, "I'll be go to hell and back, you've just joined up with a slaver!"

I chuckled at her words and said, "Sue, many men out here are runnin' from the law, broken marriages, death, creditors, or a thousand other reasons. Often these men have been on the other side of the thin line that separates a good man from a bad one. Wilson and I aren't the only black men here who are runaways, and we won't be the last. As long as the west remains untamed and then once tamed, blacks will continue to come. This is where any man can be what he wants to be, if he's strong enough to do the job."

"Sounds like bullshit to me." She replied.

Her mood pissed me off, so I said, "Enough, he rides with us. Iffen ya two have a problem with each other, ya wait until this mess is over, and then settle it. Right now, let's pull together and finish the job we've started."

Days passed slowly, and each morning I'd wander over by the camp of the slavers and look the place over. Blackie was con-stantly pissed and kicking at people, because so far they'd only found two horses. I moved in closely one morning and heard a conversation he was having with an unknown man.

"Look, iffen we don't find more horses in two days, we'll leave as we are. We'll head back to that little trading post and buy some horses from the man."

"What iffen he ain't got no horses or don't want to let none of 'em go?

"Simple, then we'll kill the sumbitch and take what we want."

"Yer a coldblooded bastard, Blackie. I feel the need to warn ya though, ya keep up the killin' and one day ya'll end up stretchin' some hemp rope."

"It'll never happen, because I never leave a witness alive. When I kill, everyone and everything dies."

"Did they find any sign of Wilson yet?"

"Hell no, and they won't. See the Injuns who attacked us, must have taken him, and from what I've heard about these red bastards, he died hard. They usually carve on a man and then burn 'em to death."

"Good God, what a horrible way to die."

"Ain't no good way to die, but some are rougher than others. Get the men up and clean this camp up a bit. When it's time to leave, I want us ready to go right then."

"I hear ya, and I'll get the job done."

As they separated, I moved back and entered the deep woods. *We have to move against these men again tonight, or they'll head back to Butterfield's. If they get to his place, it's likely they'll kill every damned body there.* I thought, and broke into a slow jog toward my camp. *We need to get organized and do the job now. We have some men to kill.*

Once back at camp, I explained what I'd heard and then waited.

"We cain't let 'em go to Butterfield fer horses, they'll kill the old man." Cotton said and then continued, "So, let's kill as many as we can now, then make a beeline to the trading post. We have horses, so we'll get there way before Blackie."

I looked at Wilson and asked, "And, yer thoughts on this whole mess?"

"Well, they won't give killing nobody a second thought.

They're cold men, and Blackie is the meanest of the mean."

Sue gazed into my eyes and said, "Let's send 'em all to hell. They owe me and it's time they pay for what they've done."

"Whoa, hold on here a minute. Ya go off like a loose cannon, and I'll leave yer rear here. Revenge has it's place, but remember, it won't change what was done to ya. It's only to payback for a wrong you've had done to ya, but iffen ya let yer emotions control ya, you'll be dead in a minute."

"The Bible says an eye for an eye." Sue came back.

Cotton laughed and said, "What ya gonna do, rape him back? Nate is makin' good sense to me. Keep yer anger under control or it'll get ya killed dead as hell."

"Now," I said, "iffen ya promise to do what yer told, I'll let ya go with us. Do ya think ya can do that?"

She nodded, but that wasn't good enough for me or Cotton, because he said, "We didn't hear ya?"

"Yes, I'll do what I'm told."

"Sue, let me tell ya story about a mountain man friend of mine. Bear as he's called now, or George Alwood, come out here about the same time I did.[2] He's a white man, and a good friend of mine. He married an Injun woman and they traded some goods for gold from a group of Injuns on the way to Fort Atkinson. Well, once at the fort, they sold the gold, and some men thought George knew where the mother lode was located. One day when George, Hawk, and another feller were out hunting buffalo, a group of men raped and killed his pregnant wife, attempting to get her to tell them where the gold was. Hell, no one in the group could have said where the gold came from, because they didn't know. Well, like I said, his wife was pregnant at the time, and Bear almost lost his mind over the whole thing. So, he started out for revenge."

"Did he finally get it?" Sue asked.

"After about a year of trailing the ole boy, Bear finally put a ball in his ass, and do you know what he told me after that?"

Sue smiled, "He felt good to have his revenge, right?"

"With tears on this cheeks he looked me right in the eyes and said, 'I wasted a year of my life seeking revenge, except when it was all said and done, my wife and unborn baby were still dead. Killing Red brought me no peace or satisfaction. I gained not a damned thing when I killed that worthless piece of

---

2   War Paint, © 2012 by W.R. Benton, soon to be a feature movie.

shit.' Now, ya think on that a spell and remember it."

The next few hours were spent repairing gear, cleaning guns, and preparing for our attack later. We ate early, got a little sleep and it was a couple of hours before dawn when we moved toward the slavers. I hoped to end the whole thing this day, but often what we plan doesn't go the way we think it will. I knew, from experience, something would go wrong.

It was hard walking to the camp, because of darkness and we had overcast skies, which blocked any light from the moon. I heard Wilson and Sue fall a couple of times and heard their low curses in the dark. Finally, I had to stop as we neared the camp and whisper, "Keep the noise down. We're close now, and they might hear us."

Sue mumbled something I didn't hear and Wilson replied, "Okay."

At this point, Cotton, who'd been out in front, returned and whispered, "One guard near the horses, but the rest are sleeping. I saw a number of whiskey jugs on their sides, so it's likely they're roostered. The fire is still blazing, which is a pilgrim thing to do out here."

Keeping my voice low, I said, "I'll take out the guard. When ya hear an owl hoot, I want each of ya to shoot into the sleeping slavers. Save yer pistols in case we have to fight to get out of this mess. I'll try to run off any horses they may have found, too."

Now, some may consider shooting men as they slept murder, only we didn't see it that way. There were only four of us and at least seven of them, so we were simply lowering the odds a bit. Besides, these men were slavers, which most folks, black and white, thought were the lowest form of human life on earth. It's ironic, while I didn't hate any of these men, what they did for a living disgusted me.

"I'm movin' now, and listen for my hoot," I said.

"Watch yer ass and take no chances." Cotton whispered.

I noticed the night sounds were gone, but guard hadn't noticed. I moved slowly so I could approach the man from behind. When I could see the man's outline clearly, he was between me and the flickering campfire, I lowered my rifle to the grass. I pulled my skinning knife and slowly made my way toward him, hoping I'd make no noise. He started moving, so I instantly froze in place, and I know I grinned when he raised a clay jug of whiskey. *God Lord, these fools are askin' to be killed if they're drinkin' while pulling guard.*

Once he lowered the jug, I moved for him once more. When I was near enough, I threw my left hand over his mouth, pulled him close to me, and stuck my knife up the hand guard into his kidney. At that point he bit my finger hard and my hand slipped from his mouth. A loud, but pitiful scream sounded in the cool morning air. I quickly stabbed him three more times and then tossed him to the side. *Sumbitch, the dance has opened a bit early,* I thought as I looked at the center of camp.

Two rifles fired, one barrel of a shotgun blasted, and more screams were heard, but from the center of their camp this time. Blackie stood and moved toward the captives, so I squeezed off a shot and saw the man go down. I reloaded as fast as possible and saw another man running near the campfire. I sighted him in, pulled the trigger and down he went. He was jerking and twisting as he screamed, and at one point his left leg must have got too close to the flames. His buckskin pant leg caught on fire.

I heard more rifle shots and another boom of a shotgun, as I scanned for more targets. I saw the man near the fire jump to his feet and the flames were now moving upward. Then, as the flames engulfed him, he began to stagger around like a drunken man, lighting up the darkness. His horrifying screams of fear and pain were loud and continuous, until Sue's shotgun fired once more and most of the man's head disappeared. His body collapsed, still in flames.

The smell of burnt flesh filled the air and most of the slavers were down, or so it seemed to me. I heard someone on the other side of camp upchuck and knew it was Sue. I could hear an occasional moan or groan but the screamers were either dead or passed out, so we'd wait where we were a bit longer.

I'd just reloaded my rifle when I caught movement in the corner of my right eye. Three men were mounting horses. *Damn me,* I thought, *I forgot about the horses.* One of the riders was lost in the darkness within seconds, his horse moving at a fast run, but the other two men were having trouble mounting without a saddle.

I selected the bigger man of the two, he was on the left, sighted my rifle in and took a deep breath. As I released the air from my lungs, I slowly squeezed the trigger. The hammer dropped, my flint sparked, the powder in my pan ignited, which in turn caused the main powder load in the barrel to fire. I watched the man fall as I was pushed back by the discharge. I quickly dropped the butt of my rifle to the ground and began reloading.

I heard a shot and when I looked toward the last man at the horses, he was not seen, but the horse was still on the picket line. Then I heard screams. Both of the men down by the horse were screeching and thrashing around.

I called out, "Sound out with yer name iffen yer okay!"

"Sue!"

"Wilson, but I'm hit in the arm!"

"Cotton!"

"Wilson, try to stop the bleedin' by wrapping a rag around yer injury. No one move from yer positions until full light! We'll wait for sunrise."

Over the next few minutes the moans and groans in the camp stopped completely and one of the men by the horses gradually grew quiet. The last man continued to scream and beg for help, so I ignored him. I had an uneasy feeling about the man who'd gotten away on horseback. *I just know that bastard Blackie was the rider,* I thought. *Iffen it was, he'll head to Butterfield's place for sure.*

Just as the sun started over the mountain behind me, I shouted, "Move for the camp. Leave the captives alone until we make sure the camp is safe first. Don't take any chances at all, so watch each other closely. If he's a threat, kill 'em."

Chapter 9

I moved slowly as I stepped from the cover of the woods. I saw five men down in camp, and I knew there were two others near the horses, because one I could still hear groaning. I heard a man moan as I neared, but the smell of the burnt body was getting to me. I pulled out a bandana and tied it around my face to keep the smell down a mite. I made my way to the injured man. He was face down, so I pulled my pistol, cocked the hammer back and used my right foot to turn him over. He'd taken a slug in the lights and his breathing was ragged. I knew he'd go under, because I'd never known a man to take such an injury and live.

Squatted beside him, I asked, "Ya make peace with yer maker yet?"

"Y . . . yes. I . . . prayed."

"Do ya want to say anything?"

"H . . . how come . . . yer a . . . black . . . man?"

"God decided Nate Grisham would be a man of color. Now, ya done?"

He nodded.

I put my pistol back in my sash and pulled my knife. Suddenly and without a word, I stuck it deep under his ribs and jerked it violent.

The man screamed, but his voice quickly lost volume and he died a few heartbeats later, his feet drumming on the grass.

"May ya rest in peace," I said, but thought, *another black man in this bunch. This must have been the other man Wilson was talkin' about.*

Wiping my bloody blade clean on the dead man's trousers, I shook my head over the killing.

I stood and saw Cotton near the supplies, "Cotton, come and cover me as I check two men down by the horses."

He joined me and we moved to the animals. I could see right off, one of the men would likely live, but the second would go under, due to bullet hitting him in the center of the back. It was likely his spine was destroyed.

I said to the downed men, "Make any moves at all and I'll send a ball into yer head. Remain still and let me look y'all over."

Checking the badly injured man first, I discovered his spine was severely injured, so I moved to the second man. I pulled a pistol from his sash, a knife from his boot, and a tomahawk from the ground near his left hand. He'd taken my ball in his upper back, but seemed to be breathing fine, so I must have missed his lungs. *Good,* I thought, *he and I will have us a talk, Injun style in a bit.*

I tied his hands behind his back with a strip of rawhide from my possibles bag and said, "You'll live, except I can't promise how long."

"What about the other man?" Cotton asked.

"He'll go under."

Nearing the fatally injured man again I asked, "Have ya prayed yet?"

"No . . . there ain't . . . no . . . God."

I placed my pistol against the side of his head and pulled the trigger. His head jerked once as blood, brains and gore sprayed the ground beside him.

Standing, I said, "I think ya know there is a God by now, because yer talkin' to 'em."

"Want me to help ya get this other jasper by the fire?"

"Why sure. We'll need a big hot fire for what I have in mind for this no account. He'll die poorly, I do believe." I watched a puddle urine form under him and knew I had him scared enough to talk now.

"How do ya want to move 'em?"

"Hell, ain't no need to gentle with 'em, so ya take a foot and I'll take a foot, and we'll drag his nasty ass to the flames. Once there, take a look see at Wilson, then I need ya to take one of these horses and move the burned body off a ways."

"I hear ya, the smells a bit ripe."

Once by the fire, I knelt, added some wood, turned to Sue and asked, "Would ya check all the pockets of the dead men and find the keys, so ya can release the captives?"

"Sure."

"When ya've done that, fix them some food. I'm damned sure these sorry bastards didn't feed 'em much or regular."

Cotton neared with Wilson and said, "Light injury to his left arm. Hell, I don't even think it needs cauterizin' or sewin' up."

"Clean the injury good and see if ya can find any whiskey to pour on it to keep 'em from turnin' sour. Then wrap it in clean cloth and we'll change the bandage every evenin'."

I pulled a small half pint bottle of laudanum from my possibles bag and turning to the injured man, I raised his head and gave him just a little.

A couple of minutes later he asked, "Why did ya give me the medicine, if yer just goin' to kill me anyway?"

"I might not kill ya, if ya answer my questions. If ya don't, then I might just turn ya over the captives, who I know damned good and well, will take care of ya."

"Are ya Nate Grisham?"

"I am, and I hear ya boys been lookin' fer me a spell."

"Yer all Blackie talks about. He wants yer ass bad, too. Seems there's a big reward for ya and ya killed his brother, too."

"So, the man shot in the leg made it back to y'all, huh? I thought fer sure he'd go under."

"When he got back to us, his leg was rancid and we cut 'er off."

"I'll bet that helped the man a lot. Ya damned fools likely killed 'em, huh? I don't see him in this bunch."

"He bled out before we could cauterize the stub. Blackie is pure mean, he is, and he wants yer ass."

"Blackie had his chance earlier, but lacked the sand to do the job. Ya got a name?"

"John, is my name."

The captives neared the fire and all eight of them looked rough for wear. The white woman looked as if they'd raped her countless times. I counted two other black women and five black men. All were frightened and I knew they were happy to be free, but doubted they knew what to do now. I quit speaking with John, so my new friends could rest in peace.

Turning to the group, I said, "Y'all need to decide what yer goin' to do now that yer free. We'll get y'all back to the trading post, but then yer on yer own. I'll warn ya, if ya head east and back to the states, it's likely you'll be slaves again within a few days. Ya can all live free out here, but you'll have to work pretty damned hard just to stay alive. I know a black feller in the mountains named Abe, and he's talked of starting a town where his cabin is located."

I got no response and didn't expect one. *Give 'em some time and then talk to them later.*

Sue said, "I found some bacon and beans I can warm up."

"That'll be fine, and I don't think they'll care much what they eat right now. A hungry person ain't real particular about food. Did ya find any bread with that?"

"Slab of cornbread."

While I'd been speaking with my captive, Cotton dragged the burnt body off, but the odor was still overpowering.

Wilson neared the fire, grinned and said, "Howdy, John, yer in a world of shit right now, but I guess ya know that already."

The man didn't reply.

"Wilson, how bad is the arm?" I asked.

"Not bad, now. Cotton had me take a few long snorts of whiskey and that helped the pain."

"I want ya to walk around camp and collect every gun, knife, powder, or ball you can find and put it all over with the supplies. Strip these dead men of all their clothing and I mean every stitch. We'll eventually wash it and let these folks make use of what fits 'em. Oh, take their boots too, so maybe we can use them as well."

"I can do that, but some of the boots will be bloody."

"Look in the supplies and see if you can find some cloth to wipe the blood off. If not, don't worry about it much. The clothing and boots we'll have to wash anyway."

"Hats, too?"

"Yep, anything we might be able to use, place it with the supplies."

Cotton returned, tied the horse to a low limb and made his way to the fire. Once seated on the ground he said, "Lawdy, what a nasty smell. I pulled the man out about a mile and left 'em."

Sue'd given each person beans and a small slab of cornbread. She smiled at me and asked, "When will we bury these men?"

Cotton chuckled, because he knew my response.

"Good God, we won't bury these men. They dealt in tradin' and sellin' of humans, so they'll get no Christian burial from us. Besides, wild critters have to eat, too. I just hope eatin' these jaspers don't make 'em sick."

"So, when are we havin' our talk with yer prisoner?" Cotton asked.

"Sue, take all of these folks over to were they were kept before and take the food with ya. Let 'em eat their fill and keep 'em over there no matter what they hear."

"Are you goin' to hurt this man?"

"I for damn sure will, iffen he doesn't talk. Now, all ya folks go with Sue." I took my knife and placed the blade in the fire.

Cotton pulled his knife and handed it to me. I checked the blade for sharpness, making sure John could see me, and said, "John, we can do this one of two ways. The first way is for ya to tell me all ya know about Blackie and this slavin' operation he runs. Or, I can take to cuttin' on ya a bit. Now, I've watched the Sioux torture captives, so I can keep ya alive fer days."

The man looked in my eyes and said, "Kiss my ass, ya black sonofabit—"

My knife blade flashed once in the morning sunlight and his nose fell to the ground. John gave a loud scream as his body jerked and quivered. Turning to Cotton, I said, "Hand me that hot knife."

I grabbed John by his long filthy hair and held his head in place as I placed the red-hot flat of my knife blade against his severed nose. There came a loud scream as his flesh burned, but the bleeding stopped instantly. I pulled the blade away, handed it to Cotton and said, "Place that back in the fire."

John was whimpering like a hurt puppy and I almost felt sorry for the man, only I knew the kind of scum he was deep inside. *He'll do anything for a dollar. Anything.*

"Cotton, pour us both a cup of whiskey, because we'll be here a spell."

He left and returned few minutes later with a clay jug and two cups. Pouring us both a drink, he said, "John, Nate here ain't playin' with ya. Now, unless ya want to die in a lot of pain, I'd suggest ya get to talkin' and do the job now."

"I'll . . . talk, but no more cutting on me, please."

"Ya talk, and I'll let ya live. Now, who does Blackie work fer?"

About an hour later, I said, "That's enough, John. Sue, I'm leaving ya and Wilson here while we go back for our horses. While we're gone, see iffen any those folks need any clothing."

She nodded, so leaving John secured by the fire, Cotton and I returned for our mounts.

As we walked, Cotton asked, "How are we goin' to travel to Butterfield's place with only five horses and twelve of us?"

"I've been thinkin' on that and don't have an answer yet. The good Lord knows the captives have walked their tails off, but they'll have do some more iffen they want to live."

"Hell, ain't none of those folks, Wilson included, that weigh much. Let 'em ride double, and we can travel by shanks' mare."

"I hate to walk, but it may be our only choice. You'd better pray we don't run into any Injuns, or we'll have serious trouble," I said.

"Do ya reckon any of those black folks know how to shoot?"

"It ain't likely, from what I know. When I was on the plantation, it was against the law for a black man to even touch a gun, and I heard stories of men having their hands cut off for doin' just that."

"I picked up some shotguns among the dead, so we'll hand them out once we get back. All they'll have to do is point and pull the trigger."

"I'll tell ya what, that Sue's pretty rough with her scattergun."

"We need to cut the chatter, we can talk later."

"Uh-huh, talkin' right now is pretty dumb."

We remained silent for the rest of the walk and when we neared our camp, everything looked normal. "Let me walk into camp while ya cover me." I said.

I stepped from the trees and looked for tracks in the dirt, but saw none. I checked our supplies and horses, and everything looked fine. I motioned Cotton to enter.

"Let's get some ropes, canvas, and take all of our horses with us. We'll bring those folks back here, spend the night and leave in the morning. We'll use these horses for the supplies, so once we go through it all here, hell, we all might have to walk."

"What are ya goin' to do with John? I mean, ya promised not to kill 'em."

"I won't kill 'em. I'll take all his clothes, but his pants. Let him have one pistol and rifle, and enough powder with balls for

6 shots each. Then, I'll run him out of camp."

"He'll go under."

I pulled two horses from the rope and as I pulled them away at a walk, I replied, "Yer words may very well be true, but iffen he dies, it will not be by my hand. Unless I see the man again."

Morning was beautiful and although we'd been up late sorting supplies, I felt good. We dug a deep pit to cache some of our supplies to pick up later, when we returned to the area. I'd kept all the clothes, threw the manacles in the woods, scattered the keys, and then went to sleep. I awoke feeling like a new man. I had energy to spare.

I walked to the tied up John and asked, "What happened to the pack of dogs y'all had?"

"Some died after we got out here and some ran into the woods, but they never came back."

"On the ground, straight behind ya, you'll find a rifle and pistol, with powder and balls in leather pouches. I want all yer clothes off, except yer pants and boots. Head east as soon as I let ya go." I pulled a pistol and aimed it at him, then cut his bonds.

He was up and gone, quickly.

A simple breakfast of cornmeal mush and coffee was behind us, so I said, "We have five horses and two of those are loaded with supplies. Now, that means all the men will walk and the women will ride. Here directly, Cotton will give each man a shotgun, powder and shot for the guns. Now, I know most of ya men ain't never touched a gun before, so Cotton will show each of ya how to load and fire yer guns. Remember, no matter what is happenin' around ya, after ya shoot yer gun, reload and I mean every damned time."

Cotton looked at me, so I nodded as he said, "Men, come with me and I'll get yer guns."

As soon as they'd left I ask Sue, "Are all the men up to walkin'?"

"I think so, and the only one to keep an eye on is named

Frank. He's well over sixty, in fairly poor condition, and I'll be surprised if he can walk long."

"And, the women?"

"May is pretty weak, and is still bleeding. Those men took a whiskey bottle and stuck it— "

I shook my head and interrupted her, "I don't need the details. Will she live?"

"Yes, I think so, but she might not ever have a child."

"I think childbirth is the furthest thing from her mind right now."

"Well, there's another possibility, ya know."

"Huh?" I asked, confused by her talking in circles.

She shrugged, shook her head and said, "It's possible she's pregnant, if all those men raped her. But, if they hurt her inside, she may never have another child. While that seems unimportant now, once she meets the right man, she'll want to have his baby."

"Damn, how's she goin' to take havin' a baby after all of this? Did ya talk with her about what might happen?"

"Some, and she swears if a child comes she'll keep it and love it. She feels it won't be the babies fault, so why punish the little one."

"She's a fine woman, then."

"There are many fine women in the world, just as there are decent men, but both are hard to find, or they're already taken."

"If there's one thing I don't need in my life right now, it's a woman. Well, enough talk, help me get this group herded and let's move toward Butterfield's place. I should have gone on ahead or sent Cotton, but Blackie is alone and Butterfield can take care of himself."

Two hours later as we moved down a mountain trail, I saw an old man, who I guessed to be Frank, staggering along as if drunk. I walked to his side and asked, "Ya doin' okay?"

"I'm keepin' up, ain't I?"

"Sure ya are, but ya ain't walkin' very straight."

"Don't ya pay no never mind to how straight I'm walkin', as long as my ass is movin' ya should be happy. I'll not ride no hoss and make a woman walk. By God, I'll not do 'er."

"Yer a tough old man, Frank."

"Son, way back when I grew up in Africa, my daddy was a big chief and life was good. When I was about fourteen, a mixed bunch of white and black men came to our village and put us all on a ship. Ya know the rest of the story. But, what I meant to say and forgot is this, I was once a strong man and while my body has gone to hell, my mind still works. Son, I think ya have a mess on yer hands now."

I scanned the countryside and asked, "How's that?"

"What are most of these people in this group gonna do now? How are they gonna live? They need work, a place to stay, and a whole lot of things."

"I have a buddy, high up in the mountains and he's a big man, like me. He's also a black man, not that it matters out here, but he talked one day of starting a town just fer black folks. Now, most of that is bullshit thinkin', but if y'all join up with 'em it might work."

"It might, but what are we gonna do fer a store or other things we'll need?"

"It was his idea, not mine. Really, I have no idea what he's got in mind, but he's a sharp man. Do ya think ya can keep this walkin' up? Be honest with me when ya answer."

"I'll try, but I really don't know. My mind says to hell with the pain and keep walkin', only I think at some point I'll have to ride or be left behind."

He's tough, and I hope the others with us are half as tough, I thought. "I'll keep an eye on ya, and here in about an hour I'll let ya ride fer a bit. Now, we need to stop talkin' because there might be Injuns out."

We walked until noon, took a short break and as we nibbled on cold biscuits, Cotton ran to me and said, "Injun's coming and a hell of a lot of 'em, too!"

Chapter 10

I quickly moved my people into the brush along the mountainside, and knew we'd be discovered. The question was not if, but rather when, and I prayed just above a whisper, "Lord let it be a friendly tribe." Cotton and I got along with most tribes, except the Ree and Blackfoot, only hell nobody got along with them. But the red man is a notional man and subject to more moods than a full time wife.

I looked at Cotton and signed, "Can you tell the tribe?"

"No, too far."

I was about to sign him again, when I felt a movement behind me. When I turned, I saw Broken Bow standing on a huge rock behind me.

He smiled and asked, *"How is my brother on this fine day?"*

"Nobody move, I know this Injun and he's a good man." I said in English; then in Shoshone I replied, *"I am fine and it makes my heart happy to see my brother."*

"There will not be a fight, so get your people on the trail. The warriors below are my people. Man Killer and I watched your fight with the white eyes and you have much honor."

"It was but a small fight and against poor men."

"Most white men are easy to kill, but there are so many now that I can kill one today and two hands will be in the same spot tomorrow."

"You speak with one tongue."

"We have come for you. You and your friends are to come to the village with us."

"My mountain man friend and I must go to the One Who Trades. His life may be in danger. One of the white men escaped and will be looking for the old man."

"I will tell my chief of your fight and why you have gone to battle against the lone man. May the Great Spirit protect you

on your trip and in the coming battle. Do not worry about your people, we will care for them as if they are our own."

"*Thank you, my brother.*" I replied in Shoshone and then said in English, "Y'all go with these Injuns, they're my friends. Cotton and I have someplace to go."

"Can I come?" Sue asked.

"No, I want ya to stay with these folks. Once I'm done with Blackie, we'll come to the village for all of ya. Then, we'll decide what to do with every one of ya."

"I can fight and ya know it, too! Let me go with you."

I grew angry, "Damn it, Sue, I said no and I mean no! Take these people with the Shoshone and if ya need something tell Broken Bow. He's the man I'm talkin' with now, and don't argue with me over this. This old red coon speaks English, but his accent is pretty thick."

I turned to Broken Bow and said, "*They will go with you. The young raven woman will speak for the group if they have needs.*"

He nodded and then walked away.

"Grab a horse, Cotton, let's get to Butterfield's."

Over the next two days, we rode hard and long, wanting to reach the trading post before Blackie, but we both knew it was unlikely we'd arrive in time. The man had a full day ahead of us, so we tried to make up the difference by riding about eighteen hours a day. I figured a man like Blackie would ride about eight hours and then make camp for the night. I looked for light as we rode at night, hoping to catch the sonofabitch asleep or drunk, but saw nothing.

It's dark now, as we move over the plains and quiet now. Gazing at the stars, I figured it was around midnight. Cotton dropped back beside me and asked, "Do ya smell smoke?"

I sniffed the air, smelled nothing, then turned my head and sniffed again. There, I picked up a faint smell of woodsmoke. "Uh-huh, but I can't tell where it's at, can ya?

Before I could react, hands came from the darkness and pulled me from my horse. I heard a pistol shot, a scream, and then what sounded like a fight. I reached to my sash, pulled my pistol and fired. I heard a grunt and then a body fell. Dropping my now empty pistol, I pulled the second one, saw a man's torso in the dim moonlight, and fired. He was close, less than three feet and I heard him scream and felt a warm liquid splash on my face. I knew it was blood, because it had a coppery smell. The man went down hard. *Damned Ree, I'll bet. Looks like wet powder and no place to dry 'er. Ya'll go under this time ole son,* I thought.

Glancing to where Cotton had been, I saw he was still mounted and held his skinning knife in his hand. He suddenly yelled, "Nate, mount behind me and now's the time to do the job, because more of these bastards are coming!"

Penetrating war cries sounded all around us, and I know there must have been a good two dozen warriors within a few yards of our horses.

I ran full speed toward his horse and when I neared that critters rump, I placed my palms on the horse's rear and up I went, landing right behind Cotton. "Go, go, go!"

Cotton's big mare shot out so fast I almost fell off, but my deep fear of being taken alive by Injuns made me much stronger than I usually am. My heart was working overtime, and I could hear it pounding loudly in my chest. *Damn me, almost captured by those Injuns.*

After running his horse for about a mile, Cotton slowed down to a canter, and after a bit, a slow walk. He spoke over his shoulder, "One of us will have to dismount in a few minutes, because our weight is too much for Molly to take fer long."

"Stop, and let me walk a spell. I'm a big man and Molly did all we could've asked of her—she saved our asses! Remind me at Butterfield's to buy her a big bag of oats."

Cotton stopped his horse, we both unforked his horse and started walking. He was holding the reins in his hand as he said, "Damn me, but I thought we were goners. I think we rode right through a big ass camp of Ree."

"If we'd done that four hours ago, when most of 'em were still awake, it's not likely we'd be talkin' right now. Scared the livin' hell right out of me."

"Ya shot two of 'em, didn't ya?"

I gave a nervous chuckle and replied, "I shot twice, and know I hit my targets, but have no idea if the shots were killing shots or not."

"What now? Do ya want to keep walkin' or hole up someplace?"

"Hole up? Have ya lost yer damned mind? We'll keep walkin' now until we get to the trading post."

"I'm bleedin' some, from my left hand, but I don't think it's much. How ya doin'?"

"I'm okay, I think, but we can't treat yer injury until the sun comes up. Any light out here now and they'll come to finish the job they started."

"It'll wait."

We walked for a few miles in silence, then Cotton asked, "Nate, ya know killin' Blackie won't stop yer old master from sending other men out here, right?"

"I know that, but right now killin' Blackie will stop things fer a year or two, maybe. I'll worry about others coming after me when they get here and not before."

"I'd take the fight to Mississippi and kill that useless piece of shit. Ya know my feelin's about slavery, but fer a man to gather up just *any* black folks he can find and then sell 'em is wrong. Some of those folks are free. Now, I think a man has a right to fetch his property, but stealin' is wrong."

"Yer the best friend I have, but ya and me don't always see eye-to-eye on things, which is alright in my book. I don't expect us to agree a hundred percent on all things, all the time. But, how far do ya think I could get into Mississippi before slavers caught me? I'd not get close to Grisham or his plantation and ya know it, too."

"Why you'd keep his last name once ya ran to the mountains? Ya could have changed it, and no one would have known the difference."

"I kept the name because it reminds me of what I once was, as well as what I am now."

"Makes sense to my mountain mind. Let me think on how to get to Grisham's plantation fer a spell."

I gave a low chuckle and replied, "Ya do that."

Neither of us would ride now, because I knew our minds well. We'd both ride or neither of us, because that was the kind of men we were. We weren't really very far from Butterfield's Trading Post, but unless Blackie had been sittin on a stump scratching his ass, he'd be there way before us. I figured we'd be at the post around daybreak, which was another four hours.

The sun was just starting to come over the mountains

when we spotted the trading post in the valley before us. Smoke was reaching for the sky from the chimney in the store, so I knew Butterfield was up and moving around.

Cotton said, "Ya know, this place ain't much but for some reason it brings a smile to my face at times like this."

"Let's get down there and see if Blackie has been here yet or not. I'll even buy ya a cup of whiskey."

A few minutes later, as we stepped onto the porch, the door opened and old stepped Butterfield holding a shotgun. The old man looked rough, with a busted lip, a black eye and bandaged around the middle. I knew we were too late.

"Oh, it's ya, Nate. I was hopin' ya was Blackie, 'cause I've a score to settle with the sumbitch."

"When did he get here?"

"Late last night. He come in here claiming Ree had attacked and killed all his men, but him. I'll explain it over coffee or whiskey, but it'll be a stiff drink for me. I'm hurtin' pretty good right now."

We walked to the table, I noticed a jug was already on the table, and took seats. Butterfield joined us a minute later with two tin cups. He filled ours with the strong amber colored drink, took a long gulp of his, and then asked, "Why only the one horse?"

I gave a smile and said, "Ree caught us out on the plains."

"Yea? Well I've heard that shit before from ya two and recently, too."

"So," I said and knew he had more to say, "what happened here?"

"That Blackie sumbitch come in here and robbed me, that's what happened. He showed in the door in the middle of the night bangin' on my door. When I let 'em in he pistol whipped me as soon as I turned my back on 'em. Took most of my money, except what I had hid, stole me blind and in the middle of the process Moses came in here. I guess he heard the noise and came for a look-see."

"How'd Moses make out?" I asked, but suspected not very good.

"Ya'd have been proud of the man, Nate, he got a shot off before Blackie and put a bullet in the man's right leg, up high."

Cotton smiled and asked, "So, did Blackie leave then?"

"I don't really know. See, I passed out at that point and when I come around again, Moses was on the floor with three bullet holes in the middle of his chest. But, the bastard wasn't happy just killin' the man, he scalped 'em and cut his throat, too."

I suddenly had a thought, so I asked, "What of April and Thad?"

The old trader lowered his head and said, "He took 'em, Nate."

"What!" Cotton yelled and started to get up.

"Sit back down, Cotton, we're goin' no place until mornin'. I guess ya ain't got no idea which way he headed, do ya?" *Damn me, he took two kids,* I thought after speaking to Cotton.

"This all happened the night before last, but yesterday mornin' I tracked him fer a couple of miles and he's headin' to Fort Atkinson, or so it looks to me."

"Ya up to gatherin' us up some supplies this evenin'? If not I can fetch 'em and write down what I take. Ya tell me how much I owe ya and I pay ya out of this season's plew take."

"Hell, let me knock off a couple of glasses of this painkiller and I'll get it all fer ya. Iffen yer goin' after Blackie, what ya need won't cost ya a penny. He took over fifteen hundred dollars from me and I'm a mite pissed right now."

"We're in no big hurry, but I want to leave at first light."

Throwing his drink back, the old man poured himself another one and then asked, "Nate, do ya think it's safe fer ya to go back east, I mean since yer a wanted man?"

"I'll go wherever Blackie goes, because this has to stop. I won't spend the rest of my life lookin' over my shoulder wonderin' if slavers are behind me. I'll kill Blackie and then brace the man behind it all."

"Nate, I ain't a man that normally gets into another man's business, but iffen ya kill white men the law will want ya then. Even in a fair fight, ya know what'll happen."

This has to end, one way of the other, I thought. I took a sip of my drink and looking over the glass I said, "The man behind all of this, and Blackie, need to be stopped and, by God, I'll do the job."

"Oh, I have no doubts about ya puttin' a stop to 'er, but watch yer ass or they'll lynch ya."

Cotton said, "He won't be alone, so I'll cover his back. If we work this right we can stop all this foolishness on one trip."

"Well, I'm here to tell ya, when ya brace Blackie have yer shit together or he'll kill ya dead as hell and do the job quick like, too."

"Butterfield, get me a pen and ink, so I can write out a list of what we'll need for the trip. Oh, do ya still have horses?"

"I have a number of 'em, but only about six that are worth a damn. In the mornin' pick ya out three or four fer yer trip. I let y'all have two pack-horses, if ya need 'em, and a ridin' mount."

A week later we were out on the open plains and it was as flat as my sisters chest. I could ride all day, look behind me, and see where I'd camped the night before. I don't like the open-ness of the plains and feel vulnerable when moving across the flatness. I knew Cotton didn't like it either, because he kept scanning the horizon. The prairie may look flat, but there were enough gullies and stream-beds to hide an army or a full tribe of Injuns.

The weather was warm, with no breeze that I could feel, and clouds were gathering overhead. *I hope we don't get any rain, because this is perfect weather fer a twister,* I thought while looking the sky over closely. *If it rains, we'll have to camp on high ground, to avoid the runoff and yet be close enough to a gully or low place in case a whirlwind decides to come visit.*

Cotton spoke for the first time since we'd left our morning camp, "I don't like the looks of those clouds. Let's keep an eye on 'em, and if it turns nasty we'll be in fer a rough time of it."

"I was just thinkin' on the same thing. It might be smart, once the rain starts to hunt a hole. I don't like winds out here because they'll blow stuff all over the place."

"I hear ya and while there ain't no winds now, iffen it rains, they'll come quickly enough."

"Well, stay away from these damned gullies, because I've seen walls of water move down those things ten feet high and they wash everything away as they pass, too."

There came loud *crack* of thunder, which made my horse prance a bit, and I glanced up again. The dark clouds were rolling inside of each other and it was looking rough to me.

"Move off to the left there and let's get a shelter up iffen we can. Near the creek, but not within a hundred feet of the damned thing. There, to the left. See those cottonwoods?" Cotton said.

Lighten flashed across the horizon in front of us and as I watched, it exploded into many smaller white fingers that went in all directions. A second or two later, a loud boom was heard.

At a canter we neared the trees, quickly pulled up, and dismounted. We immediately started working on a shelter, a crude looking lean-to that would have to work until the storm passed. We'd no sooner got the shelter up and supplies under the canvas when hail started popping on the material. Laughing, we moved under the canvas and watched the hail strike the ground around us. At first the hail stones were small, about the size of a half-dime, but over a few minutes, they grew to the size of a walnut. It was impossible to hear with the loud tattoo on the material, so we sat in silence as the storm approached.

There came three loud cracks of thunder, the horse danced wildly on the line, and then they were gone. Cotton started to leave the shelter, but I grabbed his arm and shook my head. *Hell, those horses will be halfway to Butterfield before they'll settle down some. This storm spooked 'em pretty bad.*

The wind was so high the corners of the shelter flapped up, and down and I expected to lose the whole thing any minute. I felt Cotton touch my shoulder and when I looked at him, he pointed to the west. I shuddered when I recognized the funnel shape of a twister.

"Leave it all, but bring yer possibles bag and gun! Move behind me at right angles from the twister!" I had to yell to be heard, and I was right beside him.

We left the shelter at a hard run and I saw no low ground to use for shelter. I continued to run until I felt Cotton tapping me on the arm. I looked at him and he pointed to a buffalo wallow with the water in it. It was old and only about two feet deep, which I prayed was enough. We ran to the wallow, jumped in and lowered our heads.

I heard the wind howling, pebbles and small sticks struck me on the back, and I felt the lower half of my body lifted and then lowered gently back into the water. I prayed and prayed, until suddenly, it grew quiet. The silence was loud to my ears.

"Ya okay?" Cotton asked.

"Other than rocks and sticks beatin' me half to death, I'm

fine. How about ya?"

"I'm fine, I guess. Scared the livin' hell right out of me."

I glanced toward the funnel and it was returning to the sky, it's destructive path finished for a while. The rains continued, but the hail was gone, so I stood on weak legs. My hands were shaking, and knew death had never been closer to me at any other point in my life.

I slapped Cotton on his shoulder and said, "Lets get a cup of whiskey in us and calm down a bit. I'm about to blow up. Lawdy, the power of the Lord."

Cotton nodded, but I knew how he felt.

Back at camp, it looked like we'd walked off to take a pee and came right back. Not a thing was out of place, but not twenty feet away was the carcass of a buffalo calf. Debris and sticks were scattered to the four winds. We crawled under the canvas, I pulled the cork from the clay jug, and poured two cups full with whiskey. I handed one to Cotton and took a sip out of mine.

Cotton took a big gulp of whiskey and asked, "What about our horses? Iffen we don't find 'em, we're in one a hell of a mess."

"We'll look for 'em in a few minutes. Right now, we're both bewildered and we need to relax for a while."

"Well, there are a few tracks and the closer we get to 'em the deeper the tracks will be in the mud."

"Let it slide fer a spell. Let's finish our drinks and then look for our horses."

We were both worried about our horses, so finishing the drinks didn't take long at all.

As we walked, I said, "We'll follow the tracks and when they split, so will we. Be back at the shelter before dark, unless ya run into trouble."

A short distance later the tracks spit, but they went three different ways. "I'll take the left and ya the right. We'll search for the third horse later."

About an hour before dusk, I spotted Cotton's horse and slowly approached him. As I neared, I spoke in low tones and moved slowly. Finally, I was able to grasp a rein. I patted the horse on the neck and knew she was as happy to see me as I was her. I waited a few minutes and then grabbing a handful of mane, I swung up and on her back. She was a bit skittish on the way back, so I sang an old song about a lost love and that seem to calm her down.

When I neared camp, Cotton was back with my horse and all looked good. At least we'd not be walking to Fort Atkinson.

"Yer horse was still pretty close."

"Well, we've got two and in the mornin' we'll look fer the other one."

Chapter 11

A week later we rode into Fort Atkinson with all three horses, but we were bone deep tired. The weather had turned rough and we'd fought rain, sleet and cold temperatures as we'd traveled. It had taken us two days to find the last horse, and then we'd had to make meat. I was frustrated and angered by the delay, only there was nothing I could do about the situation. *Old man Grisham ain't goin' anyplace and neither is Blackie once he gets home, so settle down some. I know where they both live. I couldn't figure out where my anger was coming from, but Blackie taking Thad and April was a good part of it.*

We rode to the sutlers, dismounted and tied our horses to the hitching post. The ground was a quagmire of mud, and I didn't make an attempt to clean my boots before entering the store. A small brass bell *tinkled* to announce our arrival.

A middle-aged man, wearing wire-rimmed glasses perched low on his nose asked, "What can I do ya for?"

"I'm lookin' fer a man," I said.

"Mister, I get a lot of men in here, so what does this jasper look like?" He spoke and then pushed his glasses up on his nose.

"Big man, about my size, with blond hair and a beard. He might have had two colored kids with 'em."

The storekeepers lips narrowed and anger flashed in his eyes, but I waited patiently for his reply, because he'd seen Blackie.

"He come in heah, oh, mayhap two days ago. He bought a bunch of supplies and was favorin' his shoulder or arm, only I couldn't tell which. When I asked 'em about it, he said he'd fought Ree and taken an injury."

"Nice feller?" Cotton asked, so he'd seen the man's reaction as well as I had.

"Nope, mean sumbitch. Ya know how it is out here, we don't see many strangers, so when I asked a few questions, he told me to shut my yap and keep it shut. So, I did."

"Anything else ya can remember?" Cotton asked.

"Yep, he bought a pint of laudanum, fer his injury I'd think, a pound of powder and the same in lead. The other stuff he purchased were just normal things a man would want in the field."

I gave his words some thought, then asked, "Did he have kids with 'em? Ya never answered that question."

"He damned sure did and treated the both of them kids rough. I don't take much to slavery, but the law says it's okay, so there ain't much I can do about 'er."

"Talked bad to the kids, did he?"

"Beat 'em is what I saw. The youngest was a girl of about ten and she was cryin' when the man left the store. I looked out the winder and he slapped the shit out of her and threatened to beat her again with a whip. The boy, he might have been all of twelve or thirteen, threatened to kill the man one day. The feller pulled that boy from the horse and stomped the living hell right out of 'em, and nobody did a damned thing. Good God, why would a man treat children that way?"

What I heard angered me, but it'd already happened, so there was nothing I could do about it until I got my hands on Blackie. In order not to draw suspicion, I said, "Ain't nobody goin' to help a black child when a white man is punishin' them. They belong to him, so what he does with 'em ain't nobodies business. Hell, by law he can kill 'em, if he decides to do the job, and the law won't even ask a question."

The man was visibly taken back by my words, I guess because of my color, so he said, "Well, by God, I went out there with my shotgun in my hands and told his nasty ass to leave. I won't have any kids treated like that, and I don't give a damn about their color, on my property."

Cotton snickered and then asked, "What'd he do when ya braced 'em?"

The clerk smiled and said, "He did what any other man with half a brain would do when a ten-gauge double-barreled shotgun is pointed at 'em, he left. It just shocked me. Oh, I've had my ass beat with switches, razor strops, broom handles and such, but I deserved it every single time, only he treated those kids like animals. You can tell the difference when a ma or pa is punishin' a child and a man that wants to cause real deep pain. It ain't right, what he did to those two."

"Was the kids in chains?" Cotton asked.

Lowering his head, the man replied, "They had chains around their necks, and I saw chains around their little hands and ankles. They was just small kids."

I handed the man a list of supplies and said, "There ain't nothin' we can do about what that man does to those kids. Not today, but tomorrow is a new day, and ya ain't never seen us before, okay?"

The man gave me a wink and said, "It'll take me about half an hour to get this stuff ready. Do ya want to take a table and have a few drinks?"

"How much fer the drinks?" Cotton asked and then grinned.

"Well, iffen yer goin' to kill that no good bastard with the kids, hell, I'll give ya a whole bottle fer free. That bothered me, it surely did." He reached under the counter, pulled out a bottle of good Kentucky bourbon and handed it to me. To Cotton he handed two fairly clean shot glasses.

"I ain't had no good Kain-tuck whiskey in a coons age," I said as we made for the nearest table.

"I'll have to weigh some of this in the backroom, so drink, and I'll be back directly."

We were working on our second drink when two men entered.

"I'll be there in a few minutes, gentlemen, so feel free to look around." The trader called out from the backroom.

I knew, just as sure as there is a God, these two men were looking for trouble. At least the old man is out of the way, I thought as I nudged Cotton with my foot under the table. Using his hands he signed, "I see and know."

"Trader!" The tallest of the men called out, "Get yer ass in here; we need our supplies, and we need 'em now!"

"I'll be there directly. I'm fillin' another order right now."

Walking to a shelf of goods lining the wall, the man grabbed it with both hands and pulled it over, sending bottles and boxes of goods to the floor. The crash was loud.

The trader walked from the room, saw the men and then said, "Morgan, I told ya before that ya an' Joseph ain't welcome in here. Now, I'm goin' to look the goods over and if anything is broken, ya'll pay fer it."

Morgan, the biggest man, said, "Wills, what ya say don't mean shit around heah. Why are ya servin' his kind in this place anyway?" The man met my eyes.

Sonofabitch, I thought, *Blackie paid these two to take care of anyone following him. Very few men, black or white, take on a man my size.*

I stood, my chair screeching as I moved, and looked the man called Morgan in the eyes. I heard Cotton moving and knew he was standing beside me.

Morgan laughed and said, "Ya better sit your black ass back down, son, or I'll kill ya dead as hell."

Now, I don't normally start fights, but I never run from one and I finish most I get involved in, so I said, "Iffen ya think ya can do the job, boy, give 'er a try. Only you'll find I take a heap of killin'."

The fool moved for his pistol and before he'd even cleared his belt, I fired, watched the ball take him low and in the belly, and then saw Joseph going for his gun. Cotton fired and the man was thrown back to a wall, where he stood looking down at blood seeping from the center of his chest. Morgan finally gave a loud sigh, fell to his knees, and then fell forward to land on his face. He began to scream none stop.

Joseph slowly slid down the wall and ended up in the sitting position, dead as hell.

"I saw it all," the trader said, his voice filled with excitement, "and they started it. Hell, Morgan even pulled iron first."

The door to the place suddenly opened, and in walked Sergeant Major Armitage, who I'd scouted for a few times in the past while working for the army. He moved to both men, looked them over, and then called out, "Private Wilkins, get a doc and do the damned job now."

When he looked at me, I smiled and said, "Howdy, Sergeant Major, sorry this happened."

The trader said, "Sergeant Major, those two on the floor started the fight. I saw it all happen."

Walking to me, the Sergeant extended his hand and as we shook he said, "I've known Nate for years, and there was no doubt in my mind who started the trouble."

I said, "You remember Cotton, don't ya?"

"Sure do." They shook hands.

"Have a seat, Sergeant, and have a whiskey with us while we wait for the doctor."

"By damn, that's the best offer I've had all day. While we're drinkin' ya can tell me what in the hell yer doin' at this fort."

I explained what was going on, where we were headed, and why. The sergeant didn't interrupt me once as I told my story.

Knocking his drink back, he wiped his mouth off with a gloved hand and said, "Nate, ya've got big balls, old son, but if ya kill a white man down South, they'll string ya up pretty damned fast. Are ya damned sure ya want take this job?"

"I've never in my life started a job I didn't finish. I figure with Cotton along, they'll leave me alone, thinkin' I'm his slave. But, Blackie and Grisham both need killin' and God willin', we'll do the job."

At that point the doctor entered, looked at Joseph and said, "This man is dead." Then moving to Morgan he squatted, looked the man over and ordered, "A couple of ya privates get in here and take this man to my tent. He ain't dead yet, but he's headin' that way pretty damned fast."

Armitage stood and said, "If ya two stop here on the way back I'll buy ya both a drink. Right now, I need to be seein' to my boys. Ya remember what I said, Nate, and watch yer ass down South."

"Anything ya need to know about the killin's here?" Cotton asked.

Armitage shook his head and said, "If Nate and ya killed 'em, I figure they needed killin'. Nope, we ain't got any law here yet, and the army ain't got any more questions, so yer free to go."

Within an hour we were moving away from the fort and toward Missouri Territory. I feared the situation I was about to enter, but knew I was right, and understood my choice had already been made. Some things in life take a lot of balls to face, only a man ain't much of a man if fails to do what he says he will do. I had no disillusions, either. For a black man to kill a white man in the Deep South meant almost instant death, without a trial of any sort, so getting caught wasn't an option. We had to get in, kill, and then get out.

It was near dusk when Cotton said, "Let's find a camp, I'm not feelin' good all of a sudden."

"Got a fever or other problems?"

"It's my gut that hurts."

He must have some serious pain, or he'd never said anything, I thought, and pointed off our right and said, "We'll move into those trees."

"I think I have a case of the squirts comin' on."

"I'll get camp up and iffen ya have to run the bushes, take a rifle with ya."

He nodded and kept moving.

It wasn't long until I had a fire burning, a lean-to up, and all of our supplies under canvas. Cotton had run to the bushes a number of times and returned to his blankets weaker with each trip. Finally, as supper cooked, he fell asleep and I leaned back on my elbows.

I could think of nothing I'd drank or eaten that Cotton hadn't had, but I felt fine. I was worried about him, but not overly so, because illnesses hit us all at times. Our treatment was limited in most cases and we really couldn't do much, except most doctors couldn't either. Common sicknesses were left to pretty much run their course, doctor around or not. Doctors had no idea of what caused most diseases and had no real cures. If I took sick, I'd want a Injun medicine man working on me, because they knew and understood most sicknesses, with the exception of illnesses brought by the white men.

I leaned over and felt Cotton's forehead and noticed a low grade fever. I pulled a pan from our supplies and added some water. From my possibles bag I removed a small pouch of crushed willow bark and added it to the water. I then placed it on the fire to boil. I'd learned to treat fevers as a young buck when one of my partner came down sick. At the time we were wintering with the Crow, and a shaman told me willow bark cured most fevers. I didn't believe him, because we white men had nothing that worked on a fever. Nonetheless, it worked then and works every time, unless the fever is cause by a serious injury.

A few minutes later, I was attacked by a foul odor and knew Cotton had messed his pants. If he was too sick to run to the bushes, this was no normal case of the squirts. I tried to get 'em to move, but it was if he'd passed out.

I walked to the creek and returned with a bucket of water. I then pulled his buckskin trousers down past his knees and cleaned him, but I'd not even pulled his pants up when he went again. This time I noticed blood mixed with the watery waste from his body. *Lawdy, bleedin' but the blood is fresh, so maybe his rear is irritated from goin' so much today. If the blood had been like tar and dark in color, his belly would be the problem,* I thought. I tried to remember what I could about folks that bled from their rear, but only knew small pox caused it, and at times so did bad water. I knew he didn't have small pox. For bad water I knew of no cure, and the only treatment was to force good water down him.

To keep the smell down and keep him as clean as possible, I removed his trousers, placed a wide sheet of canvas under his butt and kept a container of water near. I then forced about a cup of water down him. He didn't throw up, but if he had I'd been able to see if his gut was injured. A man with a belly injury can't eat or drink, because they puke it up. Also, when they puke, if they're bleeding inside you'll see the blood. The blood will either be fresh, which usually means it's a throat injury or look like coffee grounds, which means the belly is bleeding.

Near midnight I started feeding him whiskey and water, mostly whiskey. I wanted him to sleep and rest; I'd keep him clean. If you want to worry about someone you really care about, let 'em start passing blood and it scares the hell out of you. I felt helpless and, really, I was. He'd grunt, squirt, and I'd wipe him clean.

At some point, I fell asleep. Hearing a noise, I jerked awake and when I look around I spotted Broken Bow and Man Killer sitting beside me at the fire.

"You need sleep, my friend, so rest. We will care for the ill one."

I went to my robes and didn't remember closing my eyes.

I awoke a couple of hours before sunup and the first thing I did was check on Cotton. He was clean and appeared to be breathing deeply and evenly. I felt his forehead and the fever was gone, so the willow bark must have worked.

I glanced at Broken Bow and asked, *"Where is Man Killer?"*

"Hunting. If we have one sick, much meat will be needed

until he can ride once more."

"What you speak is true. How do warriors of the Shoshone come to be with me?"

"Our shaman had a dream. In the dream he saw much danger for you until you get to the land that touches the wide muddy river. The shaman said we were to go to you, but only go so far."

"Missouri, is the name of the land that touches the muddy river."

"We are to turn back once you are there. The dream said it would not be wise for us to travel over the lands owned by the Quapaw, Kansi, Fox, and Osage tribes."

"What of my friend? Did he awaken?"

"No, he has not opened his eyes, but he is no longer hot and has not passed blood again. He drinks freely when given water and he has drank much."

"Good, rest will make a man stronger when he is ill."

"Snow on Head has taken bad water. The spirit that lives in the water must pass through his body before he will heal. This, my brother, will take time."

"Then we will wait. He is my brother and he would wait for me, if I were sick."

"Of course, warriors must care for each other when no shaman is with them."

A couple of hours later, Man Killer rode into our camp with a deer tied to the back of his horse. He immediately made weak soup with the heart and liver of the animal, along with a few tubers and other plants I didn't know the name of. As I watched him prepare the simple meal, he glanced at me and asked, *"So, how are you this fine morning Big Raven Man?"*

"I am fine."

"Our shaman asked me to speak for him."

Likely some injun gibberish about a dream or vision, I thought, but said, *"And, what are his words for me?"*

"He saw your fight in a dream. You were fighting two white men and while you may be seriously injured, you will bring much honor to yourself. You will kill both men, but will not take their scalps. Watch for a dog. I do not know what this dog looks like or it's size, but it will save your life."

"A dog? I do not understand. I do not have a dog."

"You will meet this dog on your journey, but I cannot say how, because I do not know."

"I understand."

"You must heed his words about the dog, because without the animal you will die."

My thoughts were confused and while I believed some of the things Injuns dreamed, I thought this dream about me was pure bullshit, but I couldn't say that to Man Killer. I was quiet for a long time, to show I was given his words much thought, but finally said, *"When you see your shaman, speak for me. Tell him I have taken his dream into both my heart and mind. I will keep the dog safe and care well for it, once I have the animal."*

"Remember, my brother, to go against the Great Creator would not be wise. You must follow the path my shaman has given you to walk, or you will die."

Chapter 12

Three days later, Cotton was awake for breakfast, but still very weak. He was sitting up and eating a small bowl of stew, his first real food since he'd taken ill. He was eating slowly, like a starving man does, enjoying the texture and juices from the food. He'd not be able to eat much, because his stomach had shrunk and it would take a day or two before he would eat a normal meal.

"We have been watched by others." Broken Bow said flatly.

"What tribe and how many?" Man Killer asked from the fire where he was placing meat skewered on sticks in the ground, so the meat would cook without burning. He tilted each stick near the dancing flames.

"I saw two fingers of tracks, but that means little. The tracks were not known to me, and I do not know the tribe."

I said, *"Let us hope it is not the Oto or we will fight, and it will be a hard battle."*

Man Killer replied, *"The tribe matters little and if we must fight, we will do so. It is a good day to die."*

I don't think it's a good day to die, my friend, I thought, but said nothing.

"The Oto are our enemies and to have a Oto scalp would bring a man much honor."

"Oto are ferocious warriors, but we are south of where they normally are found. I think it may be Osage," I said.

"These Osage, I do not know of them." Man Killer said.

"They are friendly to white men."

"We are friendly to some white eyes, but not all. A tribe must pick friends carefully or they will lose their lands."

Cotton said, "The Osage have lost much of what they once called theirs. The white men take more and more of their lands with each new season."

Broken Bow met my eyes and said, *"They must be a weak nation to allow their lands to be stolen. True warriors will give no land and will fight for what the Great Creator has given them."*

I thought for a second and then said, "I do not know the hearts and minds of the Osage people. Their shaman may have been warned by The One Above to not fight white men. It is easy to sit and talk about fighting, when we do not know the feelings of the people or the words from The Creator."

"This is true." Broken Bow said.

Out of the blue, Man Killer said in a voice barely above a whisper, *"There are others watching us. I see   "*

I heard a sound like a hand slapping leather and when I looked at the noise, Man Killer had an arrow in his left arm. Everyone went to ground and moved behind anything that would offer some protection.

"This arrow is Oto." Man Killer said and then broke the shaft off, leaving about three inches sticking from his arm.

A warrior broke from the trees, gave a bloodcurdling war cry, and ran toward us. I saw three others coming from the right and two from our left. I raised my rifle, fired and saw a man go down, but seeing I didn't have time to reload, I pulled a pistol. Arrows flew from both Shoshone and men dropped, some fell quietly while others screamed in pain. Cotton's rifle fired and a man nearest our camp went down, the top of his head missing. I'd just turned to check behind us, when I heard a scream and glancing at Man Killer, I saw he was down with a spear in the chest.

At that point a man struck me from behind, knocked my pistol from my hand and buried a knife in my left arm. We both fell to the ground and I instantly noticed this was no normal Oto. The man was close to my size, maybe a couple inches shorter, and his eyes reflected deep hatred. I rolled on the ground with him, and at one point he attempted to roll me into the flames of our fire. I was able to kick myself away.

The meat, get a stick! I thought, because the longer a fight lasted the more blood I would lose. Eventually, I'd grow weak from blood loss and when that happened, I'd die. I felt my left hand touch one of the sharpened wooden skewers our meat was cooking on, so I grabbed it with my hand. The next time we rolled and I found myself on bottom, I stabbed hard with the sharpened wood and grinned when it entered the Oto's left eye.

I heard Cottons rifle *crack* once again and heard the *twang* of Broken Bow's arrow being released. The Oto screamed and let go of me, placing both of his hands to his face. Blood was flowing freely from his eye. I looked around in desperation and spotted my pistol within easy reach. I grabbed the weapon, pulled the hammer back and placed the barrel against the warriors belly. I promptly jerked the trigger, felt him knocked away and off of me, and then heard him screaming.

It was quiet, with the exception of the injured screaming and the dying moaning softly.

"They have gone." Broken Bow stated, as I wrapped some cloth around my injury.

I stood on weak legs, walked to the fire and plopped down, stunned by my fight. I could feel blood running down my arm freely, but for right now I needed to calm down. I reached by the log, pulled a clay jug around, and pulled the cork. I then raise the container and took a long gulp of the raw traders rotgut whiskey. I followed that drink with two more long ones.

Cotton crawled from behind the log and asked, "Are ya okay? Hell, yer covered in blood."

"I'll live. *Broken Bow, how is Man Killer?"*

"He is not long for this world and will cross to the other side in less time than it takes to smoke a pipe."

"And ya?" I asked looking at Cotton.

"Arrow through the upper left arm. I jumped behind the log when the whole shebang started."

"Does it hurt much?" I asked and then tightened the knot on my injury.

"Like a sumbitch, but I'll survive."

I heard Man Killer singing his death song and knew he wouldn't last much longer. To me, an Injuns death song was like our praying before we died. We knew, and most importantly, he knew, he was dying.

The alcohol fortified me, so I stood and said, "Come Broken Bow, we must make sure our enemies are truly dead. But first I must reload my guns."

After I finished loading my rifle and was working on my pistol, Man Killer stopped singing in the middle of a sentence. I heard a loud rattling from inside of him, followed by a long sigh. Man Killer of the Shoshone Nation was dead.

"Come, we must now check our enemies." I said to a

grieving Broken Bow.

I counted four dead, saw pools of blood where others had fallen, and Broken Bow took one man captive. I dreaded what was about to happen, because this wounded Oto would soon pay for the death of Man Killer. After tying the wounded mans arms and feet, the Shoshone began to mutilate the dead. When he noticed me watching him, he asked, *"You do not mark your enemies?"*

"The Great Creator has told all white men not to mark our enemies."

"Do you not take the scalps of those you kill?"

"The path I walk does not allow me to scalp my enemies. If I do so, my power will be weakened."

"My path does not stop me from taking hair."

Walking to the wounded Oto, Broken Bow grabbed the mans oily hair and pulled his head up. The Oto, suspecting he was about to be killed, tilted his head back and closed his eyes. The Shoshone quickly ran the edge of his knife around the man's head and then grasping the hair in front, pull the scalp back. When the scalp pulled loose, I heard a sucking sound, followed by the scream of the captive. Broken Bow pushed the wounded Oto to the ground, smiled and then placed the scalp in his sash. I noticed blood dripping from the hair ran down the warriors shirt, as the captive rolled on the ground.

"A Shoshone would not have screamed, Oto, while being scalped! We are The People and our men are brave and fearless! Oto are like women."

According to tribal law, since the Oto was Broken Bow's captive, he could do what he wanted to the man. *He'll be tortured to death at some point today. If nothing else, to avenge the death of Man Killer. Him and Broken Bow were good friends and it's expected of him,* I thought. But, we needed to move and do the job now, if Cotton could ride at all. Those Oto that escaped might go for more warriors.

"Cotton, can ya ride?" I asked, concerned about the blood he'd lost from an arm wound.

"Sure, but tie me on. I ain't got the strength to ride under my own power. I lost a lot of blood durin' the fight."

"Broken Bow, we must leave. The Oto may have gone for more warriors."

"I will prepare my dead brother, whose name I cannot speak, according to our customs. He was a great warrior and

this must be done, even at the risk of my own death. Take the captive when you leave. I will meet you before the sun dies this day."

"So be it. You must do what is required. We will leave quickly."

"Cotton, get yer ass over here and let me wrap up yer arm. Yer slingin' blood all over the place."

"Just wrap it, because we don't have the time to treat it yet. We can do that tonight."

Pulling his possibles bag around, Cotton pulled out some material, and I then wrapped the arm tightly. This will have to do until we can stop for a spell, I thought, and then said, *"Broken Bow, help me load the captive and Snow Top on a horse. Because of my injury, I cannot do this alone."*

"I am sorry, my brother, I should have known, but my heart feels much pain for the death of my lifelong brother."

"It is as it should be when a brave man dies."

Broken Bow nodded, and I could see his tear-stained cheeks.

Cotton was tied over the back of his horse, belly down, because he looked faint. Then, taking the reins to the packhorse, captive, and Cotton, I moved toward Missouri. My partner didn't made a sound for over four hours, then he said, "Nate, I can't take much more of this shit. I need to ride sittin' up. My chest is hurtin'."

I stopped, cut his bonds and then helped him into a setting position. Once in the saddle, he asked, "Can I have a drink of whiskey? That belly ridin' will kill a man, given enough time."

I handed him the whiskey, moved to the Oto and checked him. He was awake and glared at me when I checked the ropes tying him to the horse belly down. I was tempted to pull my pistol and shoot him in the head, but just couldn't do it. He belonged to Broken Bow, but I sure dreaded tonight. Injuns are experts at torture and I'd be expected, as a brother to Man Killer, to watch.

As I walked by Cotton on the way to my horse, he said, "Be

rough at camp this evenin'.'"

All I said was, "Uh-huh, and keep the whiskey with ya."

By dusk, Broken Bow still had not caught up with us and I began to worry. The Oto may have returned, but I doubted that happened. We'd hurt them badly and they're not a stupid people by any stretch of the mind, so most likely they'd gone back to the village to lick their wounds. The captive had not been given water or food, but at this point I allowed him a long drink of water. However, I wasn't going to feed him.

A few minutes later, Broken Bow entered our camp and dismounted. He walked to the fire, squatted and said, *"It is finished. My brother is now on the other side. His death will bring much sorrow when I return to the village."* He then picked up a stick with meat on it and began to eat.

"He died in battle, as a true warrior and should be honored."

The brave nodded.

"What of your captive?" I asked.

"When I finish my meat, we will prepare to ride. While this should be done with much torture, I do not have the time. The Oto were near our last camp when I left."

"And, how will you send your enemy to the other side?"

"By fire, my brother, and we will see if he dies well. Few die well with fire."

Broken bow finished his meal and then started cutting limbs from pine trees and placing them on his captive. The Oto, laying on the ground, must have had an idea of what was to come, but he was a tough bastard and said nothing.

"Since I do not have a burning pole in place, this will kill the Oto well enough. Now, pack the horses and prepare to ride. Once the Oto dies, we will ride all of this night and tomorrow."

I loaded our gear, but my arm was starting to throb; I knew it would be tomorrow before it'd get cleaned. I'm not a mean man and the death Broken Bow had planned for the Oto bothered me, and more than just a little. I could not imagine a more horrible death than by fire. I helped Cotton mount and then walked to the Shoshone's side.

"We are ready to ride," I said.

"Now the Oto must die." Broken Bow walked to our campfire and picked a burning log. Taking it to the captive, he allowed the flames to touch the pine boughs. Suddenly, I could

hear the Oto singing his death song and I hoped it was a short one. The flames grew in size quickly and soon dense white smoke was reaching for the sky.

Abruptly, the Oto began to scream like an animal as the hot flames ate at his flesh. Less than two minutes later, the screams ceased and all that remained was the snapping and popping of the fire, and the sweet overpowering scent of burnt flesh.

"Now, we must ride long and hard, because this death will anger the Oto. He did not die bravely." Broken Bow tossed the Oto scalp to the flames.

Two days later we had to stop because our mounts were staggering. We'd tried every trick in the book we knew to lose the Oto, but had no idea if it worked or not. *I'm so tired even my scalp hurts,* I thought as I dismounted in some large rocks. Broken Bow was behind us and scouting our back trail. I hope he kept his head out of his ass, or the Shoshone would be short a good warrior come sunup. As near as I could tell, we were about a half days ride to Missouri Territory, and our Shoshone friend would leave us at that point. He'd have to use every skill he had to avoid the Oto on the return trip, unless he rode south and then west for a long ways. Once far enough west, he could turn north. I rubbed my tired eyes, which felt like they had sand in them, and said, "Let's get some hot food in us. I'm tired of jerky and pemmican. That damned lard in pemmican upsets my gut."

Cotton chuckled and said, "It ain't lard, it's buffalo fat, but even I have a hard time eatin' the nasty shit. I only eat it when I ain't got a choice."

"I'll put on a pot of beans with bacon in it. Then, I'll see what kind of plants I can find to add to the whole mess. Ya'd figure there would be some Injun taters or other roots 'round here."

"Keep an eye out, 'cause we still don't know iffen we lost them Oto or not."

I grinned at him and replied, "Ya can slide, old son, because I always keep my eyes open. That's why I've lasted as long as I have as a mountain man. Besides, we have to eat."

"I'd rather sleep right now, but I'm smart enough to know eatin' comes first."

I yawned and replied, "I hear ya, and my ass is draggin' too. Well, I'll be back directly." Picking up my Hawken, I moved toward the creek, hoping to find a mess of watercress for supper.

In less than an hour I gathered a mess of dandelion greens and watercress and while they were slim pickin's, they'd fight off scurvy. *Most folks back east live soft lives, with good but simple food, and they're never happy with what they have. Let 'em come out here fer a spell, and they'll discover it's poor bull at times,* I thought as I made my way back to camp.

When I neared the camp, Broken Bow was by the fire and he nodded at me. For some reason the man looked better than me and Cotton, which I chalked up to his way of life. See, Injuns are tough people and the life they live is hard. Things that wore our asses out, well, didn't seem to bother them at all.

"Our back trail is clear." Broken Bow said.

"That is good." I replied to the man and then turning to Cotton, I asked, "Can ya take a look at my arm now and clean it up good?" It'd not been cleaned since I was injured, and the bandage had not been changed. We'd been living in our saddles, so my wound had to wait, as had Cotton's.

"Sure, pull yer shirt off and let me clean 'er up."

Just the simple act of removing my buckskin shirt hurt like hell, and I knew then there was a problem with the injury. Once my shirt was off, I sat in the dirt and waited.

Cotton brought his possibles bag, sat beside me, and unwrapped the injury. I knew my injury had soured because the cloth not only had blood on it, but also a greenish-yellow pus. *Damn, I'm in fer some real pain in a few minutes,* I thought, but said nothing.

Handing me the bottle of laudanum, Cotton said, "Take a sip of this and then have a cup of whiskey. I'm gonna have to clean your knife wound here in a bit."

I'd forgotten about the painkiller and smiled as I took a sip. I handed the bottle back to him and then picked up a cup of whiskey he'd poured for me. *I won't feel nothin' directly,* I thought and then smiled.

I threw the drink back, wiped my mouth off with the back of my hand, and said, "Go ahead and let's get this over with right now."

"*I will keep watch.*" Broken Bow said and moved toward the trail.

Cotton pulled his knife from the fire, waved it in the air to allow it to cool, and said, "Give me a minute or two fer the blade to cool down."

I refilled my drink, not trusting the laudanum to kill the pain, but I was already feeling the drug. I took a small sip of whiskey and waited.

"Okay, let me get this over with or we'll be here forever." Cotton took his knife and prepared to pry the scab off my arm. He placed his knife blade against my arm and then in one quick sweep, bringing the blade down, keeping it ninety degrees from my arm, scraped the injury. The scab fell to the dirt. I'd closed my eyes expecting pain, but felt only the pressure of the blade. *Thank God for laudanum, or I'd just lost mind when that scab came off.*

He laid the knife down and poured some alcohol on my wound. Then, he began to squeeze the pus from the injury. Occasionally he poured more whiskey on the wound. When I glanced at my arm, I saw a mixture of blood and pus slowly moving the length of the limb. I shuddered and found the foul smell offensive.

Finally, he soaked some cotton material in whiskey and wrapped my arm.

"Thanks," I said and then added, "I'm a bit under the weather and think I'll take me a short nap."

The next time I opened my eyes, Cotton was placing a pot of coffee on the fire. He must have heard me move, because he asked, "Ya feelin' better?"

"Stronger is what I feel. How about you?"

"My injury is healin' just fine. But, you should feel stronger. Hell, ya should be, ya slept for almost two days."

"No?"

"Well, ya slept through the first night and last night, so what do ya think? Ya were weak and treatin' an injury like ya have takes a lot out of man, laudanum or not."

"Where is Broken Bow?"

"I told 'em to go on back to the village 'bout an hour ago, and that you'd be fine in a few days. He didn't want to leave, and likely would have stayed, but I reminded him he'd have to leave anyway and soon. We're close to Missouri Territory, so I saw no need for him to continue waiting. Once he saw yer arm was healing clean, he left."

"He's one hell of a man."

"Yep, I have a fondness for the whole tribe, myself."

"Near mid-mornin', ain't it?"

"Not yet. I'd guess lookin' at the sun it's just a hair past daylight."

I yawned and said, "We need to ride this mornin'. And, before you say anything, iffen I get tired I'll say something to ya."

"Okay, we'll ride, but go easy with that arm. Ya tear it open and there will be hell to pay."

"I'll be fine."

CHAPTER 13

The next five days were slow moving because we'd entered Missouri and once we hit the Ozarks, it turned hilly and rough. The trees were mainly oaks and hickory, with a few scatter pines and cedars. The lazy streams were ice cold, many spring feed, and while not deep, they were filled with trout. Now, I'm not much of a fish eater, don't know many mountain men that are, but at odd times I like a mess of fish for supper.

This evening we stopped by a slow moving stream and within an hour caught six nice trout for supper. Back at the fire, after we'd gutted the fish, we stuck them on sticks, inserted through their mouths, and placed them beside the fire to cook. As we shared a pot of coffee, the scent of our simple meal was wonderful and brought back a few fond memories of my childhood. *My daddy, now there was a man who loved to eat fish,* I thought.

"What are ya grinnin' about?" Cotton asked.

"Thinkin' is all, and about my daddy. He surely loved a mess of fish and the kind didn't matter. He'd always have cornbread with fish."

"My pa was the same. He'd wash it all down with a fruit jar of buttermilk that had about a quarter of an inch of pepper on top. And, hot peppers, man, he loved those things."

"Yer pa still alive?" I asked and then thought, *Damn, how many times has Cotton sat by the fire talkin' about losin' his family to Injuns and I have to forget how they died. I must be more tired than I realize. I need to keep him off this subject, or he'll talk my damned ear off all night. I really don't want to listen to him all night again.*

"You know he's not, and I've told ya before how he died—Injuns killed my whole family. Hell, if he was still alive he'd be seventy or so and most folks die around fifty. But, no, pa's gone. How 'bout yer-un?"

"I'm sure he's dead by now. My pa was one hell of a special man and spent a lot of time just doin' nothin' with me. I didn't realize, not until years later, each time we did that he was teachin' me something. I forgot about yer family and I'm sorry."

"Hows that? I mean about yer pa teachin' ya?"

"Let's say we were whittlin' on some wood, why he'd teach me how to keep my knife blade sharp. Or, iffen we were fishin', he'd teach me how to tie knots and such. He taught while we had a good time."

Silence filled the camp with the only sound the crackling fire and bugs making noises just outside of camp. The crickets were much nosier than usual too, but they comforted me as I sat by the dancing flames.

To keep his mind off his dead family, I asked, "Have ya ever been down this way? I mean to Mississippi?"

"Nope, but iffen that's where ya want ta head, by God, that's where we're goin'."

"Am I crazy to try to stop this slavery stuff?"

Turning his head and gazing into my eyes, he replied, "Nate, we already had this discussion, and I'll not kick a dead horse. Ya seem to think Blackie and Grisham need killin' and that's all I need to know."

"Ya realize ya won't be able to come back east for years, right? I mean iffen we kill those two."

Cotton laughed and said, "What in the hell do I care? I don't intend to ever come back anyway, unless another good reason, like this one, comes up again. The odds are, in five years me and ya will be dead anyway, kilt on some mountain or out on the plains."

"Ya ever think about death much, I mean really think about it?"

"Nope, because I think thinkin' on somethin' like that could drive a man crazy. I do believe in God and that's all I need."

"I believe too, but neither one of us are good Christians."

Cotton laughed again and replied, "No, I guess we ain't. How-some-ever, we can't go to no church, like these pork eaters do, but we live in Gods livin' room up in the mountains. I pray almost everyday, and God knows my thoughts. I'm like ya are most of the time. I live my life with honor, try to do what I say I will, and try my damnedest to be the best man I can. I honestly cain't do no more than that, no matter where I live."

"I believe and I was baptized when I was 'bout ten or so. I think most of us in the —"

"Movement and no night sounds." Cotton interrupted.

Acting normal, I picked up the coffee pot, and as I filled my cup, I realized the sounds were gone. "When I say now, go to ground, okay?"

"Yep."

"Now!"

I rolled over a log and then crawled behind a large oak tree. When I'd left camp, I'd taken my rifle with me. I scanned the area, but saw no sign of Cotton. It seemed darker than normal, only I knew it was because I'd been by the fire too long. After a man has been near light it takes time for his eyes to adjust to darkness.

Long minutes of silence and then Cotton called out, "It's a white man, and he's been shot!"

"Where are ya?"

"I'm right in front of our shelter, maybe fifty feet into the woods."

I cursed as I stumbled over roots and rocks making my way to Cotton. I fell a number of times, but finally I spotted movement in front of me. "Is he alive?"

"He's breathin' and bleedin', but other than that I know nothin'."

"Let's get 'em back to camp and by the fire; we'll check 'em out.'

"Ya take his feet and I'll take his shoulders."

We packed the man from the woods and once at camp, we placed him on Cotton's blanket. The front of his homespun shirt was bloody, except that meant little.

"I'll get the whiskey," I said and moved to the shelter.

"He's got two bullets in 'em. One is in his shoulder and the other his head. The head injury ain't much, only it's the more dangerous of the two."

I returned to the fire, handed the whiskey jug to Cotton and then asked, "Any idea where he came from or what happened?"

"He was sayin' somethin' about a horse was all I caught, and a big man."

"I guess we'll have to wait."

Suddenly from the woods came a loud warning growl. We looked toward the sound, and saw a huge dog, maybe a wolf mix of some sort, standing just within the light of our fire.

Looks like this feller might have had a dog, too. A big ass dog.

Pulling a big piece of meat from a stick near the fire, I threw it to the dog.

"Is that big thing a dog or wolf?" Cotton asked.

"Mix, and I think it belongs to this feller. Don't bother it, unless we're attacked, because having a dog around might be a good idea."

Cotton looked at me, tilted his head to the left and asked, "Ya reckon?"

"Sure, they can smell, hear and see things we can't. Leave 'em be and throw 'em some meat now and again to show 'em we're friendly. Given time he'll come to us." Then I remembered the shaman's warning that a dog would save my life. I shuddered and thought, *nonsense.*

Over the course of the evening, Cotton and I would throw pieces of meat to the big dog and finally, it was time to get some sleep. He took the first guard and I went to sleep almost immediately.

Seemed like I'd just closed my eyes, when I felt a light touch on my ankle. I awoke, glanced around and saw Cotton squatted beside me.

"It's quiet and not much moving, except bugs and night critters. The dog moved to the injured man's side once ya went to bed, and I moved into the woods to guard."

I sat up and asked, "Hows your patient?"

"He was okay the last time I checked 'em, but that was over an hour ago. I haven't tried to look 'em over again with the dog beside 'em."

I stood and said, "Let me see iffen I can get near the man. We have to be able to keep an eye on him or the dog will have to go."

I approached the man slowly and speaking low even tones I said to the dog, "Hey, big feller, I need to look yer master over and see iffen he's still okay." *Lord, don't let this big beast attack me or he'll tear me apart,* I thought.

About a foot from the man, I stopped. I picked up a pan of water and placed it in front of me as I neared. Squatting beside the man, I placed the water as close to the dog as I could without moving from where I crouched. The animal looked at me and I forced a smile. *So far, so good, but he might move when I try to touch the man.*

I grew worried when the animal slowly approached the

water, sniffed it and then began to drink. I waited a few minutes and then, slowly, I checked the bandages on the man's head and then his shoulder. The dog didn't growl or move, but I damned sure keep an eye on him as I worked. The injured man was breathing deep and regular, so I suspected he'd survive. But, with a head injury, I had no idea how he'd be when he came around. I'd known a man in Mississippi that'd been kicked in the head by a mule, and he'd spent the rest of his life drooling down his shirt and making baby sounds. Head injuries were dangerous.

All was going well, until I reached for the gallon clay jug of alcohol, when I heard a low growl from the animal. Once again I smiled and said, "This will help yer friend by killin' his pain."

I poured two cups, and the growling stopped.

I lifted one cup and placing my hand under the man's head, I raised it and allowed some of the amber colored liquid to enter his mouth. As I fed the whiskey to the man, I constantly rambled on and on, in even tones, to the dog. Finally, when the cup was empty, I placed it by my side. I then raised the other cup and downed it all in one drink. When I finished, I wiped my mouth off with my hand and looked at the dog. His head was tilted and he was watching me closely. I think that critter knew I was trying my best to help his friend.

Cotton moved toward me and the dog gave a warning growl, bared his teeth, and his hackles rose. "I have some meat for ya, big guy." Cotton said, but the growling continued.

"Hand it to me, Cotton, and let's see if he'll take it from my hand."

I took the meat from him and handed it toward the dog.

"Iffen he snatches that meat, ya better count yer fingers, because that's one mean-ass critter."

"Cotton, move off a ways and let's see what he does."

After he'd moved, the dog watched me and growling stopped.

"Here, big feller, want this?" I asked, still holding the meat.

Minutes passed, but finally the dog cautiously moved toward me and it took all I had inside not to show fear. *This mutt must weigh well over a hundred pounds, has teeth like a grizzly, and is scared, so take this slow like,* I thought.

When the dog was within a foot of me, he extended his head and snatched the meat from my trembling hand. I gave him another smile and said, "Good boy!"

Cotton asked, "Ya 'bout done playin' with old Blue there? I'm sleepy and it's yer turn to guard fer a spell."

"Go on and hit yer robes, I've got it. I'll move to where ya were watchin' fer my shift."

As Cotton moved toward his bed, I picked up my rifle and moved to the trees.

About an hour before dawn it turned cold as hell and the wind picked up. I glanced overhead, but saw no clouds or bad weather moving in, so I was confused. *It'll warm up once the sun comes out,* I thought and then glanced at the dog. He was sleeping, as near as I could tell, and laying right beside his master. I hoped the man lived, or I suspected we'd end up shooting the dog and I didn't like that idea much. Bad People I can shoot, dogs or other animals, well, it is always hard on me. Animals trust us to care for them and they're so loving. Each time I've had to put a good horse down, I've cried after doing the nasty task.

Once the sun started peeking over the hills, I moved to the fire, and was happy the dog stayed beside his master. The animal watched me closely as I put a pot of coffee on to boil. I woke Cotton and then moved to our injured man. I was surprised to see his eyes open and when the dog growled the man said "Baxter, that's enough."

The animal watched, but remained quiet.

"How ya feelin' this fine cold mornin'?" I asked.

"I've got a hell of a headache and my shoulder throbs."

"Hell, I'd guess so, ya took a ball to the head and one to the shoulder. The ball went completely through yer shoulder and the head ain't much of a wound, but they can be tricky at times."

He was moaning and looking like his eyes were bothering him, so I filled a cup with whiskey and handed it to him. "I don't think one cup will kill the pain, so when yer ready fer more, let me know."

"Thank ya kindly fer the corn squeezin's."

"Ya from around here?" I asked, then pulled out the bacon.

As I sliced the meat, I watched the dog and knew my side of fatback wouldn't make a snack fer the big guy.

"I had a cabin near the Big Piney River, but I ain't sure what's there now."

"Ya got a name?"

"Yep, but I don't go by it much these days. Just call me Grits."

I chuckled and asked, "Now how in the hell did ya get a name like that?"

He downed the rest of his drink and handed his cup out toward me as he said, "When I was a kid, I loved grits. It was a good thing too, because we were dirt poor and didn't have much. Hell, I still ain't got much but at least it's mine."

"I know that feeling and well."

"Yer 'bout a big sumbitch, where's yer master?"

"I don't have a master and my friend is doin' his mornin' business. He'll be back directly."

"A freeman, huh? I ain't met many black folks that are free. I ain't seen ya 'round here before, so where do ya call home?"

Cotton was walking from the woods and I saw the surprise in the man's face when he noticed my partner was a white man. "My name is Nate, and I'm a trapper from out west in the shining mountains. Cotton Top, my buddy, is usually just called Cotton. It's due to all that white hair he's got."

"Ya doin' okay this mornin'?" Cotton asked as he neared the fire.

"I'll live, but feel like hell warmed over."

"There's plenty of whiskey, so drink until the pain goes away."

"I'll do that."

"Grits, what happened to you?"

He blinked rapidly a few times and then said, "I was sittin' down to supper when this feller rides to my place and asks if he can water his horses from my well. I said sure and didn't give it much thought. I did notice he had two black kids shackled, but I kept my mouth shut. Hell, I got enough troubles staying alive without askin' fer more. When I turned to go into my house, he shot me in the back and then while I was on the ground, he shot me in the head."

"We'll," Cotton said, "Yer a lucky bastard, because iffen he'd been payin' attention, he'd seen the head shot wasn't a killin' wound. It just grazed yer noggin, but yer goin' to need to be careful with yer head for a long spell."

"Where were ya headed out here?" I asked.

"I have a half-brother, by the name of LeRoy, that lives about three miles from this spot and I wanted to get to his place, I think. Honestly, I don't remember much after that head shot."

"Yer dogs been by yer side most of the time, once he learned that me and Nate wasn't out to hurt ya. We fed 'em some meat and while he never turned friendly enough fer us to pet 'em, he quit lookin' like he wanted to eat us."

Grits laughed and replied, "Baxter is a good dog and I found 'em town, oh, maybe five years back. He was just a young pup then, but he's grown a mite since that day."

"Well, he's loyal to ya, I can say that much," I replied.

Cotton filled the man's cup with whiskey again and asked, "So what now?"

"As soon as I'm shed of this headache, I've a back shooting sumbitch to kill, that's what. Hell, he had no call to shoot me, I would've fed him and given 'em the shirt off my back. I don't take this shit lightly, and he'll regret the day he met my ass."

"Ya need to heal up a bit before ya tackle any man," I said and then thought, *maybe Grits and his dog would like to go to Mississippi. I'd draw less attention with traveling with two white men.*

"Besides, I think we know the man yer after. Was he a big man, 'bout Nate's size?"

"Yep, had a black boy and a cute little girl with 'em."

"We're lookin' fer 'em too, but we know where he lives."

Meeting my eyes, Grits asked, "Those yer kids, Nate?"

"Nope, my dead friends, but I'll take 'em home with me, just as soon as I skin Blackie's ass alive."

Chapter 14

There was little left of Grits' place, except ash and burnt logs. The farm animals were dead, a dead cat was discovered floating in the well, and not so much as a bean could be found. His horses and one mule were gone, which is what I think Blackie wanted to start with, because his mounts were tired. If he took care of his horses like he did people, they were likely in sad shape.

Grits walked around cussing to beat the band, and I could tell he'd do what it took to make Blackie pay, but first we had to get near enough to the man to do the job. I knew where he'd be once on the plantation, or thought I did, but the key player in my mind was ole man Grisham. He was the one responsible for sending out dozens of slavers to enslave folks that were free and steal those that weren't. I'm sure he'd made a fortune over the years and if not for Blackie's greed and his thought that he could take me, I never would have known. This, all of it, must end.

Cotton and I had already discussed this with Grits, so when the man asked, "Are ya sure ya know where this man lives?"

I gave a dry laugh and replied, "Pretty sure, since I grew up there. But, it ain't even close and we have a good ride ahead of us to get there."

"Where is the sumbitch?"

"Mississippi."

"Mississippi! Hell, that's over a month of ridin'."

"Then, we need to get started, huh?"

"We?"

Cotton said, "Look, we're lookin' fer the same man. It'll be safer for all of us iffen we travel together. Do ya want to go into cahoots with two old mountain men?"

"Hell, yes, if it means I get to have my revenge!"

"Well, get mounted and let's ride. The longer we talk the more time he has to travel."

Three weeks later we entered Mississippi and I no longer rode with a rifle on my horse, nor carried a gun where it could be seen, but I had two on me at all times. Over the weeks, Cotton and I had grown close to Grits and his dog. Baxter was really a big baby in a lot of ways, but very protective of his clan, which included Cotton and I now. We shared our meals with him, pulled guard with him, and more than once I sat by the fire and talked with him, too. But, I've always talked to critters, with horses being the most common.

Tonight after supper, Grits asked, "Where's this plantation Grisham owns?"

"Just west of Jackson and not far from where we are now. We'll be in the area by this time tomorrow, unless the weather turns rough."

"Nate," Grits asked, "ya sure ya want to see the place again? It'll bring back some bad memories and it might prove to be rough on ya."

I stared into the flames and said, "The memories I have already, so that's not a problem. My ma and pa are both dead by now, or sold down river. I have no one there that's family, and I have to get those two kids back. Moses was a good man and all he wanted was for his kids to be free. By God, I'll see they get the chance."

Cotton asked, "Do ya know the layout of the big house?"

"Yep, even the very room Grisham sleeps in with his wife. Now, I don't want no women folks hurt, iffen it can be avoided. I plan to visit him one night this week and take 'em fer a walk."

"Ya goin' to kill 'em?" Grits asked.

I gave a mighty laugh and replied, "Do ya think I come all this way just to talk with 'em?"

"What about Blackie?" Cotton asked.

"He's likely livin' in the same small house the oversee man lives in. We'll get rid of his ass, after we get those two kids back and take care of Grisham."

"Yer goin' to give Grisham a chance, ain't ya?" Grits asked.

"Depends on the mood I'm in at the time. I don't cotton to murder, but sometimes a man just needs killin'."

Cotton laughed and then asked, "Grits, are ya goin' to give Blackie a chance?"

"No, none, and it don't matter what damn mood I'm in either. He's a dead sumbitch."

Turning to Nate, Cotton asked, "Do ya have any idea where the kids mighten be on the plantation? Big place like that might take some time to find two little kids."

"Well, iffen they ain't change things, new slaves were always kept in the barn fer a month or so, to let them learn their places. They feed 'em like hogs and treat 'em rough. They'll be chained to the stalls, so we need to get our hands on a chisel and big hammer."

"They'll have tools in the barn, won't they?"

"Yep, but we can't be sure what we'll need will be there, so in the mornin' ya two will ride into town and pick up what we need. We'll also need to resupply, so when we leave here we'll have no reason to stop before we get back home. I won't go into town, because I don't want to risk anyone recognizin' me, but it's been years since I was here."

"Will they form a posse, ya think?" Grits asked.

"Not if they don't know what happened fer a spell. If we're noticed while on the place and things go to hell, yep, a posse will come and fast, too." *Hopefully, we can kill these two and be long gone before anyone is wiser, but that's not likely to happen,* I thought.

"When do ya want to do this?" Cotton asked.

"Tomorrow night, after midnight."

I smiled as I hunkered down in woods behind the big house, and it still looked the same after all of these years. The lamps and other lights had been off in the place for over two hours. Nothing stirred that I could see and even the dogs were gone. I wondered about the dogs, could be they're in the barn or kept near Thad and April, or I just don't see 'em. Running into a dog at the wrong time could cause some serious problems for us.

Earlier I'd seen clouds moving in from the west and hoped we'd get rain on this night, because it would wash away all tracks once we finished and it'd cover any noises made doing our revenge attack. I felt no remorse or shame for what I was about to do and knew if I didn't stop Grisham, other innocent people would suffer, and I didn't want to spend the rest of my life looking over my shoulders. I saw a bright flash of light on the horizon and it instantly exploded into may small fingers as a loud crack filled the cool night air. I donned my oilcloth, knowing it would keep me dry from most of the rain. There came a slight gust of wind and then rain began to fall lightly. I moved forward.

I'd learned a great deal about stealth in the mountains, mostly from Injuns, but I stayed in the shadows as I moved and froze with each flash of lightning. I carried no rifle, but had three pistols on me, two in my possibles bag and one I now carried in my sash, under my oilcloth. I spotted no one and didn't expect to see anyone this time of the night. Most workers on a plantation or farm went to bed early and were up before the crack of dawn. Besides, the workers, with the exception of Blackie, don't worry me. I suspected most the slaves would be happy to learn Grisham was dead.

I was wearing moccasins, because they allow me to move silently, especially once I entered the house and moved over the hardwood floors. I wondered about Cotton and Grits, who were to take the kids and skedaddle back to camp. I'd shown them the barn, and then moved away, planning to kill Grisham and take Blackie back to camp with me. We had plans for the slaver.

I stepped onto the porch and froze as the night was lighted up by a flash of lightning. I waited patiently for the thunder. My wait was short and loud boom was heard. I could hear the rain pounding on the roof as I moved toward the door. I pulled out my pistol, turned the knob with my left hand, and found it unlocked. I entered and closed the door quietly behind me. The inside of the house was dark, but I needed no light to find Grisham. I moved to the staircase and very slowly, pausing and listening on each step, began moving toward his bedroom. At the top of the stairs, I move to the left and stopped in front of the door to the master bedroom.

I stopped, bowed my head and said in a whisper, "Lord, forgive me for what I am about to do. I'm not killing for personal gain or because I hate this man, but to protect others who this man would press into bondage or kill. This I say in the name of Jesus, amen."

I opened the door, praying the hinges would be quiet, and they made not a sound. I made no effort to close the door and moved to the bed. Grisham was sleeping on top of the covers, wearing a long night gown and he'd aged a great deal since I'd seen him last. I was tempted to just shoot the sonofabitch where he slept, but changed my mind. He'd go back with me and we'd deal with him there. I pushed all of my hatred for Grisham out of my mind and thought once at camp we could have a mini-trial of sorts. Then, following the trial, we'd hang the man.

I moved to him, put my left hand over his mouth and the gun barrel against his head. His eyes immediately flew open. In a voice slightly above a whisper, I said, "Yer comin' with me. Keep quiet, or I'll kill your wife if she wakes up and makes any noise."

I saw him looking at me, attempting to see who I was, but it was too dark. Suddenly, there was a bright flash of lightning, and I saw his eyes widen in fear—he knew who I was.

"It's me, Nate. I hear ya been lookin' fer me, so I come to see ya a spell. Me and ya are gonna talk a bit."

He violently shook his head, so I cocked the pistol, which I should have done outside the room because the sound was loud. I glanced toward his wife and saw her looking right at me. I waited for a response from her, because I knew sometimes folks didn't see well when they first woke up and maybe she'd fall back to sleep. Regardless of what I'd told Grisham, there was no way I would harm his wife.

She screamed, just as a loud *crack* was heard from lightning, and old man Grisham twisted his head away from my hand. He reached under his pillow, where I knew he kept a loaded pistol, and before I could stop him, he had it in his hand. His wife screamed again and jumped from the bed.

I still had my pistol pointed toward his head, so I lined it up better and jerked the trigger. At the sound of my shot, blood, brains, and gore spatted on the headboard and far wall. Grisham fell back to the bed, his body jerking the twitching violently as it shut down. To make sure the man stayed dead, I pulled my knife and cut his throat. More thunder cracked and boomed, so I had some hope my gunfire would not be noticed.

I scanned the large room and spotted his wife squatted in a darken corner, near a dresser. I reloaded my pistol, moved to her and said, "My name is Nate Grisham and yer husband was an evil man. Ya tell the law yer husband stole black folks, even free folks, and sold them down river. I've finished what I come here to do."

She didn't respond, so I was sure she heard not a word I'd said, and I think her mind snapped at the death of her husband. She was quivering and her head was moving in all directions. I turned and walked from the house.

I moved into the shadows and listened, but heard nothing except rain hitting the roofs of buildings. It looked like my gunshot wasn't noticed with all the thunder, so I started through the rain and mud for the overseers house.

The door to the house was locked, unlike at the big house, so I moved to a window. The first two were locked, but the third opened without a sound. I climbed inside and discovered I was in the kitchen. This house, unlike the other, only had one floor, so I moved toward the master bedroom. As I neared, I heard voices behind the closed door.

"Blackie, I'm tellin' ya, I heard a gunshot."

"Ya heard thunder, ya damned fool. Who in their right minds would be out in this downpour?"

"It was a gun, now ya don't have to believe me, but there'll be hell to pay around here if ya don't look into it."

"Where did this gunshot come from?"

"I don't know. I was asleep and it woke me up."

"Sands, I'm goin' to dress and we'll both go look, but so help me, iffen this is a bunch of bullshit, I'll have ya whipped."

I placed my hand on the doorknob and it turned slowly. Then, I opened the door and stepped inside. Blackie was sitting on the edge of his bed and a middle-aged black man stood near. Water was dripping from the blacks clothing and old hat. I noticed a lamp glowed dimly on the night stand. Before I could move, Blackie reached for a pistol on his nightstand and the black man moved back against the wall, with his hands out from his sides, palms open.

"Blackie, don't!" I yelled and then heard a clap of thunder.

His pistol came up and he pointed at me. I raised my gun, lined up the sights, but before I could squeeze the trigger, I felt a hard slap to my left arm and smoke filled the area in front of Blackie. The sound of the gunshot was loud in the small room. I was knocked against the door frame but remained standing. Seeing the man through the smoke, I fired and heard him scream. I saw a flash of flame as the lamp fell and burst open.

Since I was wounded, the black man moved toward me, with a huge knife his hand. I pulled my knife and when he neared I faked a move to the left, went right, and them buried my knife to the hilt in his lower belly. I viciously twisted the blade and felt his intestines fall in loose strands over my hand. I heard yells from other rooms in the house and had to leave now! Pulling my knife from him, I ran from the room, and was out the kitchen window in seconds. I then ran hard for the woods and my waiting horse.

The rain increased its tempo and was falling in buckets. The wind was high and mud was already ankle deep, which tired me after a spell. I slowed down to a walk once in the trees and made my way toward my mount. Thunder continued to boom and crack as lightning helped light my way. It was during a bright flash of light, I saw my horse. I knew a response would be slow in forming, because Grisham's wife was a mental wreck and the only witness to me shooting Blackie was dead. I may not have killed Blackie and that worried me some. Nonetheless, once back at camp we would leave as soon as humanly possible. I hoped in a few days to be too far away for them to track us and into my mountains within a month or so. We'd travel hard and long.

Nearing camp, I saw no light, which was good and I knew no campfire would burn on such a wet night anyway. I pulled up short, just outside of camp and yelled, "Cotton, it's me Nate."

There was flash followed by a boom a few seconds later.

"Come." I heard his reply.

I move to the picket line, tied my horse and made my way to the shelter. As soon as I was under the canvas, I asked, "Did ya get the kids?" I heard Baxter growling and then when he got my scent he quieted.

"Yep," Grits said and then continued, "but we had to kill a guard to do the job. He was outside the door."

"I see ya brought extra horses, too."

"We did and it was Grits' idea. Hell, I'd forgot all about mounts fer 'em."

"What kind of condition are they in?"

"The boy has had the shit kicked out of 'em pretty bad, but it looks worse than it is. The little girl I'm worried over."

"Why's that?" I was puzzled.

"Nate, she was whipped by Blackie."

I felt a sudden rage, but fought it down, "He whipped a ten year old girl?"

"She had dried blood all over her legs and back. She told me Blackie hurt her with a whip. Hell, it don't take a doctor to figure out what happened. How'd your talks go?"

I explained and the sat in silence for a few minutes. Finally, Grits asked, "So, ya don't really know if Blackie is dead or not?"

"I hit 'em, fer sure, but no, I can't say he's dead."

"Shit!" Cotton let out.

"Cotton, Blackie wasn't the brains or money behind gatherin' up people, that was Grisham's doin' and he's as dead as it can get. Now, can both of these kids ride?"

"Yep, I know they can. April was hurt by Blackie days ago and she was movin' fine on the way here, but the boy will sit crooked in the saddle."

"We need to move and an hour ago wouldn't have been too soon. By daylight, every lawman and slaver in the country will know Grisham was killed, along with a couple of hands, and whatever the status is of Blackie. Now, we're lucky, because they don't know about the two of you. Hell, the only one who can identify anyone is Grisham's wife and her mind snapped. I just couldn't kill no woman."

"Well, lets move then, but Nate, if we get stopped, ya and the kids belong to me. I guaran-damn-tee ya, ain't nobody goin' to touch none of ya either. Keep yer pistols hidden, but ready to use, until we hit Missouri Territory."

I grinned and replied, "Come, lets get the hell out of here, but ya need to wrap up my left arm before we ride."

Four days later, after riding eighteen hour days, we were in southern Arkansas and on a meandering trail that led to Missouri. The weather was clear, no winds, and it was a pleasant morning. I was relaxed and humming a no-named tune, when four riders broke the brush and confronted us. I could see right off they were mean no account men, lookin' for easy money.

"Hold up!" The biggest of the group ordered.

"Says, who?" Grits asked.

The big man gave a puzzled look and said, "I do."

"Well, just who in the hell are ya?" Cotton asked and his rifle was laying in his lap, but the barrel was in the general direction of the riders.

"I'm John Hobbs and by God, when I give an order, people jump."

I moved my hand to my saddle where I had a pistol under my buckskin jacket. It'd been cool this morning, and I had a pistol resting between my legs with the jacket on top. I smiled when I felt the smooth wood of the handle, and moved my finger to the trigger. Two of the men carried shotguns, so I knew Cotton and Grits would take them out first. A shotgun can do serious damage.

"Ya see anyone jumpin' now, dumbshit?" Grits asked.

"Ya ain't got no right to be callin' me names, I've half a mind to kill ya!" Hobbs replied.

"Yer right, Hobbs, ya got half a mind. I strongly suggest y'all turn yer horses and ride out of here, before ya piss one of us off. Iffen we get mad, we'll kill every damned one of ya."

"Where'd ya get the black folk?" Hobbs asked, suddenly deciding he didn't want push the two men.

"At a gettin' place, why?"

"Neither one of y'all look like ya got two dimes to rub together in your pockets, and yer ridin' 'round with thousands of dollars in slaves. Maybe me and the boys will just take them folks from ya. See, I heard tell of some folks looking fer two black kids and a big man."

Grits grinned and said, "Hobbs, why are ya so determined to get killed today? Ya make one move toward any of us, and you'll be the first to die."

Hobbs laughed hard and then as he laughter died, he yelled, "Kill my ass, iffen ya think ya can. Take 'em boys!"

The gun Cotton was holding spat lead that struck Hobbs in the forehead. The big man's hands flew up for a few seconds just before he fell from his horse. Grits fired at a thin man, who carried a shotgun and down he went, screaming in pain. I fired, hit the other man holding a shotgun and saw the dust fly as my bullet hit him in the middle of his chest. The last man's horse was rearing high in the air, when Cotton's pistol ball knocked him to the ground. Baxter instantly had the man by the throat and was shaking him violently. He was screaming as Cotton and Grits dismounted, pulled their knives, and moved toward the men.

Grits ordered, "Come, Baxter." The big dog dropped the man and moved toward his owner.

Minutes later the screams ceased, replaced by choking.

"Take their guns, especially the shotguns, powder, and lead. We need to get movin' in case anyone heard our shots."

"Ya know," Cotton said a few minutes later when he mounted, "that Hobbs is the first man I've ever shot that actually asked me to kill 'em."

CHAPTER 15

The days turned into weeks and finally, we crossed onto the plains and knew were getting close to home. We'd had no problems along the way, once out of Arkansas, and I wondered how Sue, Mary and the rest were doing with the Shoshone. We'd been gone for months and surely they'd given us up for dead.

I rode up beside Cotton and asked, "What ya workin' yer mind on so hard?"

"Blackie. I keep wonderin' iffen he's dead or just injured."

"It's likely he's dead, but iffen he ain't, he damned well will be the next time I see 'em. I got a good solid hit on 'em, fer sure."

"Well, I don't think we've seen the end of the sumbitch."

"We'll deal with that problem when it comes around again. He's white trash, we both know it, and I'm more worried about a posse on our asses than I am of Blackie."

"I don't understand how a posse could still be follerin' us."

"The word is out on us, and I'm sure that feller Hobbs we killed in Arkansas knew about us. Why else would he forced the issue?"

"Maybe he was just an ass or thought Grits and I captured y'all. Did ya think of that?"

I laughed and replied, "Mayhap he was an ass, but I think he knew the killers were at least one big black man and he was likely travelin' with two blacks kids. Hobbs said something about that before ya killed 'em. I think there is a sizable reward for all of us, only I don't think they knew of you and Grits."

"What do ya think of Grits?"

"He's got bark on 'em and a dependable man. I've thought of askin' him to join us this coming plew season, why?"

Cotton smiled and said, "I had the same idea. Hell, he

didn't head home when we passed through Missouri and I thought he would."

"He ain't got a place any longer. It's just him and Baxter right now and I like 'em both."

"We can ask 'em tonight. I figure iffen he didn't want to go with us, he'd gone back to Missouri and rebuilt his place."

"Who knows what's on his mind. A feller spends years making a place work and then has some back shooter come along to burn 'em out. While that ain't right, it's part of life."

"We'd better stop with the naybobbin' 'cause it ain't a smart thing to be doin' right now."

We rode in silence for the remainder of the day and the only sound heard was the *"clip-clop"* of the horses or occasionally metal striking metal as someone repositioned a gun. All of us were alert, and Grits rode out front with Baxter the whole day. The dog amazed me, because he always obeyed every command given and instantly, which I'd never seen a dog do before.

At dusk, we made camp in a shallow valley that had a small creek running through it, which was lined with cottonwood trees. None of the trees were big, but we'd found enough wood to keep a fire burning all evening. Our meal would be a buffalo calf, downed by Cotton near noon, and I was hungry enough to eat the thing raw. My stomach rumbled and growled at the thought of food.

Grits placed a cast iron pot on the hot coals, once the fire burned down, to warm up our beans and fatback from the night before. The buffalo roasted on sticks beside the fire, as usual, as we relaxed and cleaned our guns. We always cleaned our guns one at a time, never all at once. We kept most of our guns ready for use, which was the only smart way to do the job.

Before long, we sat in the grass and ate our simple meal, washing it down with hot coffee. Suddenly, Baxter stood and gave a low warning growl. His ears were standing up and his teeth were bared. Saliva dripped from his snarled mouth.

"Somethin's out there." Grits stood and cocked his rifle.

There came a loud growl from the darkness and Baxter started barking. Over the dog, I heard Cotton yell, "Grizz!"

There are few things in life that honestly scare me, Blackfoot Injuns, a drunk cowboy with a loaded gun in his hand, and a grizzly bear. I stood, cocked my rifle, and squinted to see into the inky darkness. I grew more worried as each minute passed, especially when both of the kids screamed in fear.

Finally, the bear moved from the darkness, near the horses and gave a mighty growl. I swallowed my fear and moved forward. I knew we had to move in close to kill the big beast, but it took all the courage I have to move forward.

Baxter was charging at the bear, nipping at his legs, then moving out of reach when the bear would swing a big paw toward him. The dog was fast, but I figured in a few minute, Grits was goin' to be shy a dog.

Grits fired, then Cotton, but I held still for a second to see what effect the shots had on the animal. Dropping to all fours, the grizz moved toward us, with Baxter zipping all around in front of bear. I figured the bear was ten feet tall and good thousand pounds, except I may have been off a bit, but not by much. I moved in close, waited until the bear stood once more, aimed for his open mouth and fired. I heard a loud scream of anger from the animal, felt myself struck hard, then flying through the air, and I hit the ground hard. I turned my head, only to see the bear moving for me. I pulled my pistol and wondered, *how'd my hand get bloody?*

Baxter made a mad dash, biting at the bears rear hamstring, and I saw the beast turn from me and move toward the dog. Baxter had just saved my life, just as the shaman had said. I didn't believe it and when I tried to move, my body didn't obey my mind. I was unable to move, but could still hear the kids screaming in the background. *Lord, protect those young-uns.*

I heard two rifles and then two shotguns fire, saw the bear stand and heard a loud scream come from the brute. As I watched, the bear dropped to all fours and Baxter ran in and caught the animal by the throat. Once again the animal stood, with Baxter hanging from his neck, and shook his head violently. The dog must have locked his jaws, because he was going to stay right where he was for the time being. I heard another shot, then saw Cotton move toward the bear, which dropped to all fours again. When the bear opened his mouth to growl, Cotton pushed the barrel of a shotgun near his teeth, and jerked the trigger. The big creature dropped instantly and lay unmoving. I just knew Baxter was one dead critter as well.

"Come, Baxter!" Grits yelled, and the dog moved from the bear limping.

Cotton approached the beast, pulled his skinning knife and

touched an open eye with the point, but the bear remained still. It was dead. Sheathing his knife, Cotton moved to my side, squatted and asked, "Can ya move?"

"No, but I don't feel any pain, either."

"Grits, come and give me a hand with Nate!"

Soon they had me by the fire and Cotton cut my shirt off. By the light of the flickering flames, I could see my chest was soaked with blood.

"Grits, bring me the whiskey and some of that white cotton material in the shelter. Hurry."

It was the word hurry that caught my attention, only there was nothing I could do. A few minutes later, Grits arrived, squatted and handed the supplies to Cotton. He glanced at my chest and said, "Damn, are ya goin' to be able to stop the bleedin'?"

"Yep, get me the laudanum now too. I forgot to tell ya a while ago."

"Am I tore up, Cotton?"

"Yep, four deep cuts across your chest. I'll fix ya up, only ya won't like what I'm goin' to do."

I gave a dry laugh and replied, "Hot knife, huh?"

"Yep, just fer starters. You've also got some broken ribs, a broken arm, and I'm not sure why ya can't move on yer own. I just hope ya ain't got spine problems."

"Here." Grits handed the medicine to Cotton.

He poured a bit in my mouth, fed me a cup of whiskey and then said, "I'll start on ya in a few minutes. Just as soon as Grits and I finish our whiskey. Good God, who expected a bear out here."

"Ya . . . need to . . . give Bax . . . ter a big . . . steak." I said, my words wouldn't form, because my tongue seemed too large, so I knew the laudanum was working.

"Try not to talk Nate, yer hurt bad, old son." Cotton replied.

I kept quiet, but listened to them talk. Maybe they'd thought I'd passed out, but I heard Cotton say, "The bone on that arm is stickin' through the skin, the ribs are cut right to the bone, and I think he hurt his neck or spine when he landed. This ain't good."

"We'll go nowhere for a spell then. I reckon, after a few days or a week, we might have to make a travois to move 'em." Grits replied.

"Nate's tough, so iffen anyone can survive this, it'll be him.

But, lawdy, what a mess. Okay, put yer knife in the fire."

At that point, I must have passed out, either from the drug or my body just shutdown, because when I next opened my eyes, it was dawn or sunset. Moving my neck to the east, I saw it was dawn.

"Water?" I asked.

As I expected, Cotton replied, "Here, let me lift yer head and give ya a little. It's got whiskey in with it to help yer pain."

I swallowed, grinned and said, "It's my turn . . . to stay drunk . . . a spell."

Cotton laughed and I heard Grits bustin' a gut on the other side of me. I felt a movement by my legs and when I looked, I saw Baxter. I'd swear that dog was grinning at me at the time.

"Okay, are ya well enough to think right?" Cotton asked.

"I think so. Damn me, I hurt all over."

Grits said, "Hell, ya should. Ya have broken ribs, a broken arm all wrapped up, a twisted ankle, yer cut all the way across yer chest, and Cotton spent about an hour sewing part of yer scalp back on."

"Yep, yer not as bad off as Huge Glass, but by God, yer close. Do ya think ya could sip a little meat broth?" Cotton asked.

"I ain't hungry, need whiskey fer the pain. How are the kids?"

"Nate, it's been four days since the bear attack and ya ain't ate a thing. Now, I'll give ya whiskey, but only after ya drink some broth. And, don't worry about the kids, they're fine."

"Give me the damned broth, iffen that's the only way I can have my whiskey." I said in anger, but thought, *four days? I've been hurt worst than I feared.* I moved my leg on my own, my good arm, and then raised my head.

I smiled.

"What in the hell are ya doin'? Yer movin' all around." Grits asked.

"I couldn't move at all the last I remembered and didn't want to spend the rest of my life layin' on my ass in some bed waitin' to die. I'm goin' to try to situp now."

"He's movin'," I heard Thad say.

"Praise Jesus!" April shouted.

Cotton placed an arm on both sides of me as I raised my head and shoulders. He figured to catch me if I didn't have the strength and fell back. I quivered like hell and it hurt like a sumbitch, but I did the job.

"Now, lay back down and drink this broth."

I sipped a cup and then asked, "Any sign of festerin' yet?"

Cotton placed the empty cup on the ground beside me and replied, "Nope, nary a bit and I've changed your bandages twice a day. Here's yer whiskey."

I coughed as the straight whiskey slid down my throat, but once the burning from my belly spread, I could fell the pain start to lessen. "Any of the rest of ya hurt?"

"Couple of scratches and marks on all of us, except the kids, but nothing like ya have. Hell, when that huge beast slapped ya, I just knew yer head would roll off. Damn, I heard the smack, saw ya flying through the air and thought, that's the end of Nate." Grits said as he poured himself some coffee.

"I don't remember much once he struck me. Baxter is what saved my ass. If not fer our dog that nasty-assed bear would have chewed on my hide."

Cotton chuckled and said, "Didn't that old Shoshone shaman say a dog would save yer life? Well, by God, he was right on the mark."

"I . . . need sleep," I said, and my world turned gray and then slipped into black.

Ten days later, I was in the saddle and moving, but had the jug of whiskey tied to my saddle horn. We were moving across the plains fairly quickly, because none of us like the openness. The sky was a clear blue, from horizon to horizon, and the winds were light. The grasses were now longer and the short grasses were miles behind us. As I rode, I looked through the ears of my horse and saw an endless sea of bluish-green long grass. I was still as sore as a whore a day after a payday rush, only we had to move, our lives might depend on it. *There was a good chance someone was on our asses,* but I thought, *iffen they knew what they were doin', they'd have caught up to us when I was hurt. Could be a posse is just heading toward the mountains and they have no idea how to track.*

I caught movement out of the corner of my eye and when I

swung my rifle around, Grits said, "It's a coyote." Baxter, who was out front with Cotton, growled and then barked a couple of times at the other critter, but didn't leave our group.

We made a good twenty-five or more miles on this day and when we stopped for a the evening, the kids began to gather firewood, Cotton cared for the horses, as Grits cook our supper of meat and beans. Since I was still hurting, I laid on my blanket and sipped my strong corn squeezing for the pain.

I'd almost dozed off, when I heard a loud scream, and then Thad yelling for help. I stayed where I was, knowing Cotton or Grits would be there in half the time I'd take hobbling toward them. With my twisted ankle and broken bones, I was a slow mover, and my ribs still hurt when I took a deep breath.

I sat up, pulled my rifle around, and waited.

A few minutes later, Cotton walked into camp holding April in his arms. He placed the little girl on a buffalo robe, turned to me and said, "Snakebite. I killed a good sized rattlesnake where they were and the bite was to her right hand."

"Ya know how to treat it, so have at it. Odds are it won't kill 'er anyway, but do what needs to be done."

Cotton fed April a cup of our whiskey, pulled his knife and had Grits hold her down. He made two cuts across each fang mark, about 1/4 of an inch deep, and then began sucking the poison out. Every few minutes he leaned to the side and spit out blood and poison. Her hand and arm were already double in size, but that was typical of snakebite, if the snake was a dangerous one. Unless she had a weak heart or some other problem, she'd live. *She must be scared to death*, I thought, *because it'd scare the living hell out of me and I'm five times her size and years older.*

About twenty minutes later, Cotton poured whiskey on the cut, which brought a scream from little April, and then he wrapped up her hand.

"It's up to the Good Lord now." Cotton said and then added, "We'll go no place for a day or two, at least until we can see how she'll do with this bite. Snakebites are strange doin's most of the time anyway. It's like some rattlesnakes ain't got a full load of poison and others seem pretty deadly. I have no way of tellin' what'll happen now."

Grits said, "She's sleepin' now, so we'll have to keep an eye on her overnight. This first night is when we'll learn iffen she'll be okay or not."

"Snakes scare the livin' hell right out of me," I said.

Grits said, "I ain't scared of 'em, iffen I can see 'em, but I respect 'em a great deal."

"Well, I don't like 'em, but I don't kill every single one I see, neither. I figure the Lord put 'em on earth for a reason and I'll only kill those that are a threat to me or mine."

Thad, who'd been quiet most of the trip asked, "Is she goin' to die?"

He was standing beside his sister and while I felt his concern, I was honest when I said, "Ain't a one of us that can say yep or nope. It all depends on how strong she is, especially her heart, and iffen she's healthy. We'll keep 'er drunk for a few days and see how she fairs. Most folks will live."

The young man looked at me, his eyes shocked, and asked, "Drunk? She ain't but ten years old."

"Son, it's all we have to kill her pain. Now, we have laudanum, but I don't want to use that except for really bad hurts, with bleeding and such, and don't have any idea how much to give a kid."

"Cain't ya give 'er the same y'all take?"

"Nope, because too much will kill 'er. It's a good drug, when a body is hurtin' bad, but too much will kill ya fast. She ain't as big as a man or woman, so how much do I give 'er? We cain't take the risk."

"Well, keep her drunk then, even if it don't sound like the right thing to do to my sister."

"Aye, lad, we'll do that." Cotton said.

"Thad, can I ask ya a question?" I asked, hoping the boy would talk to me.

"I reckon, since we owe ya our lives."

"Did Blackie really take a whip to April?"

"Yep, he did. It was about the fourth night out from Butterfield's when he did it, too. I wanted to help my sis, I really did, but I was chained to a big oak tree. All I could do was watch and cuss the man. When he'd finished with her, he beat me about half to death. Iffen ya didn't kill the bastard back there on the plantation, when I grow up, I'll do the job."

"I'm goin' to stay up all night and care for yer sis. Do ya want to stay up with me?

"Yep, I'll do what I can, because we have to care for each other now that pa is gone."

"Well, come over here and sit by me on my blanket. It'll be

a long night."

A little over an hour later, Thad fell asleep and I expected it. He was determined to help me, but he was still a young pup, and the moving had worn him out. I let him sleep and covered him with a blanket. Glancing around, I noticed Cotton in his robes and Grits off a ways standing guard.

It's been a rough trip, between the bear and this snake. I hope it gets a hell of a lot smoother from here on out, I thought and then took a sip of whiskey.

I spent the night dozing on and off. A couple of hours before daylight, I moved to check on April, and discovered she wasn't breathing.

CHAPTER 16

We buried April on the plains, and Cotton read some words from the Bible. Thad didn't shed a tear, but I did enough crying for both of us. Burying women and children always brought tears to my eyes and after all the little girl had suffered, I didn't see any justice in God taking her home now. But, as my momma used to say all the time, God has His reasons. My only choice in life now, was to accept her death and move on with my life. The same was true with Thad, only his lack of tears concerned me, and more than just a little. See, I knew he loved his sister, so why the dry eyes?

Moving to the fire for breakfast, I sat next to Thad and asked, "Are ya doin' okay?"

He didn't reply.

Grits started to speak, but I shook my head at the man. I suspected he was goin' to jump Thad's ass about not answering me.

"Thad, I asked ya a question and expect an answer."

"No, I'm not okay with this! Why did God let my sis get kidnapped and beaten half to death by Blackie, only to let a snake kill 'er? What kind of God would do this?"

"I ain't got an answer fer ya, boy. I've been askin' myself the same question fer years and still don't have a good reason to give ya. I do know it was time for April to go to God and everything He does is fer a reason. He makes no mistakes, none."

"Well, I don't need a God like this one, then."

"Mad at God, are ya? Well, I've been like that a few times myself in the past. But, after a spell, I started to see that everyone died eventually. It hurts to lose somebody we love, only it's suppose to hurt, iffen we've been raised right."

Suddenly the boy burst into tears, and I let him cry for a

while. Finally he said, "My family, pa and April are dead, so what am I goin' to do? Where will I live? How will I eat? Nate, I ain't got nobody left."

I took my left arm, put it around his shoulders and pulled him close. I said, "Ya still have a family. Why, ya got me, Cotton, Grits, and Baxter. We won't let ya go hungry or lack fer a place to live. See, young pup, we take care of our own and yer one of us now."

He quit crying, wiped his nose with the back of his hand, but still sniffled. Long minutes pasted before he was able to get his emotions under control. Then, he asked, "Why do this for me?"

Grits said, "Son, we'd help anyone who needed help. See, most of us out here ain't got two dimes to rub together in our pockets, but all of us will help someone that needs it. Why, some day, years from now, I might need yer help. That's why we help each other."

"Did ya enjoy bein' around Mr. Butterfield?" Cotton asked.

"He was nice to all of us. I know he got shot when Blackie killed pa. Why would a white man try to help my pa? Blackie said we was only good as slaves."

"Well," I said, "Blackie was wrong. Son, don't ever judge any man by his skin color, or you'll be wrong in almost every case. Ya look at us. Me and Cotton been ridin' together almost as long as you've been alive and either one of us would die for the other. Just keep in mind, all blacks ain't good and all white folks ain't bad. Ya have to judge each person by their actions and if they have a sense of honor."

"What's that word, honor, mean?"

Cotton said, "To me honor means iffen a man says he's goin' to do somethin', he does it because it's the right thing to do, even if it's hard to do or other people don't like him doin' it. See, when we come to Mississippi after y'all, it was an honorable thing to do at the time."

Wiping his nose again, the lad thought for a few minutes and then asked, "So, iffen I kill Blackie someday, it'll be an honorable thing to do?"

"Yep, because ya have a God-given right to avenge what he did to ya and yer sis."

"I think I understand. I'm goin' to have to think on this a long spell."

I chuckled and said, "Now, let's eat and get ready to move.

We have a full day of ridin' to put in today." A few minutes later I thought, *I hope my pain stays low enough I can stay off the panther piss today. This will be my first full day in the saddle without drinking any of the strong liquid, and I have to do the job.*

Later, as we left camp, I caught Thad looking over his shoulder at his sisters grave. I felt his pain, but death was part of life and the earlier a man realized that, the faster he'd grow up.

Weeks later, as we neared Butterfield's, the bottom fell out of the sky and rain fell in buckets. We moved into a thick grove of pines and made camp. Since the death of April, I'd taken to reading to Thad at night and while the boy could read, he didn't do the job well enough in my opinion. After handing out leather tough jerky for supper, I asked, "Thad, how'd ya like to learn to read better?"

"Ya know how to read pretty good, but where'd ya learn to do that? Pa said slaves didn't have no learnin'."

"Well, yer pa was right, we never had a school house, only we had schools late at night after the white folks went to bed. My momma and an Uncle Ben of mine taught me how to read, do my sums, and some other stuff. Only they did it in our cabin. See, slaves were punished if they knew too much or iffen they got caught teaching others."

"We ain't got any books, except that Bible ya tote all over the place in yer saddlebags."

"It'll do a good job, until we can get some other books. But, a feller has no excuse not to be able to read or write some, no matter his color. I could do some when I first come out here, only I've picked up a lot of learning in the mountains."

"They got a school in the mountains that teaches black folks?"

"Sure and it's called The School of Shining Mountains."

"Yer teasin' me, ain't ya?"

"Kind of, but not really. See, all of us mountain men know different things. Some of the boys were doctors, lawyers, preachers, teachers and the list goes on and on. Now, that's a lot of knowledge and when the weather turns nasty, like it is now, we teach each other things to pass the time. Only, it ain't a schoolhouse full of teachers."

"I understand."

"Tonight we'll not start any learnin', because we're close to the trading post. Iffen ya decide to stay with John, that's Butterfield's first name, he can teach ya a lot, because he went to some fancy university back east. He's a learned man, but he doesn't act like one most of the time."

"How come?"

Cotton interrupted and replied, "Because he's usually talkin' with a bunch of ignorant trappers."

I laughed and added, "John speaks like we do so most of us will understand what he's sayin'. Not all trappers have an interest in learnin' and more than just a few can't read a bit and mark their names with an X. So, you'll find all kinds of men out here."

"Can ya read to me a bit tonight?"

I nodded and pulled out my Bible.

The next morning we arrived at Butterfield's place just as the sun was coming up. The air was cool and clouds were moving in from the west. I expected rain, but snow wasn't out of question. The old man opened the door with a big Greener shotgun in his hands, saw us and smiled.

"Did ya get the bastard?" He asked.

"Before I answer that question, do ya have any food and whiskey in your place?"

"Can a duck swim? Hell, yes, so come on in. It's fixin' to do somethin' out here in a little while, only I ain't sure iffen it's rain or snow."

We entered the trading post and a potbelly stove in the corner was glowing red-hot on the sides. I found the heat overwhelming, but knew it was from spending weeks on the trail. We all took chairs at the closest table and Butterfield soon arrived with a good bottle of Kentucky bourbon. Sitting, and then placing the bottle on the table, he said, "Now tell me about yer trip. Oh, just grab one of the cups and have at 'er."

I took an empty cup from about six on the tabletop and poured my cup full. I took a big gulp and then told my story. Butterfield didn't ask a single question as I was talking, so I knew he was giving my words deep thought.

He took a healthy gulp of his drink and then asked, "So ya don't really know iffen Blackie is dead or not, right?"

"No idea if I killed the man. I hit 'em hard, but that's all I know."

Turning to Thad, Butterfield asked, "Ya ever given thought to being a store clerk?"

"What kind of job is that?"

"Keepin' stuff on the shelves, givin' customers what they want to buy and learnin' how to keep books. Yer pa was a good man with books. He was an accountant and they're hard to find; well, a good one is hard to find."

"I think I'd like that. Nate said I need to keep learnin' so I can grow up to be somebody."

Giving me a wink, Butterfield replied, "He's right. A feller can never know too much, because the more he knows the easier it is to get a job or make more money. Now, money ain't everything, but all of us have to have enough to live on and get the things we need."

"Does this job of yers come with money?"

"Sure it does and yer pay is the same as I'd pay a man to do the job. It's hard work and you'll earn every penny of it too."

"I'll try my best, but how much does this job pay?"

"You'll get twenty dollars a month, room and board included. That means, free food and a dry place to sleep. Hows that sound?"

Thad looked at me with questioning eyes, so I nodded.

"I'll do it. Only, I don't have to live down where I lived with Pa and April, do I?"

Knowing the place would bring back painful memories for the boy, Butterfield replied, "No, my store help, since it's just ya, gets a room in the tradin' post. How's that?"

"Great, can I see my room now?"

"Ya sleepy?"

"No, I ain't never had a room by myself before. Our cabin in Missouri was just one big room."

Butterfield knocked back his drink, wiped his mouth off,

stood and said, "Come with me, Thad, and I'll show ya yer new room."

The next morning, as we moved north by west, I realized what a special friend old John Butterfield was to all mountain men. His prices were a bit high, he was cantankerous as hell and blunt, only he had a soft heart for each of us. I knew Thad was in good hands and if Butterfield raised 'em, he'd be one hell of a fine young man. Now, not many folks would turn a youngster away, but it was harder to find someone willing to take a black kid in, especially back east. By workin' alongside Butterfield, Thad would learn not all whites were bad, like old man Grisham or Blackie. He'd learn and come to understand what I meant about judging each man by his actions, not his color. He'd grow up a better man, instead of a bitter man.

"I have movement off our left side." Cotton whispered from in front of me. Grits was riding out front with Baxter.

"Keep ridin'. If they want to fight, we'll know in a little bit."

Suddenly, Grits stopped, but waved his hand for us to meet him.

Cotton said, "I'll stay here. I don't think it's smart fer us to bunch up."

I rode forward, stopped beside him and asked, "What do ya see?"

"Absolutely nothin' and the birds stopped singin', too. Baxter is nervous, only he's not growled or anything."

"Cotton picked up movement on the left of us, so it's likely Injuns."

"Who's land are we on now?"

"Shoshone, but that doesn't mean shit. See, out here the Injuns go where they want and when they want. Let's pray it's not Ree or Blackfoot, or there will be hell to pay."

"What do ya want me to do then, keep movin'?"

"Nope, you drop back with Cotton, but leave Baxter with me."

"I'm glad to hear ya say this. I don't know shit about Injuns, and they make me a bit antsy."

"Yer a smart man then." I replied with a dry chuckle.

Once Grits was in place, I moved up the trail, suspecting the Injuns were friendly or we'd be up to our asses in a fight right now. I relaxed a bit in the saddle.

About a mile further on, Baxter growled, and when I looked where the dog was looking I saw a warrior standing in the brush. He was, however, not Shoshone, but Sioux. I speak Sioux, almost fluently, but this man was a bit north by west from where the Sioux are usually found.

"Hello my brother, it is a good day to travel."

"You are known among my people as Tall Raven Man, are you not?"

"Yes, I am called Tall Raven Man."

"I am known as Bloody Blade, and I am a dog soldier of The People."

The dog was still growling, so I said, "Baxter, hush." Once he quieted I replied, *"What brings the Sioux far from home to the land of the Shoshone?"*

"Our village was attacked by Ree and many of us died. I was told to bring a small band of my people to the mountains to hide. This I have done, but I do not know if the fight went well for us or not."

"Has no one from your village come for you?"

"No, we have seen no one."

"How many people are with you now? I have food, but only a little."

"Three hands of us are here. I only have two other warriors and I worry about keeping my people safe."

I nodded and replied, *"It is as it should be for a dog soldier. Your people must come first, or you would not be an honorable warrior of The People. Do you have hunger?"*

"We will eat with you."

"Come, bring your people and we will eat."

I looked over my shoulder and said, "Move off to the right; we'll share our meat with these folks."

What the warrior forgot to tell me was, he had about a dozen kids, too. Cotton soon turned the meat over to the women and joined us at the fire. The warrior was worried and rightfully so, but I had no idea how to help him.

One of the woman approached and said, *"There is only enough meat for the children."*

"The little ones must eat, because they are our future. Feed

them and what is left over is to be shared with the women." Bloody Blade ordered, looked at me and then shrugged.

I turned to Grits and said, "Get all the jerky and that nasty pemmican we have and turn it over to the women. I'll not have these folks go hungry."

Grits returned a few minutes later and said, "Nate, we've a damned serious problem right now with these Injuns. Now, I'm not sure, but one of the men has what looks to me to be small pox."

"Good God, no." Cotton spurted.

I felt a wave of fear, but pushed it aside, and asked Blood Blade, "Have some of your people been sick?"

"Yes some have the spotted disease. They were not sick before the Ree attacked us. Is this something they will die from? We have never seen this illness."

"Many of your people will die, if this is the spotted illness from white men. I will move among your people and see this sickness with my own eyes. How many suns have you been away from the others of your people? I will tell you then what must be done."

Bloody Blade suddenly turned to me and said, *"I am a warrior, not a shaman, but as a true man, I want to keep my people safe and strong. Look among my people and tell me what your eyes see. We have been alone for seven suns."*

Turning to Grits, I asked, "Me and Cotton have been around the illness before and neither of us will catch it, but how about you?"

"Nate, my pa was a horse doctor. Just before I left home in Saint Louis, to settle in the Ozarks, he gave me what he called an inoculation or something that sounded like that. He scraped my left arm and it scabbed up after a spell. He said it'd protect me against small pox and at times the disease hit folks hard. He didn't want me over a hundred miles from him without the procedure done."

"Well, you'll not get it for sure then. Cotton, ya come with me and let's look these folks over closely. I hope ya both know, we'll not see the Shoshone for a month or better, if these people have the pox."

About an hour later, Cotton said, "Nate, we're in a world of shit. I'm guessin' a good seventy-five percent of these folks have the pox. A couple of the littler kids were so sick they can't eat. We need to do something with these folks."

"Hell," I asked still fighting my earlier fear, "like what? I need to ask Bloody Blade a few more questions and maybe we can figure something out."

"Bloody Blade, do you know where the main group of your people may be?"

"We scattered like the winds, in all directions and in many small groups, so I have no idea. We were to meet near the wide cold river three days ago, but when I went searching for them, no one had been there."

"Someone should have been there." Cotton met my eyes.

"Unless the whole damned tribe is down sick and stuck out in the woods someplace."

"What can we do?"

"Nurse this bunch and that's about it. Shit, I just thought of something."

"What?"

"Iffen the Sioux have the pox, then the Ree do too by now, since they were exposed to the disease first. Hell, it's just a matter of time before most of the tribes get it."

"Ya go warn the Ree, I'll not even try."

"No, I'm just telling ya the way it is. The Ree will kill anyone not a Ree on their lands. But, what about the Shoshone?"

"Lawdy, Nate, do ya think they're in danger?"

"Any Injun out here is at danger, or so I think. They're always fightin' each other and all it takes is one exposed warrior to return to the village and it'll hurt 'em all, and bad, too."

"What in the hell can we do about it?"

"Cotton, I need ya and Grits to stay here and care fer the Sioux. I'm goin' to take two horses and ride in relay to the Shoshone. Once I meet a guard or warrior, I'll stop far enough away to tell them of the danger."

"That's a long ride fer a single man."

"When these folks come down with the pus-filled sores, the squirts, fever and then start passin' blood, ya two will be needed here. I'll get back as fast as I can to help."

Grits, who'd been quiet said, "Ya do what needs to be done. First thing I need to do is take Baxter and make some meat. We're goin' to need soup cookin' twenty-four hours a day, seven days a week, and that's just for those that survive."

I looked the Sioux over and felt deep pity for them, because by the time I returned, at least half of them would go under. I stood, picked up my gear and said, "I will return as soon as possible. If I'm not back in a week, I'll never be back."

155

CHAPTER 17

By riding my horse and leading Cotton's, I could ride relay, which meant when my horse tired, I'd switch to Cottons, and lead mine as it rested. I hoped to cover the distance to the Shoshone in a couple of days, barring any problems. I'd need to sleep a little, maybe as little as two hours a night, and for food, I had pemmican.

"Lord, I never ask ya fer much, but please keep the Shoshone, and our people with them, safe. I ask ya to protect all of them. I never ask ya fer much, and I know I don't pray as much as I should, only I try to live my life based on the scripture, God. Please, let me get to these people in time. This I ask in Jesus' name, amen." I prayed as I rode, but found myself praying often as time passed.

I have no idea if any of the black folks with the tribe have been around the pox before or not. Hell, I could end up losing all those folks and there's not a thing I can do about it, either. What a damned mess and all because the Ree got a wild hair across their butts and decided to attack the Sioux, I thought and then kicked my horse into a faster walk.

Three hours after dark, I pulled into the trees for some much needed rest. As I lay on my blanket, I looked up at the stars and thought about the life the red man live and how it would soon end, all in the name of progress. Oh, I knew I'd likely not see it, but iffen I had a son, he surely would. A few minutes later, I was asleep.

I awoke a couple of hours later, wiped the sleep from my eyes, and move north a few minutes later, hoping I'd arrive in time. All day I rode until one horse got tired, then switched horses; by dark I thought I'd been born on a horse. I moved in some large rocks, cared for both mounts and then went to sleep. I awoke four hours later and once again mounted my horse.

It was near noon, when felt I was being watched and that alerted me, because my feelings have never been wrong. More than once I'd saved my ass by listening to my inner voice or a tingling of my scalp. Someone was near, but I had no idea who it was. It wasn't until I stopped to change horses that I made contact.

"Big Raven Man, you have returned to your people." I heard a voice say in Shoshone.

I smiled, because I knew the voice well, *"Broken Bow, are you well?"*

"I am well, but many in the village are sick with the white man's illness that causes them to die by passing blood from their body." He was standing in the brush near the trail.

"I have come to warn the people, but your words mean I am too late. Have many died?"

"Many, but I do not know how many yet. I was out hunting and saw your movement. You ride quickly and I am on foot."

I had a thought, so I asked, "Are the Shoshone friends with the Sioux?"

"Sioux, I do not know this tribe."

"You call them the 'Cut Throats'."

"I have no reason to fight them, if they are not on Shoshone lands."

"I have some with me, with Cotton Top and another white man. The Sioux are sick, with the same sickness your people have. They were attacked by Ree, which gave them the sickness. Can I bring them to your village?"

"That is a question I cannot answer, as I am not chief and do not know. If you will let me ride a horse to the village, we can ask Many Coups. We only grew ill after a battle with a small group of Ree. But you will get the sickness if you come with me."

"I cannot get the sickness, I am protected. Why do you not have it?"

"I had the illness when I was but a small child, and my mother said I almost crossed over, but the Creator had other plans for my life."

I smiled, *"How are your mother and father?"*

He walked from the woods, met my eyes and said, *"They crossed over to the other side, one sun ago. My mother's last words to me were, 'hunt and care for your people.'"*

"Come," I said, "let us ride to your village."

Two hours later, I was sitting in a dim lodge speaking with Many Coups. The discussion was sober and solemn as we discussed the illness. Many Coups was on the high side of fifty, still muscular and in good health. He's had the pox before, so he was not ill. His coal black hair was streaked with white and on his cheeks where the scars of his previous battle with the disease.

"I do not understand how the Ree have a disease of the white man. The Ree are not white, so how can this be? Why do my people grow sick from the Ree?"

"Father," I said using an informal but respectable title for him, *"this illness travels from warrior to warrior, no matter the color of the man. By touching the weapons, clothing, or scalps of the sick warrior, you become ill. While it is a white man's illness, it sickens everyone."*

The chief nodded and then asked, *"How can we stop this sickness? I worry about my people."*

"It cannot be stopped. But the lodges, clothing and all things the sick have touched must be burned."

"What of our dead, are they to be burned as well?"

"Yes, but I know that is not the way of the Shoshone."

"No, it is not the way we treat our dead, but I will give this burning some thought."

"If you do not burn all things, the disease may stay among you for many suns."

"I hear you well, Big Raven Man, only to burn our dead is new to me and I must give thought to not only the living, but our dead as well. Those who have crossed-over, should be honored."

"Have you decided on the Sioux?" We'd discussed them first, because Broken Bow had immediately brought it out for discussion. *"I know I am rude to ask in this manner, but many lives depend on your answer, father."*

"I have no fight with the Cut Throats, and they will be brought here. They must understand, once they are well, they

must leave. Our mourning will be for many moons."

"As it should be when good people pass-over."

"I know you worry about your friends and the Cut Throats, but as we speak, I have sent Tall Badger for them. You must rest from your ride and grow strong. I fear in the coming suns, warriors like you and I, will be making soup for our sick."

"Have any Raven's died from this illness?"

"One, an old man, who I think was called Frink."

Frank, he was a tough old coot, I thought but said, *"The Ravens are lucky."*

Silence filled the lodge, then Many Coups said, *"Broken Bow will show you to a lodge you may call your own while you stay with us. Many of our women are sick, so you must cook your own meat. Now, go to your lodge and wait for Spirit Helper, our shaman to visit you. I am sure he will seek answers you do not have."*

As we moved through the village, I noticed no women scraping hides, cooking or gathering wood for fires, which was unusual for a village. Usually from dawn to dusk an Injun village was a busy place, but this one looked deserted. Two warriors rode in with a horse piled high with buffalo meat and I saw Broken Bow smile.

"They have found meat." I said.

"Yes, it is enough for a day or two. Many of our sick do not have hunger."

"The white man has this sickness too, and it kills many."

He turned, glared at me and replied, *"As long as one white man lives, it has not killed enough."*

We walked in silence a few minutes and then he said, *"I was speaking from my heart, Big Raven Man, and not my head. I was wrong to speak to you in such a way."*

I smiled and replied, *"You are my brother. I know both your heart and mind. I have forgotten your words and hope you have forgotten mine."*

"Good, here is your lodge, but as Many Coups said, you will cook and care for yourself, as all the women are busy with our sick."

"I can do that."

"I will have some buffalo meat brought to you soon. I must go and check on my wife and son."

"Go, my brother, all is well with me. You must care for others."

Not ten minutes after Broken Bow left, I heard Wilson at my entrance, "Nate, are ya in there?"

"Yep, come on in." I'd just started a fire and had a pot of coffee boiling.

When he entered, Sue was with him, and they sat on a blanket beside me. Wilson said, "Most of the Shoshone are sick with the pox, and we lost Frank a few days back. He come down with the illness and was dead in less than a day."

"He was old and lacked the strength to fight it off," I said.

Sue gazed into my eyes and said, "Was your trip a good one?"

I filled them in on our trip and when I was finished, Wilson said, "Iffen Blackie ain't dead, he'll come fer ya. He's rattlesnake mean."

"Mayhap he will, but it won't be fer a year or longer. While I may not have killed the bastard, I hurt 'em bad at the very least. Any other black folks come down sick?"

"We've been lucky, and all of us are okay. I think many of us have been around the sickness before, so we won't get it. I had a brother die from it, but it never bothered me at all."

"I never got it either, but it killed my ma and pa when I was a little button, near on five or six." Sue said.

"We need to do all we can to feed and care for these people. There are two reasons for doing this and the first is the most important. It's the Christian thing to do, and God expects us to help these folks, plus, the tribe will feel they owe us when it's all over. That means, the Shoshone and Sioux will never bother any of us again. If we're goin' to live out here, then we need all the friends we can get."

"I like the first reason best." Sue said, and then smiled.

"Sue," I said, "ya need to find the largest pot ya can find and get some buffalo meat broth cookin'. Wilson, ya'll join me in a buffalo hunt here in a bit, after I speak with the village shaman."

"Who has meat?" Sue asked.

"A couple of warriors just brought in a pile of meat, so take a look and get the soup goin'. The sick folks won't be able to keep most of it down, but those that do have a better chance of livin' through all of this. Wilson, ya go and get yer weapons. I'll meet ya down by the horses."

After they left, I knew we'd be lucky if we only lost about half of the village. Small pox was nasty and the victims died leaking blood from every hole in their bodies, and with terrible grimaces on their faces. Some plantation owners down South, the smart ones, had their slaves inoculated against the disease. They didn't do it out of kindness, but to protect their investment.

I heard a light scratching on my entrance and heard a male voice ask in Shoshone, *"Big Raven Man, we must talk. I am called Spirit Helper by The People."*

"Enter."

An old man entered and I guessed his age to be around seventy, but I'm here to tell ya, that's old no matter what people he lived with. Most folks were dead by fifty. I indicated with my right hand for him to be seated on my right, an honored position.

Once he was beside me, I said, *"I have no pipe to smoke or tobacco. I have no meat or food worthy of a medicine man. I only have dried meat and not much of that, but if you hunger, I will share. Many Coups said you would want to speak with me."*

"My son, I have no hunger. In these times the pipe is not needed as we speak. Many are dying and the Great Creator knows our hearts."

"What can I do for you, Grandfather?"

"I seek knowledge of the spotted disease and need to know how we can stop it from killing more. Last night we lost one hand of warriors and today we've lost four fingers. This dying cannot continue or the Shoshone will soon be no more. Tell me what you know of this sickness."

"The illness is a white mans sickness, but it can kill all people. If a person who is ill meets someone healthy, the healthy one will become sick. The guns, clothing, scalps, and all things the sick ones have will cause the disease to spread, even if only touched by healthy people. I have heard words that the Shoshone fought with the Ree and scalps were taken. This is how the illness visited your village."

"How can we stop the illness?"

"Do not allow anyone into the village that is not sick. Only allow other ill ones to enter, so they may be cared for and fed. The belongings, everything, that belongs to a person who had died, must be burned in hot fires."

"Many Coups spoke of burning the bodies of the dead: is this true?"

"Yes, all things that have the illness or the ill one has touched must be burned. There is no other way."

"This will stop the sickness?"

"Grandfather, there is no way to stop the illness. Once it has touched everyone in the village, it will die."

"How many Shoshone will die? It has touched all."

I met the old mans eyes and replied, *"From two hands of people, one hand may die. I have seen one hand and two fingers die from two hands. It is not like a warrior that we can kill if we fight long and hard enough, but the illness is as deadly as a Blackfoot warrior. When it is finished life will go on, but not as before."*

The shaman's eyes grew large as he asked, *"What of my people? Will the Shoshone be no more? Will all die and there will be no one left to remember us? What can we do with those that are sick?"*

"Feed them broth from meat and plenty of water. They will soon start to form red sores on their bodies and then passing blood from all holes. Those that do not pass blood may live and the sores will crust over with a scab. Those that pass blood have little hope, because out of two hands, only one may live"

Standing, Spirit Helper said, *"I must go and help my people. I will share your words with others and do as you think is proper. It will be hard to burn our dead. It is not the way of the Shoshone people. I thank you for sharing your wisdom with an old man. May the Great Spirit protect and guide you for your act of kindness."*

I nodded and the old man left. *I wonder how many of the Sioux still live,* I thought as I leaned back on my blankets. I was tired and was asleep in seconds.

This morning, early, Wilson stuck his head in my lodge and said, "The Shoshone have a couple of trappers near that want to come into the village. Broken Bow ask ya to come and talk for the people."

I put my hat on, grabbed my rifle and exited the lodge. The last thing we needed was to expose trappers to the sickness, but the Shoshone may not know the words needed to explain the disease and the trappers might not speak good Shoshone. I ran after Wilson until we neared the trail I'd been on and I saw Broken Bow standing to one side speaking with another warrior.

As I neared, he gave a faint smile and said, "The takers of the one who swims, do not speak Shoshone well. While one of the other Raven people could speak for us, we know you speak with one tongue. Tell the white men they are not wanted here, our people are sick.

I moved toward the trail and spotted Deacon, James and Buffalo waiting impatiently. Deacon I'd known for years, James was a new man to the mountains and I'd heard nothing but good words about the man. Buffalo I'd know since my first year in the mountains. He liked it down near Taos and was rarely this far north, but mayhap this season he wanted a change in scenery.

"Howdy, boys, it's me, Nate!" I called out.

They moved toward me, but I added, "Stop and don't come any closer. The village has small pox."

"Good God, no." Buffalo said, obviously shocked.

"Have y'all been around the disease or had the inoculation?"

"I ain't in either case." James said.

"Me neither." Buffalo replied, shook his head and added, "Ya doin' okay, Nate?"

"I've been around the disease before. How about ya, Deacon?"

"Yep, I've had the inoculation and been around the disease."

"Are ya damned sure, son? This is deadly serious."

"About a year back I took some furs to Fort Atkinson with Ty Fisher and Jarel Wade. A doctor there was sellin' the small pox inoculation fer fifty cents a man. I met a trapper named Bear, but his real name was George Alwood, and over whiskey he talked me into buyin' one from the doctor. Wasn't much to it really. He scrapped my arm a bit, it scabbed over and fell off a couple weeks later. Bear claimed it was needed out here."

"I know Bear and he's real beaver. Pull yer shirt off and let me see yer arm."

A few minutes later, I saw the scar on Deacon's arm and said, "Yer safe enough, but James, you and Buffalo need to get the hell out of this whole area and do the job pronto. The Ree, Sioux and Shoshone have the pox. Now, that means any damned Injun they've met, fought, or had tea with is likely infected. Iffen ya can, avoid all tribes until ya get south of Fort Atkinson."

Buffalo looked at Deacon and asked, "Ya gonna stay here?"

"Before ya answer 'em, Deacon, we have some Christian folks here, but they're black."

Meeting my eyes Deacon replied, "I'm stayin'. These folks will have need of a Christian man, and I can give a few of them comfort."

"Well said," I stated.

They shook hands all around and Buffalo called out, "Nate, Deacon, ya both watch yer top knots until we see y'all again."

We waved and the two men mounted their horses and moved down the trail.

"Who is this man who stays with the people?" Broken Bow asked as he neared me.

"He is a shaman for white men. He knows the ways of the spirits."

"This is good. Shaman are welcome now. Bring him, he is needed. We have sick Raven people, too."

Leading his horse by the reins, Deacon and I made small talk until we arrived at my lodge. "Ya can live with me while yer here, but I have to speak with Many Coups in a bit. Ya go on in and get comfortable."

My discussion with Many Coups lasted but a few minutes. He was fine and in good health, but his wife and daughter were seriously ill. I mainly wanted him to know Deacon was with us, so he could sort of bless the affair. I think his mind was elsewhere and he heard few of my words.

As I moved toward my lodge, Sue approached and said, "May is down sick and so are two men."

"I thought most have been around the pox before."

"I thought so too, but now I ain't sure they really know. They're scared to death and some were slaves and don't what they've had or not had."

"I'm sending a preacher man to ya in a few minutes, and his name is Deacon. He's a good God-fearing man, so ya can trust 'em. I've known him since he first come out here, and he ain't got any problems with black folks."

"Do you think he'd say a prayer over Frank's grave? I don't like the man bein' buried like we did with no scripture read over him."

"Let's care for the livin' first, then we'll worry about the dead."

Just then I heard a loud scream and folks began to move toward the trail.

CHAPTER 18

I pulled the hammer back on my rifle, which was usually in my hand, and moved toward the noise. As I neared the few Shoshone, I spotted Cotton Top and knew the warriors had found them, not that I ever had much of a doubt they would. I felt a great deal of relief too, because I thought we were experiencing an attack. Lord, that's all we need is an attack on these folks and it'd spread the pox to another village, I thought and moved toward Cotton and Grits. Baxter as usual, was spotted by his master.

When Cotton and the rest neared, we shook hands, cut a few jokes, and then I asked, "How many Sioux remain alive?"

Grits moved his head to the right, blinked a few times and then said, "Nigh on half of 'em. The one's with us now haven't caught the illness or have crusted scabs. I figure they'll live."

"Bloody Blade?"

"He's fine and not a sign of gettin' sick either. I suspect the sickness might not attack a strong person as hard as a weak one, and he's as strong as a bull." Cotton said.

"Listen, I know yer both tired as hell, but we need meat. I've gone out a few times, takin' Wilson with me, but we ain't seen a buffalo yet. These folks been livin' on rabbits, deer and a few squirrels. They need good dark meat to get strong."

Cotton asked, "Are you goin' with us?"

"Yep, and guess who showed up earlier?"

"Hell, Nate, I'm too tired to remember my own name right now, so just tell me."

"Deacon, and he's working with the black folks now."

"I always did like that young pup. He's a good addition to these mountains and damn fine man in my eyes."

"Well, let me pull a few mounts from the herd and we'll make some meat."

Less than an hour later, we were moving over the mountain trails and heading to the plains, with ten horses along to carry meat. We'd left Baxter behind. The weather was nice, not a cloud in the sky, and I was in a good mood. I'd spent so much time worrying over sick folks, I'd been wound up tighter than a dime pocket watch. Of course, seeing my friends helped my mood a great deal. Wilson had come with us, but I had mixed feelings about the man. He was a good enough man, but he didn't have much in the way of woods skills and that ignorance could get him killed, and quickly. I think he honestly wanted to fit in, but didn't know how.

Grits was riding out front, when he suddenly stopped, pointed to the ground and moved on. When we neared the spot he'd pointed at, I saw the tracks of about twenty unshod horses. They weren't wild, because each was carrying a weight and the tracks were deep. The tracks moved to the north and I suspected Blackfoot. *Lord, keep us safe on this trip. We have a lot of sick and dying folks in the village and I'd like to get a couple of buffalo so we can feed them proper,* I silently prayed.

Shortly after noon, Cotton rode from his position out front and said, "Over this next rise is about a zillion buffalo. Now, iffen we come at 'em from the right side, walkin' beside our horses, we can get in close before we shoot."

Grits, while an experienced woodsman, hadn't hunted much buffalo before and he laughed right then.

"Do ya have something to say about my idea, Grits?"

"Hell, ain't no horse got six legs."

Cotton grinned and replied, "Ain't no buffalo that can count either. This'll work, because I've done 'er before. Now, since there are four of us, we kill one apiece and we'll be fine."

I thought for a few seconds and added, "Cotton, ya and I will kill two. That'll give us six buffalo and then we can quarter 'em. I want to kill, cut, and load fast. The last thing we need is to run into Injuns out here. We've sick people to feed, and I don't like the thought of givin' this sickness to another tribe."

"Huh?" Wilson asked.

"If one of us touches another warrior and he gets away, or iffen one or all of us are killed, the tribe that attacks us will come down with the pox. Iffen we're killed, they'll take all of our gear and that'll spread the disease even faster."

"Let's pray the Blackfoot don't find us then, 'cause they usually hunt around here." Cotton said, and then scanned the countryside.

"I thought y'all hated the Blackfoot." Wilson said and when I looked at him, he wore a confused look on his face.

I said, "I don't like 'em much, but by God, I'd not wish the pox on the devil himself. Hell, ya saw Frank die and it was rough, right?"

Wilson lowered his head and said, "Roughest way to die I've ever seen."

Knowing the man felt bad about his comment, I said, "Cotton, ya lead the way. When we move toward the herd, don't enter it, but stay to the sides. If they stampede, move at right angles away from them, because if ya go down, there won't be enough of ya left to bury in my possibles bag."

As we moved, Wilson said, "Nate, I'm   "

"I know what ya meant and it's okay. We all say things without thinkin' at times. Let 'er slide, son, and let's get some buffalo for our friends."

From the side, the buffalo were still where we'd last seen them, so we dismounted. Cotton said, "When yer ready to fire, rest yer rifle on yer saddle, line up the sights and squeeze the trigger. Iffen ya move away from yer horse, they'll spook on us."

About twenty-five yards from the animals, Cotton raised his rifle, as did all of us, and sighted in an animal. I selected a cow, because they're always better eating than a bull, more tender to me. I squeezed the trigger, felt my gun discharge, and saw the buffalo collapse. I'd only heard three shots, all close to mine, and when I looked at Wilson, he pulled the trigger.

His horse reared, screamed in fear and took off at a run. Wilson, struck in the face by his rifle, was flat on his ass in the grass, unconscious. I glanced toward the buffalo; while they'd moved a mite, they were nowhere close to running. I quickly loaded my gun, as did Cotton and shot another cow. She remained standing, with bright red blood running from her mouth and each time she exhaled through her nose, blood would spray in all directions. I finished loading my rifle and was ready to put another ball in her, when she fell to her knees and then rolled to her side.

"That's six critters, boys, so that's enough." Cotton said, and then turning to Wilson, who was coming around, he added, "Fine damned time to take a nap, son. Why didn't ya tell us ya was sleepy?"

Wiping blood from his mouth and nose, Wilson grinned and replied, "Cotton, kiss my ass."

When we broke out laughing, the buffalo moved away at a fast walk. In a few minutes, nothing but open plains remained, and six dead animals.

Concerned about our noise, I ordered, "Quarter the animals and do the job fast. We have no idea who might have heard our shots."

Less than thirty minutes later, Wilson said, "We have visitors. Off to the right."

"Blackfoot, boys, get behind a buffalo and get ready fer a fight!" I yelled as I wiped my bloody hands on my trousers.

With the wave of a lance, the warriors rode right for us and I counted close to twenty Injuns, which is the same number of tracks Grits had pointed out earlier. *Damn, we need to get this meat back or a lot of those folks will die,* I thought as I lined up my rifle and dropped a rider to the grass.

Arrows rained around me, bullets ate at the grass, sending clumps into the air, and a spear stuck near my head.

Three more shots sounded and the Blackfoot now had four men down, but likely not all were dead. "Make this cost 'em, boys! If we injure and kill enough of 'em, they'll leave."

I fired my rifle, dropped another man, but when I pulled the trigger on my pistol, it misfired. However, the Blackfoot swerved away from us and soon gathered on top of a hill, just out of good rifle range. I quickly fixed my pistol and placed it at my side. I suspected they weren't finished with us yet. I was right, here they come again.

This time when they grew near, they began to circle and I fired my rifle, smiled when one warrior grabbed his head and fell; he landed about six feet from me. The top of his head was missing. I heard a scream and when I turned, Wilson was down with an arrow in his belly. I glanced at the Injuns again, aimed my pistol and fired. I must have missed because no rider fell. I reloaded both of my guns and pulled my second pistol out, because I'd not be taken alive.

Without warning, one horse jumped into the middle of us, and Cotton took the man down with a mad swing of his rifle. Once the man was on the grass, Cotton plunged his knife into the man's chest three or four times.

The line of circling Blackfoot suddenly moved to the hill they'd been on just before this attack. I reloaded my guns and then asked, "Everyone okay?"

"I'm as fine as frog hair!" Grits yelled.

"Me, too, but Wilson is down with an arrow in the lights." Cotton answered.

He'll die then, I thought. *Now, how can we get this meat home if the Injuns leave? I'm sure they've taken the pack-horses we had behind the rise.*

One lone warrior ran right for us. I'll swear, his headdress had more feathers in it than a Christmas turkey. Three rifles fired, he fell from his horse and slid across the grass to stop near Grits. Grits ran from his horse, cut the warriors throat and scalped him. He then held the scalp high in the air and yelled, "Come on down an' play, ya red sumbitches! We've got more bullets where those come from!" He then ran to his buffalo and knelt.

The Blackfoot must have figured they'd lost enough men, because a spear was raised and the Injuns turned and rode away. I felt my pounding heart slowing down. I glanced at the others, saw Grits about to stand and said, "Give 'em a few more minutes before ya stand. Iffen ya want to move, crawl over and check Wilson."

I kept my eyes on the horizon, but after ten minutes I said, "They're gone."

"Wilson is hurt bad, and I don't think we can do a thing fer 'em. The arrow hit him about two inches above his belly button." Grits said.

"Cotton, check on our pack-horses, but I suspect they're gone."

As he moved for the hill, I reached into my possibles bag and pulled out the laudanum. Wilson was in a fetal position and he was moaning and groaning as I neared. I broke the arrow off and pulled the rest of it from his body. He screamed loudly, but for what I had in mind, I had to give him some laudanum.

While he was whimpering, I squatted beside him and asked, "Have ya prayed to the Lord yet?"

"That's all . . . I . . . been . . . doin'."

I pulled his head up, met his eyes and felt his fear. I gently stroked his hair and asked, "Son, did you ask the Good Lord to forgive yer sins?"

He nodded.

I pulled the cork from the laudanum and said, "I'm goin' to give ya some of this to kill yer pain, okay?"

"Y . . . yes."

I raised the bottle and allowed a good amount to enter his open mouth.

"Nate," Grits said, "That's too much and it might— "

"No, it won't might, it will. I'll not have him spending days in pain like this and die in the end anyway."

I held Wilson and sang a gospel song for him for a few minutes. I was smiling and looking into his eyes when he died. His eyes lost focus, he gave a light shudder, something rattled inside of him, and his breathing stopped. I lowered his head and placed his hat over his face.

I shuddered and silently began to cry.

Cotton returned a bit later shaking his head, so I knew the answer before I even asked, the horses were gone. Once at my side, he asked, "Wilson dead?"

"There wasn't no hope, so I fed him more laudanum that he could handle."

Cotton knew me well, because he placed his hand on my shoulder and said, "Iffen ya have to do that fer me one day, do it, and don't let it bother ya none. Ain't no reason fer a man to suffer pain like that fer days, maybe, and then die anyway. This way he didn't suffer long and I know ya were with 'em when he passed. Yer a good and strong man, Nate Grisham, and I'm proud to call ya friend."

I wiped my eyes with the back of my hand and said, "Okay, let's get the meat on our three horses and we'll walk to the village. We'll stop often, so we won't wear the animals out."

It was after dark before a guard near the village challenged us, but once I said my name, we were allowed to pass. The village was different now, with some completely dark, a few with bright fires burning and some with just a dim light. I made my way to Broken Bow's lodge and said, "Broken Bow, we have meat for your people."

Baxter ran from out of nowhere and was going crazy jumping around Grits. I had to smile; just seeing their love made me happy.

When he walked out a few minutes later, I could see he'd been crying. I pointed to the meat and said, "We will cook in the big pots I have seen at campfires. When a warrior or someone feeding the sick needs soup, take what is needed."

He nodded and started to turn away, but I asked, "Is all well with your family?"

"My family is still sick, but the sores no longer have pus. I have been crying over my people and our future. We have lost many hands of people. What is to happen to us? Why has the Creator forsaken us? I do not cry because I am afraid of tomorrow, but for those who have gone to the other side."

"I understand and a true warrior should cry for the loss of his people. Being a leader of others is hard and we grow close to them. When they go to the other side, we grieve for them and that is how it should be, my friend."

Glancing at us, Broken Bow asked, "Where is the raven man that went with you?"

"We fought with the Blackfoot, and he died bravely. Grits, my friend, has a Blackfoot scalp he collected on this day. We killed some, wounded many, and there will be much crying in Blackfoot lodges this night."

"As it is in Shoshone lodges." Broken Bow replied and then walked into his lodge.

"Cotton, ya start gatherin' up big cast iron pots. Grits, I want ya to go and get Sue and any of them that aren't sick to help us. Cotton, yer the chief cook, while Grits and I'll cut meat. Sue and the rest are to take soup to every lodge and feed all who are hungry."

Four days later, a little after dawn, I stood by the biggest of the pots and asked, "How many died last night?"

Grits shook his head and said, "Last I heard was ten of 'em. None of the black folks have died, but we lost some of the Sioux and more Shoshone. Bloody Blade lost everyone in his family and is alone now."

I cut a piece of chewing tobacco from a twist, stuck it in my mouth and said, "He's a strong man and he'll come back from this. Didn't that May woman die?"

"Naw, she scabbed over and while her cheeks will be scared a mite, she's still as pretty as ever."

I stirred the soup, grinned and replied, "Sounds like yer growin' sweet on the woman."

"I ain't sure what I feel fer her yet, but she's pretty enough. Sue told me she was a good woman and was stolen."

"Ya know by law she's black."

"Nate, it doesn't matter out here and ya know it."

"Grits, what ya do ain't none of my concern, but as yer friend first and then a black man, I have to warn ya about children."

He turned to face me and looking confused he asked, "What in the hell are ya talkin' about?"

I chuckled and said, "I've been asked that before and many times. Let's just pretend ya marry up with May. Now, ya know her past and what the slavers did to her, and I respect ya fer not holdin' that against her, but let's say she ends up pregnant. It could happen and ya know it, too."

"I imagine it'd make me happy."

"What if the child was born black?"

"Hell, that'd not matter one iota to me and ya know it."

"It's not ya or May I'm thinkin' about."

"I see . . . the child is a different matter. By law the child wouldn't be black, right? I mean May is as white as I am."

"If the child had black skin, it would be legally a black child. Did the law stop Blackie and his bunch from taking May to start with?"

Lowering his head, he said, "No."

"Give thought to children and it's important. Now, I care about ya and I'll stand behind yer decision, only don't rush into this marriage. Think 'er all through before ya act."

Cotton neared and said, "The smell of burning bodies is gettin' to me this mornin'."

"They need to be burned and ya know it as well as I do. How much longer will we need to be here, do ya think?" I said.

"I'd say another month and then we can move on. We might get away with it now, but I don't want to risk it. We go back to Butterfield like this, and every trapper in the mountains will come down with the pox."

I stirred the soup again and said, "We don't want that to

happen, so we'll just wait until we know it's safe to go back. I couldn't live with myself iffen I knew my turnin' up at Butterfield's made all the trappers sick."

"Well, what's planned for the day?" Cotton asked.

"Get a count of all the survivors of this sickness. Count everyone, and I'll talk to Broken Bow."

"I'll get the numbers in a bit. But, while yer doin' all that political trash with Broken Bow and Many Coups, I'll take Grits and we'll go hunting. I think it might be healthy for us to take Sue and May along, too. May is up and moving, so mayhap they can find some roots and other stuff to eat. I grow tired of meat boiled into soup all the time."

"Ya do that, but be back before dark. I suspect a couple more will die on us over night, and they'll likely be the last bunch. We'll need the women back fer sure."

"Come on, Grits, let's go get the women and make some meat."

"What about Baxter? He's not left the village since we got here."

Cotton laughed, happy to get away for a while and said, "Hell, bring the dog too!"

I had to chuckle at the look on both of their faces. We'd been in the village a long time, and they had a serious urge to leave for a short spell. I could appreciate that, but one of us had to speak with the chief.

Seeing Broken Bow walking toward his lodge, I called out to him, and he walked toward me.

"Yes, my brother?" He asked once beside me.

"Most of the illness has finished. How many hands of Shoshone and Sioux remain on this side?" I asked, dreading the answer.

"Where there were once ten Shoshone, now four stand. For the Sioux, one hand out of two remain alive. Many have gone and no longer walk beside us."

"We will mourn, but later. Now the people need more meat, and my two friends have gone to hunt buffalo and gather plants for the healthy ones."

I knew his sadness in my heart and felt it just by looking at him, but a warrior is a proud and brave man.

"Come, I must speak with Many Coups about our losses. He knows of our losses, I feel it in my heart, but it must be told to him. He must hear from someone who speaks with one tongue."

CHAPTER 19

Night has come and my friends still haven't returned. Only that's not unusual, and I think they killed a number of buffalo, and it takes time to gut, cut, and load them on horses. I wrapped up in my robe and thought, iffen they're not back by mornin', I'll go lookin' fer 'em..

Morning dawned cold with the threat of rain low overhead. I scratched on a lodge door and Broken Bow stuck his head out.

"My friends have not returned from their hunting trip, and I fear for their safety."

He shrugged and replied, *"Often hunting takes more than a sun. Who can say what they've killed or seen."*

"Your words are true, but I feel something has happened."

"Then, come in and we will speak."

I entered and sat by his fire.

"If you have hunger, my wife will cook."

"I have no hunger."

"Have you had a dream or vision of danger to your friends?"

I shook my head and replied, *"My mind is concerned, because I know my friends. On my trip to the land of the rising sun, I killed one man, but only injured the other."*

"Do you feel this man has returned to the land of the Shoshone?"

"I have no idea, but usually when I feel like this, something bad has happened."

"It may be a warning from the Great Spirit. I do not have this gift, but we must do something."

"I am riding this morning to look for them; would you ride with me?"

"You did much for my people when all were ill, and I cannot refuse your request. To do so would make me less than

a real man. Let me prepare for the trip, and I will meet you near the horses."

Less than an hour later, we were moving down a mountain trail, heading for the plains. The weather still threatened us with rain, but regardless of the weather, we'd ride. Off in the distance, I could see falling rain on the western horizon, so eventually we'd get wet. I pulled out my oilcloth and placed it behind my cantle and tied it on.

We'd no sooner entered the plains than Broken Bow's horse reared and began to dance around and I heard the telltale sound of a rattlesnake's rattle. The warrior, superb rider he was, had the mare under control in a minute or so, looked at me and grinned. "I did not see my brother the snake," he said in sign language.

"Nor I," I signed in return.

We rode in silence for over two hours, then suddenly the brave pointed to the sky in front of us and I spotted a thin finger of smoke.

"Come." He said.

We rode to close to a hundred yards from the smoke, dismounted and then moved forward on foot. I hoped all was well and my friends were camped here, only it was unlikely a mountain man would make a smoking fire. When we neared, I saw a fire, some clothing, a shelter, but little else.

Signing to Broken Bow, I said, *"Cover me as I check the camp. I can tell nothing from here."*

He nodded.

I cautiously moved forward, scanning from side to side, expecting a rifle shot or attack at any moment, but saw nothing. The tracks in the dirt showed where a fight had taken place, a dried puddle of blood, and little else. The fire was from clothing and buckskin burning and that surprised me. I walked to the far side of the camp and heard a moan—or thought I did.

I remained in place and using sign, asked Broken Bow to circle the camp. A few minutes later, I heard the sound again. It sounded as if it came from the left side of camp. If it was a trick by some unknown tribe, it was a damned good one, because I saw nothing. I stayed in place until Broken Bow walked to me and said, *"No one is here. I saw the sign of two hands of horses moving away, traveling south. And, the big dog has crossed over to the other side."*

"The dog is dead?"

"Shot many times, my brother, more than two hands of bullets hit him."

I felt a sharp pain, because I knew the dog would die protecting the others, and it hurt me. I'd grown fond of the big beast, and I would miss him.

"Are you well? I see your pain on your face."

"The dog was like a brother to all of us."

"I understand."

I met his eyes and realized he really did understand my feelings. I didn't reply.

A few seconds later he asked, *"What did you hear?"*

"I heard a moan or groan in the grasses, but I see nothing."

"Someone who knows how to hide does not need a forest of trees, my brother. Let us search for one who has been injured."

We split and a few minutes later, Broken Bow said, *"It is Snow On His Head. He has been shot."*

Cotton Top, I hope ya ain't hurt bad, son, I thought and moved toward the brave.

He was laying on his back, his eyes open and he had a wore a weak smile. I squatted beside him and asked, "Where are ya hit? I only see blood on yer head and it doesn't look like much."

"I go for our horses." Broken Bow said and took off at a run.

"My head and a bullet burned my left calf a mite. Ya got any whiskey?"

"Let's get ya to camp first. Can ya walk at all?"

"I ain't got no idea. About six jaspers fired at me and down I went."

I scooped him up in my arms and carried him to the fire. I placed him on the grass, raised his head and said, "Grazed yer noggin', which likely hurts like a bitch, but it won't kill ya."

By the time Broken Bow returned with the horses, I had cut Cottons pant leg up past his injury, looked the wound over, and pulled the buckskin from the fire. I walked to my horse, pulled a jug of whiskey and returned to Cotton. I poured him a cup of the strong amber drink and then asked, "What happened?"

He knocked the drink back and extended the cup once again. I refilled it as he said, "Yesterday we downed two buffalo and the women gathered plants and roots. We were late starting back and darkness found us right here, so we spent the night. Sue was pulling the guard shift just after dawn, when I heard her scream, followed by the blast of her shotgun and then saw fellers run into our camp. I knocked one on his ass when I fired my rifle, but don't think I killed 'em. At that point, they all fired at me and down I went. I'd been over in the grass making water when they struck. Next think I knew, I thought I saw you walk by me. I tried to yell, but couldn't get the words out. Pour me some more panther piss, iffen ya don't mind."

"Well, they took the others, and Baxter is dead."

"By God, they was dressed like white men. One man, well, I'm sure was Blackie, but I didn't really get a good look. I'm sure they had to kill the dog, can ya imagine the ruckus he'd raise?"

Damn, Blackie may have come looking for me again, I thought. *I should have made sure the sonofabitch was dead in Mississippi. I suspect he's put two and two together, and knows I was the one who attacked his slavers now. When I get my hands on his ass this time, he'll stay dead.*

I poured Cotton a drink and then removed some medical supplies from my horse. Ten minutes later I had his head cleaned and wrapped, as well as his leg. "I think you'll be able to walk in a day or two, because all the bullet did was burn ya. Now, we both know how head injuries are, so iffen ya get to feelin' tired or sick to yer stomach, let me know."

"He drinks much of the firewater. His mind will soon leave him." Broken Bow said.

Grinning, Cotton said, "Naw, I'll be fine, just hurtin' is all."

"Yer goin' to have to ride, even iffen I have to tie ya to a horse."

"My brother, were the horse tracks you saw of white men or another tribe?" Cotton asked.

"The horses wore the metal shoes. Unless the horses were stolen, the riders were white men."

I explained to Broken Bow what had happened and he grinned. After a few seconds he said, *"There are only two fingers of men for each of us. It will bring us much honor to kill these men and it will teach others not to steal the friends of the Shoshone. For what they have done, they will be punished."*

I walked near the fire and bent over. I picked up a discarded cigar and showed it to Bloody Blade.

"White men. They will be as children when we battle them. Tonight we will look for their fire, it will be large and easy to spot. Come morning, there will be fewer of them."

I wondered, but said, *"The biggest man is mine alone. He is the one I went to kill before, and he's proving to be a hard man to kill."*

"All men may be killed, only this time make sure he stays dead —cut his throat."

"Come, let us ride after the white men."

As we rode, I glanced back at Cotton and he looked like a slight wind would blow his ass off his saddle, but he kept up and that's what mattered. How many long miles have we traveled together, with one or the other hurt and sipping on whiskey as we moved? I hope the good Lord give us many more, but a man never knows His plans. I try to live each day to the fullest, knowing well, it may be my last day on earth.

Broken Bow dropped back beside me and said, *"I will scout ahead and find the white eyes."*

As he moved forward, Cotton asked, "He scouting?"

"Yep, from our talk earlier, we'll visit them fellers later tonight. I hope he finds them before they turn rough on the women folk."

Cotton gave a dry laugh and said, "They ain't had the time to take a good pee yet, so the women are safe enough. They fig'er, in my mind anyway, that it'll be days before ya find my dead body. They'll head to where they got comforts, like whiskey, food, and shelter before the women have to worry about anything. They fig'er to use the women while they wait fer ya to come fer 'em."

"Likely yer right, but Cotton, on this trip there will be no survivors. I mean not a one."

Three hours later as I started up a slight rise in the plains, Broken Bow topped the rise, waved at us and then walked his horse to me. He smiled and said, *"The white men are but a short distance from here and are drinking the water of fire. The women and another man are safe for now and tied to a wagon. The man did not look good, so I think they have beaten him. The women, both of them, were tied to the part of the wagon that turns and moves."*

"He means the wagon wheels." Cotton said.

"I gathered as much." I said and then asked Broken Bow, *"How many men are there?"*

"Two hands, so all did not ride out to raid."

"Let us move into the next valley and make camp. No fires or moving around much. We must clean our weapons, eat jerky, and sleep. An hour before dawn tomorrow we will visit our friends."

Broken Bow abruptly gave a loud war cry, followed by a series of sharp yips, that made my body shudder. I almost felt sorry for the men we were going to attack.

Two hours before dawn, we were positioned around the camp of the white men. Cotton had demanded he come with us, but I worried about his head injury. We'd decided to catch them over their breakfast fire and take them at that point. Broken Bow was to start the dance by shooting a few well placed arrows, that would make the slavers think they were under attack by Injuns. I didn't expect to kill all of them, but we had to lower the numbers before we finished them off. *I just hope Blackie ain't got the sense to use the captives to bargain with, or it'd be a tight fight.*

In the pale moonlight, before we'd moved into position, Broken Bow signed that he would scatter the horses after shooting his bow, just so we could keep our targets in the area. *It's time to end this shit and get on with our lives,* I thought. Revenge is a nasty job and some take it to extremes, never quitting until the awful job is complete.

I heard an owl hoot, a signal from Broken Bow, and when I looked at the center of camp, men were starting to move. Blackie climbed from his blankets, stretched and walked to the edge of camp where he made water. One-by-one, all of the men did the same. An old man, black, moved to the fire and started preparing breakfast and coffee. I waited, my finger on my double triggers and fear gnawing at my gut. I knew I'd be fine, once the fighting started, but just before any fight fear was a companion.

I hoped the men weren't trail savvy enough to notice the

morning sounds were gone. Not a bird chirped, no small animals were out, and it was as still as a graveyard.

"Smith, gather up some wood fer the fire and be quick about it, iffen ya want to eat this mornin'." Blackie ordered as he sat in the grass beside the large fire.

Smith moved right for me, so I moved back into the short brush and waited. I placed my rifle on the ground and pulled my knife. Smith was a tall lanky black man, the cook as far as I was able to determine, but by riding with slavers, he'd sealed his fate.

Stopping not two feet from me, the man must have smelled me or felt my presence, because his eyes began scanning the grasses. Like a snake, I struck fast and hard. I wrapped my left arm around his throat, pulled him to the ground, and my knife blade struck him in the chest three time. I held him tightly until all movement ceased and his body went limp. I then cut his throat and scalped him. I scalped him in the event we had to run or if we were unable to kill all the men. This way they'd assume the Injuns did the killing and never suspect me.

I glanced back at the fire, but no one noticed anything or if they did, they were good actors. Suddenly a man on the far left stood from the soil and reached behind his back. Then, looking down, he saw the chipped arrowhead of Blood Blades arrow, which was sticking about six inches from his chest. I watched as the man reach up and felt the tip of the bloody arrowhead.

A big black man suddenly fell to his side in the grass and began screaming with two arrows in his back. I heard Cotton fire his rifle, followed almost instantly by his pistol. Two men fell, one lay unmoving, but the other fired in return.

I aimed at Blackie as he held the hot coffee pot, fired and saw the coffee pot fly from his hands, and at once heard screams from the men around him. Hot coffee was thrown into the air and while I'd not hit him with a bullet, I'd burned him and a few others. I pulled my pistol, aimed for the center of Blackie's chest, but when I pulled the trigger, all that sounded was a loud *snap* as my powder failed to ignite. Since it wasn't full light yet, I lost sight of the big man, as I worked to reload both of my weapons.

Out of the blue, Broken Bow ran through the camp, his tomahawk swinging left and right, and men fell. I heard screams and before the men could recover from the attack, the

Shoshone was gone.

"The horses! Get the horses!" An unknown voice yelled.

"They're after the hosses!" A deep bass voice was heard.

I hoped Cotton was able to locate and free our people, but after his first shots I'd heard nothing from him. It was then I heard a yell from the camp, "The slaves! They've got the slaves!"

I smiled.

I heard a shot from where Cotton should have been, followed by a scream.

They must have more men than Broken Bow counted, I thought as I watched the warrior run into the center of the camp once more. He held his tomahawk in his right hand and his knife in his left. I heard a loud blast of a shotgun and down the Shoshone went, without a sound.

Silence filled the cool early morning air.

I waited, hoping I'd get a chance to get to Broken Bow and help him. The men had gone to ground and slowly, as individuals, they started to stand. I noticed they walked around aimlessly, not sure what to do next, which made me wonder where Blackie was.

A tall white man asked, "Anybody seen Blackie?"

"When the shootin' started he mounted a horse with them two ladies and left us high and dry to fend fer ourselves." Came the answer.

"Sumbitch! He's a damned coward." The tall man all but screamed. He then walked to Broken Bow and before I could move, shot him in the head.

I aimed at the center of the tall man's chest, took a deep breath and as I released it, I started squeezing the trigger on my Hawken. I heard the flint strike the pan, heard a light puff, and it was followed by the main powder igniting in my rifle. As soon as I heard the shot, I crawled a good ten feet from where I'd fired, and lay close to the ground.

Four or five rifles fired toward my smoke, but I was long gone.

When I glanced back at the camp, maybe ten minutes later, the men were standing in a group talking. I heard one voice say, "Well, by God, it wasn't Nate Grisham this time, it was Injuns and we've a dead one to prove it. Only, what are we goin' to do now? We've got no horses, I'm sure the Injuns have 'em, so we're in one hell of a mess now. Lookin' fer 'em would be a waste of time."

"Silas, I know where that tradin' post is, so we start walkin' that a-way. I don't see where we have a choice now, do ya?"

"Gather up the guns, powder and food for the trip. Iffen an injured man is too hurt to walk, put 'em down. Leave nothin' for the savages, because I suspect they'll be back to check on us later." Silas ordered.

"Ya ain't gonna bury these men?"

"Manning, ya can stay and do the job, iffen ya think ya can get it done before the Injuns come back. As for us, we'll be long gone."

I slowly crawled back toward the rise and once over the top, I ran for our camp. I needed to see how Cotton had fared with the captives and to let him know Bloody Blade was know dead. We'd plan our next move together.

Chapter 20

When I walked into our camp, Cotton was bent over Grits, talking with the man, and it was full light. I looked around and saw no sign of either woman. Grits was on a blanket and from what I could tell he'd been worked over pretty hard.

"Drink this." Cotton ordered as he handed Grits some alcohol to deaden his pain. "When ya finish that, try to get some sleep. If ya need more, the jug is right beside ya."

I moved toward the horses, suspecting Cotton to follow, which he did.

"Where's Broken Bow?" He asked.

"Dead. He tried another run through camp and a shotgun caught 'em." I saw no need to mention he'd been finished off by one of the men.

"That'll do the job quick enough."

"I heard back at camp that Blackie took the women and ran; is that true?"

"Yep, it's true. See, when I finally located them, one of y'all started the dance a bit early. I found Grits first, tied over an anthill, and by the time I'd untied him, the women were gone. They were still asleep in the grasses when I looked fer 'em and not easy to see in the dark."

"Damn, did they both look okay to ya?"

"Cotton, I ain't got no idea. Things were happenin' pretty fast, and Blackie is a slick one. He scooped them two women up and was gone in just minutes."

"It's likely he had something like that planned from the start. How bad off is Grits?"

"He'll not go under, but he ain't ready fer no dance anytime soon, either. They cut 'em a mite, to attract the ants and get 'em bitin', so he's been chewed on pretty good, too. Iffen yer really

",

askin' me can he ride, well, he wants some serious revenge for the death of Baxter and fer losin' the two women. Hell, he can ride, but do him like we've both done a time or two, hang a jug of whiskey from his saddle horn. He told me he was sweet on May and has decided to marry her, so, uh-huh, he'll ride."

I walked to Grits and asked, "Ya got any bark left on ya?"

"I heard the talk, so I'll ride. Nate, they're a bunch of damn animals, every single one of them."

"I'm wanting Blackie, the rest we'll get after we take him. He is the brains and money behind this now, so iffen we can kill his ass, the situation will go away. Once we get the women back, do something with him, then we'll get the others. How soon can ya ride?"

"Let me get some laudanum in me and a few belts of this panther piss and we'll ride. Iffen he hurts either of those women, I'll skin the man alive."

"You'll have to stand in line to skin Blackie and it starts forming after me and Cotton. We've both blackened our faces, we have." I moved to my possibles bag, removed the laudanum and handed it to Grits. I watched as Cotton refilled his tin cup. We'd be riding shortly, because the painkiller worked quickly.

Lord, I prayed in my mind, *keep the women both safe. I'm not askin' for me, but for them. Listen to their prayers, Lord, and also allow us to prevent more deaths. This I ask in the name of Jesus, amen.*

"I'll get the horses ready," Cotton said, and then moved toward the picket line.

"Grits," I said, "I hate makin' ya ride in the shape yer in, but the women come first. Now, we can leave ya, iffen ya want and pick ya up on the way back."

Standing, but looking like death warmed over, he replied, "Nothin', shy of death, will keep me off of Blackie's backside. I've had enough of the man, and I'll make 'em come this time."

I laughed softly inside, because I knew the drug was talking, and he was too weak to do much. However, it didn't detract from the fact he wanted a solid piece of the man's ass. Hopefully, God willing, we'd soon have the women safely back with us.

Cotton approached and said, "I placed all the supplies on the horse Bloody Blade rode and we can use the pack-horse fer Grits."

"Let's ride."

We rode around the camp where we'd fought the men, but I'd come back and pick up Bloody Blades body on my return to the mountains. I'd take him back to his people, so they could bury him according to their customs. He was a good man, too good for the likes of those that killed him, but death visits all of us eventually.

"He's movin' toward Butterfield, or so it looks like to me." Cotton said, and then thought for a second before continuing, "Do ya think Thad is safe?"

"No, I don't think he's safe at all. Hell, Butterfield has threatened to kill the man on sight, so let's hope we can get him before he gets to the tradin' post. If we don't, I fear this time Butterfield will be killed and likely the boy, too."

"We'll ride through the night then. I don't see any other way to do the job, do ya?"

"We can do that, but we're takin' a shortcut too, which will shave about three hours off the ride."

Cotton's eyes grew large as he asked, "Dead Squaw Pass?"

"Yep, unless ya have a better idea?"

"Nate, that place is dangerous and ya know it, too. I ain't scared of much, but the rock slides and snow slides in that pass scare the hell out of me. But, iffen that's what it'll take to get the job done, let's do 'er."

"I doubt Blackie knows of the pass, so we're one up on the man, and while I know it's a dangerous place, that's the way my stick floats right now. I fear for the lives of more than just us and think it's worth the risk."

"I hear ya, but I'll be prayin'."

"I have been prayin' since the start of all of this. How's the head?"

"It still hurts, but the leg bothers me more. Next chance I get, I'll steal the whiskey from Grits."

I reached behind me, to my saddlebags, and pulled out a bottle of good rye. Tossing the quart bottle to Cotton I said, "Here, and it's good stuff."

"I'll buy ya another one at Butterfield's place."

"We need to start thinking about where we'll winter this year, too. Won't be long it'll be time fer us to head out again, iffen we can end this fight pretty soon."

He didn't reply, because he was busy pulling the paper and cork from the whiskey. I knew then he was in some pretty good pain, because Cotton was an old curly wolf and no complainer.

Hours passed and each time I looked back at Grits, he'd give me a big smile and a thumb up, but I knew he was half roostered by the strong drink.

Finally we neared Dead Squaw Pass and I stopped and said, "Grits, we're goin' to take a pretty dangerous shortcut. Keep yer voice low and no loud noises at all, if it can be prevented. See, the sides of this pass are lined with huge rocks and trees and just the slightest noise causes 'em to come tumblin' down. If we have a rock slide, ride like the devil is on yer ass straight ahead, and don't stop fer any reason. I ain't jokin' in the least, and I know of at least ten men who've died in here. But, iffen we make it through okay, we'll shave a bunch of hours off our ride to Butterfield's."

With his speech slurred, Grits said, "Let's have at 'er then, iffen it'll allow us to make better time."

I looked at Cotton and said, "Pass that bottle over here for a minute, I need some liquid courage." Once I had the bottle, I downed about an inch of the wonderful drink and then tapped my horse in the ribs to move forward into the pass.

Cotton said, "Pass that bottle back. Iffen I see a rock slide comin' I'll try to down it all before the rocks kill me."

I handed the bottle back to him and never saw any humor in his comment, because it could very well happen. I knew the pass was short, only about a mile, but it was a mile right out of hell in my mind.

As we moved, all I heard was the soft breathing of my horse and the loud sound of metal horseshoes hitting rocks on the trail. I kept my eyes on the left side, as Cotton scanned the right. The wind was light and I could hear the bird singing, but I watched an overhang and prayed it wouldn't come down. Although the temperature did warrant it, I began to sweat profusely. My heart rate increased and the sound of it beating became louder with each passing moment. Just when it sounded like a big bass drum, I heard a roar on Cotton's side and him yell, "Move, and do 'er now!"

I kicked my horse hard with both feet and shot forward at a hard run. I lowered myself as much as possible in the saddle because small rocks were already peppering us from the fall. I heard Grits scream something, but I never slowed down one beat. To slow down meant death, and I was determined to live.

Finally, at the end of the pass, I stopped my horse and placing a hand on my pommel and another hand on my cantle,

I looked behind me. I was hacking and spitting because of the debris in the air. Dust filled my view, but a second later Cotton materialized from the chalky whiteness and he was coughing as well.

For some reason, it really wasn't needed, I yelled, "What of Grits?"

"I heard 'em yell somethin', but I have no idea what he said."

I pointed toward the dust and said, "Iffen he's still in there, he's gone under."

"Let's let the dust settle a few minutes and then　"

"I'm fine, just got turned around the last few feet or so. Couldn't see a damned thing and my horse didn't do any better," Grits said as he rode from the dust. Like Cotton, he started coughing.

"What was ya yellin' about back there?" Cotton asked.

"Pack-horse got flattened and we have no supplies now. I'll swear, when that big rock hit that horse, I just knew it'd take me too, but it missed me by just inches."

I gave a nervous laugh and then said, "Cotton, pass me the bottle, I think I need a drink about now."

"Right after me," he said and then took a look healthy drink.

He then handed the bottle to me, I took a snort and then said, "Let's ride, we're burnin' daylight."

Early the next morning we arrived at the crack of dawn at Butterfield's and rain fell in buckets. I suspected Blackie had holed up a spell due to weather, only we kept moving. I knew from the start, iffen we could get to the trading post before him, we would really surprise the big man. I dismounted, walked to the door and gave a loud knock.

I heard Butterfield call out, "Hold yer horses, I'll be there directly."

A bright flash of lightning filled the sky and when the thunder cracked sharply, the door opened.

"Nate? What in the world are ya doin' out in this weather?"

"Blackie is on his way here." I turned and motioned my

friends to come in out of the rain.

"All three of ya get in here before ya wash away. Good God, Blackie? Are ya sure it's him?"

I entered the structure, slapped my felt hat against my leg to get rid of the water and then replied, "Beyond a doubt. We had a fight with the man and his group a few days back."

"Sit," Butterfield ordered, "while I get some coffee fer us all. Hell, I just woke up a few minutes ago."

"Can I skip the coffee and get some sleep?" Grits asked.

He looked weak and pale, so I knew the trip had been hard on him. I noticed a questioning look on Butterfield's face and said, "Grits was tied over an anthill fer a spell, and he's in some pain. He's had enough whiskey to float a boat, but rest is what he really needs."

The old trader nodded and said, "Go down the hall and you'll find the last room on the left empty. At the foot of the bed are some towels, so dry off good before ya climb between my clean sheets."

Grits disappeared down the hall and Butterfield brought a pot of coffee, along with three cups, to our table. After he sat, he asked, "Now, what in Sam's hell is this about Blackie?"

I explained what had happened and then waited. The old man's face turned red and his eyes narrowed as he said, "What makes ya think he's comin' here?"

"First off, he ran off and left his men to fight us, taking two women with 'em. They're the same women he took to Mississippi the last time. Second, he ran scared, so he has few supplies, if any, and you're the only place he can get 'em." I said.

"Some nerve, huh? Last time he robbed me and beat the hell out of me, and now he thinks I'll let 'em buy goods in here? It won't happen. How fur do ya think he is behind ya?"

I took a sip of coffee, shivered from the cold rain, and said, "I have no idea. It all depends on iffen he stops fer this storm. I suspect he will, because he'll want to care for the women, and he's soft. The women he'll sell down South again, iffen he gets past us."

"By chance," Butterfield said, "he kills ya two, I have a double-barreled ten gauge sawed off under this counter, and I've yet to see anyone I've fired at with it walk away. It's a wicked-ass gun."

"Well, how are we goin' to do this then to keep the women

folk from bein' killed?" Cotton asked. "I mean iffen ya fire that shotgun, the women will die, too."

I thought for a moment and then asked, "When he came in here the last time he was alone. I think he'll keep the women on their horses until he kills ya. Or that will be his plan. Seems to me it'd be too much fer him to iffen he had the women and was tryin' to kill ya at the same time."

Butterfield smiled and said, "That makes sense, but he mighten not do it that way."

Nope, so here is what we're goin' to do." I said.

Shortly before noon the rain stopped. Cotton used a ladder to get on the roof of the building while I cocked and placed two pistols under the counter. Butterfield had his sawed off shotgun under the counter as well. Our horses were in the barn, and we were as ready as we could get.

Butterfield went through his normal day to day activities, and by late afternoon as he cooked supper, we heard horses nearing. From the roof I heard a robin singing on the roof, which I knew was Cotton. I moved behind the counter, ducked down, and waited. Butterfield remained cooking, but he had sand in his craw, so he'd stand.

I heard the door open, the brass bell *tinkled*, and then Blackie spoke, "So, I didn't kill ya the last time, huh? God knows I tried hard enough."

The trader turned and said, "What in the hell are ya doin' here, Blackie, I have nothin' for ya."

The slave hunter laughed and said, "You'll give me what I ask for, or I'll kill ya."

Keep 'em talkin' Butterfield, until Cotton gets the women, I thought.

"What brings ya back here? Didn't Nate teach ya not to come out here causin' trouble?"

"Speakin' of Nate Grisham, where is the big sumbitch?"

It was then I heard three horse running hard from the trading post, and knew Cotton had the women. I picked up my pistol, stood and said, "I'm right here, Blackie."

He'd turned for the door, but stopped, turned to face me and then went for a pistol in his sash. I have no idea what he was thinkin', but he should have known better. Hell, ain't no way ya can pull a pistol faster than a man holdin' one can fire one.

I pulled the trigger, heard the loud report of the gunshot and saw Blackie knocked hard against the door. He then fell to the floor and started screaming.

I glanced at Butterfield, saw he had his scattergun and said, "Cover me, while I see how badly he's hit."

"Go, I got 'em, but don't take no chances, Nate."

I kicked the pistol he'd tried to pull away from him, saw my shot had taken him in the chest, and he was jerking and twitching. I forced him over onto his belly and checked for guns, pulling a second pistol from the small of his back and a knife in his right boot. I then tied his hands behind his back with some rawhide strands I carried in my possibles bag.

"We got 'em!" Butterfield gave a loud yell.

"Bring him over to the fire and bring me a small bottle of laudanum. We'll see if he'll talk iffen we deaden his pain a little."I knelt beside the injured man.

At that point the door opened, the brass bell announced an arrival, and when I looked, Cotton stood grinning. "Ya got 'em. Good." He placed his pistol back in his sash and said, "I'll be right back. I need to fetch the women. I hid 'em and thought I'd better find out who won the fight before bringin' back here."

"Get 'em," I said and slipped a bit of the laudanum into Blackie's mouth. After a minute or so, he sat up, glaring at me. I quickly wrapped his injury. I saw no bloody bubbles on his lips and he wasn't bleeding from his nose or ears, so he'd live.

"Give me a whiskey, Butterfield, and Cotton went to get the women." I said, very happy we had the man. *I'll have a drink and let the medicine loosen the man's tongue a little.*

Right then Grits walked into the room and said, "So, ya got the bastard, huh?"

"Where ya been?" Butterfield asked.

"Sleepin', why?"

"Didn't ya hear the gunfire?"

"Somethin' woke me up, but I thought it was thunder."

We laughed and then I looked at Blackie and asked, "Who's behind all the slave runnin'?"

"Nobody, and I wasn't lookin' fer slaves. I come out here

lookin' for yer ass and happened on some valuable women." Then glancing at Grits, his eyes narrowed and he continued, "So, ya lived, huh? I thought I'd shot ya dead when I hit ya."

I smiled and said, "Iffen you'd killed 'em, it wouldn't have changed a thing. I'd still have ya. Y'all are like kids in the woods, and yer men are heading this way right now. How about I turn ya over to them when they get here?"

"N . . . no, they'll lynch me."

Cotton walked in with the women and the first words out of Sue's mouth was, "He's the one who brought the pox to the Injuns. He bragged about it to us."

"Is that right?" I asked gazing into his drug-dulled eyes.

"Yep, the Ree wanted gifts from me to travel over their lands, so we gave 'em some special blankets and other junk. See, two of my men died earlier on the trip in Arkansas from small pox and we'd saved their blankets. All the other men had had it or wouldn't get it, so we were safe enough. I realize now just how good my gift was to the dumb-ass Injuns. They're pretty stupid, do ya know that?"

"They're people, too, Blackie, with feelin's." Butterfield said in anger.

I glared and said, "They're better folks than some whites I know, especially ya. Pox kills hard, with a lot of suffering, but ya don't give a damn, do ya?"

"Hell no, why should I care about a bunch of stupid savages? That's all they are, animals. All that die now saves us the trouble of killin' later. Why should ya care, ya ain't nothin' but a dumb-ass worthless slave and not much better than they are."

I backhanded him harder than I intended to do and he fell back to the floor.

I stood, made my way to the table and suddenly had an idea. I said nothing, but the thought grew stronger the longer I thought about it. After a few minutes, I said, "We'll all take turns guarding him over night and we'll leave in the mornin'."

"Leave?" Cotton asked, puzzled.

"Where are we goin'? Ya don't want to go after them other fellers then, do ya?" Grits asked.

"We're goin' to visit the Shoshone. Forget about the others." I replied and saw Cotton smile.

Chapter 21

It's cold this morning, as high as we are in the mountains, and all Blackie did on the ride was complain. I'd warned him a couple of times about the need to be quiet, but it'd done little good. So now he rode with a gag in his mouth. I knew he was in pain and each evening I'd give him enough whiskey to allow him to sleep, but he'd started the whole pox sickness, so compassion wasn't in my soul. He'd killed a great number of people with his earlier adventure, and I hoped the Devil had a special place in mind for him. Justice must be served. May rode behind me, leading Blackie's horse, while Grits was riding behind the big man with a shotgun. The gun was always pointed in Blackie's general direction. Cotton was riding out front and Sue covered our rear. Good people, every single one of them.

Suddenly, Blackie went limp and fell forward in the saddle. Iffen his legs hadn't been tied under his horse, he would have left the saddle. "Hold up, Cotton!"

I dismounted and saw the man was delirious with pain, so I gave him a slug of laudanum, which should keep him going until dusk. He was still bleeding, but I suspected once we got to the Shoshone, he'd be well cared for by them. They have special treatment for their enemies.

The day passed uneventful, with the weather remaining cold and while the sun came up, it never got warm. I wore my capote and pulled it around me tightly as I rode. It was near dusk when I called for an evening camp and moved back into some pines. In very little time we had a camp established, food cooking, and the horses wiped down.

We fed Blackie, untied one hand so he could drink some whiskey, and then gave him a couple of blankets. I suspected the night would turn cold and while I hated the man, I would take better care of him than he ever did his prisoners. See, I was raised to respect life, all forms of life, from insects to people and to never kill or hurt unless I had to do the job. Others, like Blackie, considered others inferior to them and treated them poorly. A human life meant little to men like him, unless they could sell the person for a few dollars.

After supper, while Cotton pulled guard, I saw a need to explain why we were heading back to the Shoshone with Blackie. I was sure they were more than just a little confused and I had to admit, it'd make little sense to someone who'd not spent a lot of time with Injuns.

From near the dancing flames of our small fire, I said, "I'm taking Blackie to the Shoshone fer justice because they were the people wronged by the man the most. Granted, stealing slaves and free folks is wrong, only none of ya died from it. I will turn him over to Many Coups and the village elders, if any yet live, and they will decide his fate."

May said, "Frank died from the pox."

"May, the Shoshone and Sioux lost much more than just one person. Normally, I'd see justice served myself, but since Blackie bragged of givin' the infested blankets to the Ree, I don't think it's our place to punish the man. His crime and sin is against them, more so than us."

"He gave the blankets to the Ree, not the Shoshone." Grits said and then shrugged.

"Ya try to get close to the Ree, and we're all dead." Sue said.

I said, "That's why we're goin' to the Shoshone instead. We'd never get close enough to talk with the Ree."

Grits said, "Well, by God, he killed plenty of Injuns with those blankets, but what will they do with him?"

"Usually they torture men to death who've wronged them. But, to be totally honest, I have no idea in a case like this."

"They'll want blood fer sure after all of the deaths he caused." May said.

Leaning forward and removing the coffee pot, Grits thought for a moment and asked, "When they torture a man to death, how do they do the job? Fire? Hang 'em?"

"When a captive is to die, they turn the man over to the women of the village."

Sue blinked rapidly a few times and then asked, "Women?"

"Yep, and believe me, they can be wicked and vicious with enemies. I won't discuss it now, but it's important fer y'all to understand, they don't torture to be mean. Now, a red captive considers torture an honor and to die well is important. The idea is to not cry out in pain while being tortured so your enemies know how strong your people are. Few die without crying out, because the pain is some kind of terrible at times."

Suddenly, Sue said, "It's snowing!"

It was, but it'd not amount to much, and while they all made a big whoop-de-doo over it, I just smiled and said, "It's the first snow of the year and it's just a bit below freezing, so it'll be gone by noon."

Grits stood and said, "I'm off to bed, I have guard in a bit and need my sleep."

I said, "It's a good idea iffen we all get some sleep, because tomorrow will come early and it's likely yer more tired than ya realize right now." One by one they headed to their shelters, and I wondered how Abe would take to startin' on his town so soon. Could be he was all talk, but I'd felt he was serious at the time.

Sue woke me near two in the morning and I gulped down a cup of cold coffee and moved under a huge pine to get out of the wind. The snow must have stopped right after we'd gone to bed, because I saw none on the ground. I heard a fox or something chasing supper in the trees behind me and then heard an owl hoot a couple of times off in the distance. I realized I loved the life I lived and wouldn't give it up for anything. Sure, it was rough and I may die tomorrow, but I'd die like a real man, fighting to the very end.

The next three hours were busy for me, as I sat under the tree and thought about all the men I'd known, both here and on the plantation, the few women I knew, and some of the good times I'd had at the annual fur roonyvoo. I'd only gone to a couple, because as Cotton said, "They don't pay the goin' rate for plew per pound, they mark up everything by five hundred percent and there just ain't any money doin' business like that." So, usually we took our plew to Butterfield's iffen we were lazy, or all the way to Fort Atkinson. Once we'd gone to Saint Louis, but it was too far and not worth the time it took to do the job.

As soon as the shadows started turning from black to gray, I awoke everyone and had the women prepare breakfast. The men loaded supplies, saddled the mounts and basically did all the heavy work. Grits was on guard as I untied Blackie from the tree and led him toward the fire. His hands were still tied behind him, but I'd untied one at the tree. I had him sit on a log as I fed him a cup of whiskey.

I'd just placed the empty cup by my foot when I heard a horrible scream and when I looked toward the sound, I saw Grits walking toward us with a spear in his chest. I moved toward him, but before I reached him he took three arrows in his back. The bloody points of all three where protruding from this chest.

"Injuns!" Cotton yelled, and everyone went to ground. I moved to the log beside Blackie. He looked at me with huge eyes and asked, "Are ya goin' to untie me?"

"No."

"For the love of God, don't let me die with my hands tied behind my back. Give me a pistol and I'll help fight."

"I think not, because I'd end up with a bullet in the back. Now, shut yer damned mouth and hope we win this fight. If we don't, some warrior will find ya a pretty easy kill, huh?"

I glanced over the log and Grits was on his knees, his head back as if looking at heaven and praying. A Ree warrior ran from the wood, grabbed Grits' hair, and made a few quick cuts with his knife blade. He then grabbed the front of my friends hair, placed his knee in his back, and pulled the scalp from his head. Grits gave a heartbreaking scream as I lined up my sights and shot the red bastard in the center of his chest. Two more braves broke from the trees on my left and another two from the trees on the right. I heard Cotton's rifle spit lead, heard the loud boom of Sue's shotgun, and a third shot came from close to where I'd seen May. Each shot dropped a warrior, but Sue's victim was screaming and thrashing around wildly. The last brave was determined to touch Grits with his coup stick, but a shot from my pistol knocked him on his ass right beside the man.

Still on his knees, Grits pulled his knife and buried the blade in the warriors chest. They both fell to the grasses.

It grew silent, except for the brave screaming that Sue had shot.

We waited, our nerves on edge.

Then, Sue's shotgun fired once more and it grew quiet again, only the screaming warrior's voice was growing weaker.

Long minutes passed before I called out, "No one move. Stay where ya are for a bit."

Finally, after over thirty minutes, I stood cautiously and scanned the woods. I saw nothing. As I moved toward Grits, I said, "Cotton, cover me while I check these warriors out."

The two beside Grits were dead as hell, as was my friend. I picked up his hat, closed his eyes, and covered his face. All were dead, except they one Sue'd shot, and I couldn't understand for the life of me how he could still be alive. The blast had torn a huge chunk from his side and by all rights, he should have died with the blast. I pulled my pistol and shot him in the head.

"I want Grits' body placed on his horse, put the fire out and let's move. There may be more Ree out there."

"Do ya think they were on point of a larger group?" Cotton ask as he neared.

"Mayhap, but hard to tell. We'll mount and not stop until we reach the village. Sue?"

"Nate?"

"What was that last blast I heard from your shotgun?"

"I happened to hear a noise and when I looked over my shoulder, a young boy of about fifteen or so was running right for me. He didn't have a gun, but he had a knife in one hand and tomahawk in the other. So, I blew him away. I didn't know he was kid until he fell."

"Young boy can kill ya as dead as a full grown man. Ya did the right thing. Okay, let's ride, people." I ordered as I moved to my horse.

Cotton said, "Ole Blackie must have been pretty damned scared, 'cause my boy peed his trousers."

From his horse, Blackie glared in anger but wisely kept his mouth shut.

At daylight, we were still moving, slowly but forward all the same. I was tired, hungry and sleepy, but knew we'd run into a wolf from the Shoshone any minute now. My eyes not only burned, but felt like they had sand in them.

I'd just wiped my right eye, when Cotton stopped and said, "Injuns, so hold up."

We waited for the tribe to make contact. I just hoped it was the Shoshone or the shit would hit the stump again. Grits, I thought, ya were one hell of a fine man. I hope you and Broken Bow are sitting around a campfire sharing jokes right now.

"*I am known as Talks Much.*" A warrior said from the side of the trail.

"*How are the people?*" Nate asked.

"*Better, now the spotted illness has passed. How are you,*

Big Raven Man?"

"I am well, but tired. I need food for my hunger and lodge for my eyes."

"I too know the feeling. Come, the village will welcome you."

Talks Much walked beside my horse as we neared the village. Finally, he asked, *"Why is one man tied?"*

"I must say that reason to Many Coups. Is he well?"

"He is well and will welcome you back again."

"Let him know I have returned."

"This I will do now."

Once we were in the village proper people waved, while some only looked, but all smiled. I stopped in the center of the village and rested. I knew all of us were beat and needed sleep, but first I had to talk with the chief.

Talks Much appeared and said, *"Many Coups asks you to come to his lodge and bring your man with you."*

"Where will my friends find food and shelter?" I asked.

"I will see they are taken care of well, so go."

"Cotton, pull Blackie from his horse and bring him with us. We're to speak with Many Coups right now. The rest of ya, go with Talks Much and he'll give ya a place to sleep and some food."

When Cotton neared Blackie he yelled, "What are we doin' here? Why'd ya bring me to a damned Injun village?"

Grabbing the man's left arm, Cotton pulled his knife, and cut the ropes tying him to the horse. He then, not so gently, pulled Blackie from his mount.

A warrior I could not remember the name of asked, *"Do you want the man with the secured hands to come with you?"*

"Yes, but he will fight and we are tired. He is my captive."

Looking around at other warriors, he asked, "Who will help me take the captive of Big Raven Man to see Many Coups?"

Since I'd helped when everyone was ill, four warriors soon escorted Blackie toward the lodge. Once there, I scratched on the hide and heard Many Coups say, *"Enter."*

I entered, with Blackie and two warriors behind me. Once inside, the chief gave me a strange look and said, "Be seated." He motioned for me to sit on his right. To the warriors he said, *"One warrior stay with the captive and the other leave."*

"I am happy in my heart to see my father is well," I said.

He nodded, glanced at Blackie and replied, *"Thanks to you*

and your raven people, my tribe survived the sickness. But, why is that man tied as a captive would be?"

"He is my captive, only not for long. He is a gift to the Shoshone people."

Many Coups nodded, but I knew he was interested when he asked, *"Why would the Shoshone people want a white man as a gift?"*

I spent the next ten minutes explaining who Blackie was, what he'd done to others, and then the fact he'd given small pox infested blankets to the Ree. The old warrior didn't interrupt or say a word and soon I was finished speaking.

It grew quiet in the lodge where the only sounds heard were the crackling fire and the heavy breathing of Blackie.

"We the Shoshone people are deeply honored by your gift. I must think on this man tonight and decide what must be done with him. He is an evil man, no good in the white or in the red world. I think he must suffer much pain before he crosses over to the other side." He said to me, then turning to the brave, he said, *"Take the captive and tie him to the post in the center of the village. Have two guards on him at all times. This one must not be allowed to escape."*

Blackie had a dumb look on his face and I knew he hadn't understood a single word spoken, so I said, "Yer to go with the nice young man behind ya. He'll see yer cared for until they decide how to kill ya."

"Ya can't turn me over to these red bastards, they'll torture me to death and it'll take days! Ya can't do this to me."

"I can do this and I have. Yer no longer my prisoner, but a captive of the Shoshone people."

"Please, dear God, don't do this to me!"

"They'll see justice is served and yer prayer is a good sign. I suggest ya do a lot of talkin' with the Good Lord and confess yer sins. Here within the next day or two, you'll get to meet Him personally."

Blackie was pulled from the lodge by the brave and continued to scream until he was out of hearing range. I knew they'd kill him slowly, but I had little use for a man who would give a disease like small pox to the Injuns and then laugh about it.

"I do not think our guest will die well." Many Coups said a few minutes after Blackie was gone.

"No, he will die screaming and praying to his God. He is

not a brave man."

"I will turn him over to the women with the coming of a new sun. I think they will play with him for many days."

Now, that I'd turned him over to the Shoshone, I began to have second thoughts. In my earlier anger, well, maybe I'd been wrong. I did know there was nothing I could do about it now, because I'd already given him to the tribe.

"Yes, they will play."

"In the old days, I would have brought your captive to stand in front of the Shoshone council, but they no longer live. I will make decisions until we are able to form a new one. You sound tired, my son, so go to the lodge you had before and eat, then rest."

"Father, I must leave with the coming of a new sun. I must move to my mountains and prepare for taking of the one who swims. For a few days, I will visit my Raven friend called Abe on the Mountain With No Snow."

"Rest, and if I do not see you before you leave, may the Great Spirit provide you with many furs this season. The moons of cold will bring you many of the one who swims. If I have need of you, I will send word."

I stood and left the lodge.

The sun was high as I moved toward my lodge. I avoided the center of the village, where I knew Blackie would be tied to a pole. It was over, in my view, and best to get some rest. Come morning, we'd move to Abe and see about his town.

Cotton joined me for supper. We had a cook, but I sent her on her way and the two of us spent hours drinking coffee and talkin'. I'd slept for over three hours, felt good for a change, and was in a talkative mood.

"I don't understand why I suddenly felt guilty turnin' Blackie over to the tribe." I said.

"It's simple, really, if ya think about it a spell. We both know how he'll die, and it won't be quick either. It's likely they'll cut on the man for days. While at first the idea sounded like justice, ya now realize it mighten not be. But, if ya try to take 'em back now, they'll kill every one of us, too."

"No, takin' 'em back is out."

"Nate, the man deserves this, and I agreed with yer decision from the start. He's a worthless piece of shit and some men deserve to die. If ever a man needs to die, it's him."

"I guess, but lawdy, what a way to go."

"Deacon is still here, too. I spoke with him earlier and he's glad ya brought Blackie to the tribe."

I grunted.

"He told me he prayed over Frank's grave and knows the old man is with God."

"Frank had bark, he surely did. I can still see him in my minds eye, stumbling down the trail, refusing help   because he was a real man. Now, by God, that's some!"

An hour later, Cotton left and I moved to my sleeping spot. I pulled the buffalo robe up, closed my eyes, but couldn't sleep.

Chapter 22

The next morning, an hour before dawn, I sat in my lodge with Deacon and Cotton. I'd been awake all night and knew I had to do something about Blackie, but damned iffen I could think of anything. Deacon assured me God would understand my situation, only he told me to ask Him for forgiveness and I'd already done that a hundred times.

I moved on my robe and the bottle of laudanum fell out of my possibles bag. I picked it up and said, "If we could give him some of this before they tortured him, he'd not feel any pain."

"Only for a few hours, then it'd be hell again. I don't think we can do anything, so I'm going to my lodge and gather my gear." Cotton said, stood and left my lodge.

I picked the bottle up, stared at it for a few minutes and then remember Wilson. He's been hit so hard I'd given him laudanum to put him out of his misery. If I could somehow get this bottle to Blackie, I could do the same thing. I could kill him without any pain.

"What are ya thinkin' on over there so hard?" Deacon asked.

"If I could get most of this bottle into Blackie, he'd die before they could torture him."

"It'd be murder in the eyes of the Lord, but the Good Book says he will forgive us of all things, iffen we only ask."

I worked the cork loose, but not all the way out. I gave thought to what I was about to do and stood. "Deacon, do ya want to pray with the doomed man before we leave?"

"Ya know I would. Only, I'm telling ya right now, I'll have nothing to do with his murder."

"I only asked ya if ya wanted to pray with the man." I picked up my capote, slipped the bottle up-side-down in my right sleeve and walked out, with Deacon beside me.

It was cold and dark when we neared the guards watching Blackie. The white man was naked, had a few cuts and bruises, and looked like hell.

"Our shaman wants to pray with the white man. Can we do this?"

The guard had three coup feathers in his hair, thought for a minute and then said, "Yes, you and the shaman may pray with him."

"Do you have a little water I can give him? Our prayer requires water."

Picking up a pan with about an inch of water in it, the guard said, "You can feed him water from this. He will get no more water on this side of the river. Once he dies, he may drink."

I knew the guard couldn't see me well, and they had no reason to suspect me; after all, I'd brought the man to them for punishment. As we walked, I pulled the cork from the bottle and let all of it flow into the pan.

We stopped in front of Blackie and I saw he was in pain, but conscious. He glared at me with hate-filled eyes as I said, "Drink this water. It has laudanum in it. I want ya to drink all of it. If ya do, ya'll go with no pain."

"Raise . . . it." He said.

I raised the pan and smiled as he drank the water. A few minutes later, the pan was empty. He met my eyes and asked, "Why?"

"I have my reasons."

He gave a light laugh and said, "Ya would have brought top dollar, too."

"Iffen ya want to pray with Deacon here, ya'd better get started."

Deacon said, "Shall we pray?"

"Yes, I've asked . . . forgiveness already."

As Deacon prayed, I bowed my head and asked God to forgive me for taking this man's life. When Deacon finally said, "Amen," I noticed Blackie was quiet. I felt the side of his neck, and I felt no heartbeat. I slapped Deacon lightly on the shoulder and said, "Come, the job is finished."

Nearing the guard, while still holding the pan in my hand, I said, *"The white man has died. I do not think his heart was strong."*

At my words, both guards ran to the pole and a few seconds later I heard one say, *"He has died. Get a burning log from the fire and let us see if he has been killed."*

I smiled, because I knew they'd find no marks on the man, not a thing, except what the women had put on his body earlier, and none would have killed him. I returned to my lodge, wrapped the pan up with my supplies, knowing even a Shoshone would smell the laudanum in the pan.

An hour later our group rode from the village and I never glanced back.

The End

ABOUT THE AUTHORS

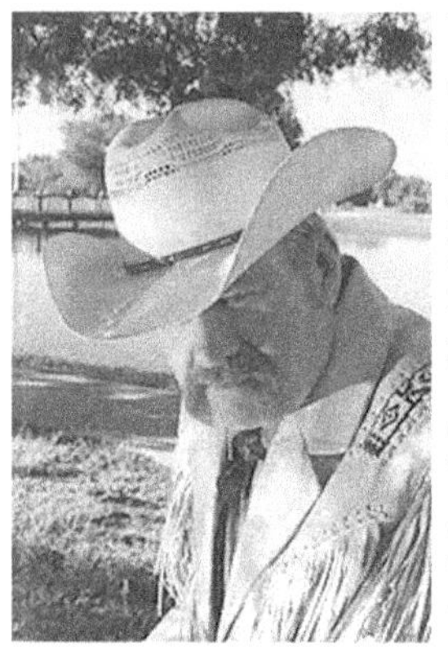

W.R. Benton is an Amazon Top 100 Selling Author and has previously authored books of fiction, non-fiction, young adult, and Southern humor. Such notable authors as Matt Braun, Stephen Lodge, Don Bendell, and many others have endorsed his work. His survival book, *"Simple Survival, a Family Outdoors Guide,"* is a 2005 Silver Award Winner from the Military Writers Society of American. James Drury, "The Virginian," endorsed two of his Westerns, *"War Paint"* and *"James McKay, U.S. Army Scout."*

Mister Benton has an Associate Degree in Search and Rescue, Survival Operations, a Baccalaureate in Occupational Safety and Health, and a Masters Degree in Psychology completed except for his thesis. Sergeant Benton retired from the military in 1997, with over twenty-six years of active duty, and at the rank of Senior Master Sergeant (E-8). He spent twelve years as a Life Support Instructor where he taught aircrew members how to use survival gear, survival procedures, and parachuting techniques.

Mr. Benton and his wife, Melanie, live near Jackson, Mississippi, with four dogs (Dolly, Newt, Benji, and Skillet) and two cats. Visit him at: http://www.wrbenton.net or on Facebook at https://www.facebook.com/wrbenton01

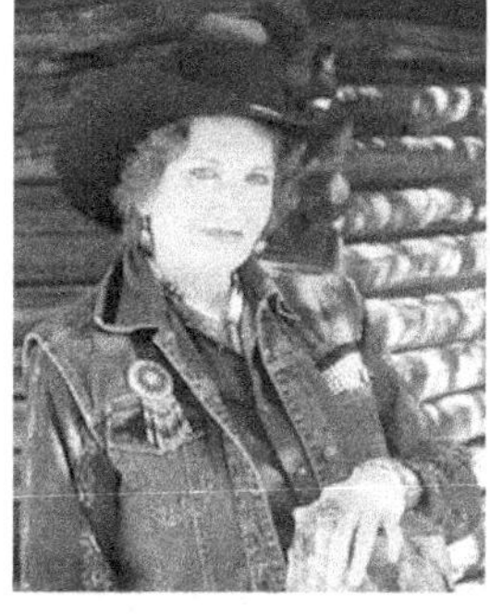**Grady Clark**, the pen name of Melanie D. Calvert-Benton, is a retired respiratory care practitioner. She now works with her first loves, photography and writing. While running a successful photography business for years, she only recently turned to writing a novel through the urging of her husband, Western Fiction Writer W.R. Benton. Melanie's photography has appeared on the covers of all four of Mister Benton's *"The Drum Series"* and soon will be gracing her own books. Her first book, *"A Southern Moon Rising,"* was released in 2008.

An avid outdoors-woman, she enjoys acting, deer hunting, fishing, camping, and of course, outdoor photography. She prefers the smell of wood smoke, the crackling of a fire late at night, and the serenity of nature, to a fast-paced life in a big city. Born and raised in Mississippi, most of it on a farm, she is a true Southern Belle.

Feel free to visit Melanie at:
https://www.facebook.com/melanie.c.benton

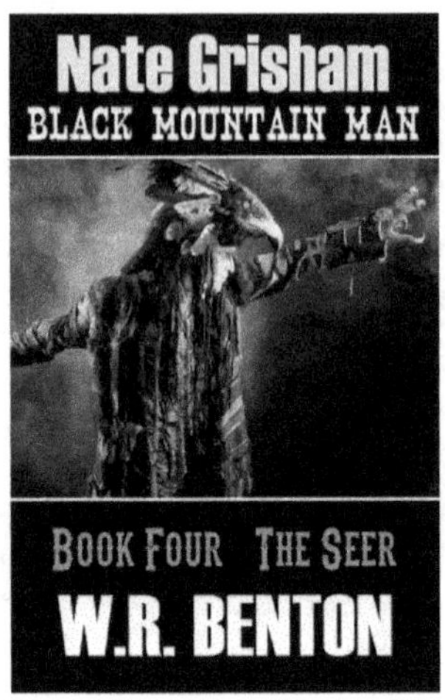

The Seer

When Nate and Cotton are hired as guides by two English military officers, they're saddled with an unusual task. They must return a kidnapped Crow squaw to her tribe. But this woman is no ordinary Indian, she is a seer...someone whose dreams foretell the future.

Spooked by the accuracy of the seer's predictions, the English officers want to complete the task and shed themselves of their challenging cargo as soon as possible. However, Nate befriends the squaw, and soon is surprised by her revelations for his future. Romantic ties are not what Nate wants, or needs, yet the squaw is confident their lives are to be entwined.

It's another exciting, page-turning chapter in the saga of **Nate Grisham: Black Mountain Man**.

Now available at Amazon and other online bookstores

On a trip to the Lake Clark area of the Alaskan bush, a sudden arctic weather system forces down the small plane of Dr. Jim Wade, and his son David. Both have survived the crash, but not unscathed. Food, fire and shelter are all a priority. Following the death of his father, now it is up to David to figure out what to do next, and how to survive, on a remote Alaskan mountain—in winter!

This is a fictional story of survival, resilience and of the spirit to live. It is both authentic and accurate, having been written by a former Air Force life support survival instructor. For ages 10 and up

Set adrift, a family of three are cast out to sea in a rubber raft, where they must find a way to conquer one terrifying tragedy after another or die in the process.

In this gripping story of survival everyone will be tested to their limits. Christian faith and hope are hallmarks of this tale that will touch your heart..

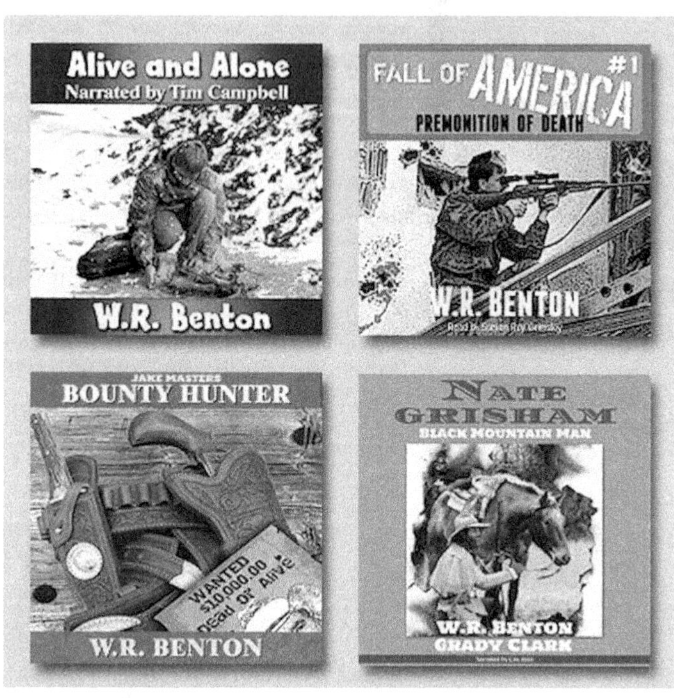

Audiobooks by WR Benton

Available at
Audible.com
iTunes
and Amazon.

www.ingramcontent.com/pod-product-compliance
Lightning Source LLC
Chambersburg PA
CBHW070944190726
48292CB00004B/1340